"Did they...hurt you?" Vin asked.

Skylar shook her head. "They drugged me, tied me up and scared the life out of me."

Those tears threatened again as she remembered the moment, years ago, that she'd seen her father's welcome face as he'd led her away from the men who'd taken her. For a moment she wanted to lean into Vin, that same feeling warming her inside like hot cider.

"Oh, God, I forgot. They took my laptop." How had she forgotten about the most important research in her life? She could only attribute it to the terror, the escape...and the rugged Agent Fitzgerald.

"One of our agents has already secured it. It'll be returned to you. Rest assured that I'll take good care of you."

She wasn't sure what scared her the most— interacting with this intriguing man who made her insides turn to water, or facing the four madmen with automatic weapons.

Dear Reader,

My To Protect and Serve miniseries continues with *Designated Target,* throwing together a brilliant navy scientist and a tough-as-nails ex-marine NCIS agent.

Dr. Skylar Baang is kidnapped right out of her home and is rescued by special agent Vincent "Vin" Fitzgerald. When the safe house she's placed in is breached by the kidnappers hell-bent on retrieving Sky, and two NCIS agents are killed defending her, Vin must take her and run, not sure whom he can trust. He takes her to a secluded cabin in Pennsylvania where sparks fly. Vin's professionalism is not only tested but compromised. Sky struggles with her own past. Her parents gave up everything to save her from the Chinese government who wanted to use her brilliance for their own purposes. She vowed to make her intelligence count and sacrifice everything to their memory, but Vin is making her yearn for more. When Vin vows to be her shield, she's terrified she'll lose him, too. They can trust only each other in this high-stakes game of cat and mouse.

Best,

Karen

DESIGNATED TARGET

—

Karen Anders

◆**HARLEQUIN**®ROMANTIC SUSPENSE

Recycling programs
for this product may
not exist in your area.

ISBN-13: 978-0-373-27896-1

Designated Target

Copyright © 2014 by Karen Alarie

Printed in U.S.A.

www.Harlequin.com

Books by Karen Anders

Harlequin Romantic Suspense

 Five-Alarm Encounter #1658
At His Command #1713
¤*Special Ops Rendezvous* #1804
Designated Target #1826

*To Protect and Serve
¤The Adair Legacy

KAREN ANDERS

is a three-time National Readers' Choice Award finalist and RT Reviewers' Choice Award finalist and has won a prestigious Holt Medallion. Two of her novels made the Waldenbooks bestseller list in 2003. Published since 1997, she currently writes romantic suspense for Harlequin. To contact the author, please write to her in care of Harlequin, 233 Broadway, Suite 1001, New York, NY 10279, or visit www.karenanders.com.

To whitenoise who serves

Chapter 1

Skylar Baang didn't know what woke her, pulling her from the heavy weight of an exhausted sleep. A sound?

After a grueling forty-eight-hour marathon on her top secret project, she was slower to react than normal.

Wait. A footstep. That sound didn't belong in the empty silence of her house.

Her gut twisted, her heart surging with the panic-soaked memories of her kidnapping as a small child. Twisted emotions accompanied every heartbeat, every breath, evoking the terror that lived in the deep recesses of her mind, always ready to spring on her.

There were monsters—and they didn't live under the bed.

The sound came again, injecting adrenaline into her system. Her eyes sprang open, her vision focused, and she turned her head toward the door.

Somebody was in her house. How did the intruder get past her formidable security? This couldn't be just any ordinary burglar. She didn't have that many valuables.

That meant they weren't exactly here to rob her. Her head whipped around and focused on her laptop.

All her research was in there.

Fully awake, she sprang into action. Jerking open the window, she released her emergency fire ladder and turned to slip down it. She stopped when she saw the black SUVs in front of her house. Were there more assailants down below waiting for her? Staccato thumps of boots on her stairs replaced the stealthy footsteps. *Crap!* That meant there was more than one somebody out there. What the hell was going on?

She raced to the bedroom door. Her first fumbling try at the lock failed. The metal slipped out of her sweaty, trembling fingers. After a few more tries, she finally succeeded. But locking the door wasn't going to stop them for long.

She wasted no time. She had to hide, and the only place for her to go was the attic. She started for her laptop, but the solid thump against the door sent her scrambling for the closet instead. Inside, she grabbed the pull cord and yanked the stairs down. As she climbed, she folded up the lower section. Once in the attic, she pulled on the stairs and the hinged door slammed as she heard them breach her room.

Crack!

The wooden door smashed into the wall, shaking her hiding spot in the rafters. She could see through a small sliver where the ladder met the ceiling. Sweat trickled in a slow track from her hairline down the side of her temple to her cheek. Every muscle in her body was rigid, including the hand she would have raised to brush at the moisture. Her heart fluttered like a tiny, terrified bird in her chest.

Her very life depended on remaining completely still. As a child, reciting the periodic table in her head had kept her calm.

Hydrogen. Atomic number 1. Lightest element. Most abundant element in the universe and makes up about ninety percent of the universe by weight. Hydrogen as water (H2O) is absolutely essential to life, and it is present in all organic compounds.

Several people clamored out of her room, the sounds of their footsteps moving off into the distance. Had her window ruse worked?

Lithium. Atomic number 3. Group 1 element containing just a single valence electron (1s2 2s1). Group 1 elements are called "alkali metals." Lithium is a solid—

There was an outburst, a curse. Was that…*Russian?*

The dim memories of another bedroom, another night, and men who'd taken her from her home, speaking a foreign language, filled her mind. Wide-eyed, she backed into the deepest corner in reaction. The wood beneath her creaked. She froze.

Her stomach sank when the doorknob to her closet rattled, then twisted, the squeak screaming along her nerves like fingernails on a chalkboard. Light glowed around the attic opening. Her heart stopped. Her breath stopped.

The unmistakable metallic sound of a cocked automatic weapon made her stomach tighten and her heart surge back into action, thumping against the wall of her chest in an almost painful rhythm.

Her muscles trembled, her brain freezing up as everything inside her urged her to run.

But there was nowhere for her to go.

Someone pulled the ladder down, and a fresh injection of adrenaline shot into her system.

Suddenly a shaved head slowly elevated into her line of vision. She pressed her back against a beam, all her muscles tensing until they were sending waves of pain to her brain. The face of a man she didn't recognize. His deep-set black eyes stole her breath, the intent in them sending fear into her blood, prickling her scalp and running like wildfire down her spine. He smiled, but the humor never touched those malevolent eyes. She sucked breath into her lungs to scream, but before she could, a hypodermic sank into her thigh. Her vision immediately blurred, her rapidly beating heart sending the drug even faster through her system. She tried to lash out, but her sluggish arm wouldn't work properly, and he easily blocked her weak attempt to knock him away from her.

He laughed as she plunged into oblivion.

Another sound worked its way into her consciousness. A scraping, tearing sound that replayed over and over until she finally opened her eyes and identified the noise.

Tree branches caught in the wind scraped against the house. Sky didn't have any trees close enough to her home to make that sound, which meant…she was no longer in her own home. *Just like before.*

She took a moment to get her bearings, her mouth dry and cottony. She had a gag in her mouth. Sodium Pentothal. That was probably what they'd used on her. The effects were quick, fifteen to thirty seconds, but kept a person out for only about ten to fifteen minutes. The room she was in was unfamiliar—a bedroom, judging by the mattress she lay on. She had no idea how long she'd been out. They could have kept injecting her with the drug. She tried to move. Her hands were tied behind her, and her feet were immobilized.

The man who had stabbed her with the needle hadn't

bothered to cover his face. That meant he didn't care if she saw it. He was confident that she wouldn't be telling anyone what he looked like.

And if she didn't do something, she would end up a statistic.

Very dead.

Special Agent Vincent "Vin" Fitzgerald eyed his steely opponent. There was a time to give up and a time to dig in and make a stand. This was that time.

Without hesitating, he reached his arm back and threw the dart at the board.

"Ha! A perfect bull's-eye, Vargas. Try and beat that."

Special Agent in Charge Chris Vargas smirked and slid a sidelong glance at his beautiful wife, Sia.

"Wait. Before you throw, let me get some victory beers," Vin said. "I know you'll want to drink to my win." He grinned as he walked away toward the bar in the wake of Chris's laughter. His cell rang, and he reached for it as the bartender caught his eye and Vin raised two fingers.

"Fitzgerald."

"Vinny, it's Lilah."

His sister's voice was subdued and she sounded as if she'd been crying. "What's wrong?"

He grabbed the two opened longneck bottles and pressed the phone between his ear and shoulder, pulling out his wallet and giving the bartender a twenty.

"What is ever right?" She sniffled. "Dad needs you to come home as soon as you can."

"Why?" The volatile mix of anger and frustration made his voice harsher than he'd meant it to be. But this was the same old stuff his dad had been slinging for years. When would he ever understand his son?

"I promised I wouldn't say." When her breath hitched, his heart tightened. "He wants to talk to both of us. I think it's about the company."

"Not this again… Lilah, it's a waste of time."

"Vinny, please don't make me do this alone." He loved his sister and his family; that wasn't in question. What was in question was how many times he would have to hash this over with his father. In the end, he couldn't turn his back on his sister. "When can you come home?"

"I'll have to see."

"Is this your way of putting me off?"

"No, I'll talk to my boss. Don't cry anymore, okay? You're an ugly crier."

"Shut up," she said with a little, watery laugh.

"Oh, Vinny, I miss you. Let me know. Please make it soon."

He went back to the table near the dartboard and set down the drinks.

"Okay, step aside," Chris said. He walked to the board and pulled out the darts, then sauntered back to the place they'd marked in the sand. He raised his arm and…his cell phone rang.

"Ah, an ass-kicking reprieve, Fitzgerald."

"You were the lucky one, boss," Vin said.

"Vargas," he said into the phone's receiver. Vin's instincts went on full alert at the way his boss listened intently, his gray eyes narrowing. "When?"

He looked at his watch as he listened some more. "We're on it."

Chris hung up and eyed Vin. He knew that look.

Vin buttoned the top button of his dress shirt, retying

his loose tie and shrugging into his suit coat. Looked as if his long day at the office had just gotten extended.

"Don't worry. I'll take a cab home," Sia said to her husband.

"No, you take the car. I'll catch a ride with Fitzgerald. Sorry to cut our night short, my love. I'll check in with you later."

"I'm just disappointed I didn't get to see Vin trump you at darts."

Chris laughed and kissed her on her upturned, laughing mouth. "Kiss the baby good-night for me."

"What's up?" Vin asked a few minutes later as his boss rattled off an address in a posh Washington, D.C., suburb.

"There's been a break-in at the home of one of the navy's brightest research scientists. A neighbor reported dark SUVs at her house and heard some commotion. The door was left wide open, and it looks like the woman was taken."

"Who's the researcher?"

"Dr. Skylar Baang," Chris said.

"Baang? She's one of the premier talents working for the navy."

"I'm always impressed, Vin, with how much you know."

Vin pulled up to the curb. Bathed in the blue lights from the flashing cruisers, an old lady dressed in a pink fuzzy robe stood on the porch with one of the D.C. cops, her hands in constant motion around her face, her long, gray hair in a braid down her back.

Pulling up to Dr. Baang's house, they got out of the car, and Vin said, "Chris, after this case, I need to talk to you about some personal time. I've got to go back home."

"Sure. Let's see what we have here, and we can work it out."

"Thanks."

As Vin and his boss approached, two more cars screeched to the curb. Amber Dalton, a tall, athletic blonde, emerged from the first car and met the second agent, Beau Jerrott, who ran his hands through his black, mussed hair and over his dark stubble.

He cut in front of her. "Hey, whatever happened to beauty before age?" Amber said.

"It's trumped by a full-fledged agent before a probie."

"I was a lieutenant in the JAG Corps before I ever started here."

"But here you're a probie."

Her eyes narrowed. "Did you have a hot date?"

"That's none of your business."

"I bet you used your sexy Cajun accent on her. *Chère*, you and me, kiss kiss." She screwed up her face and made smacking noises with her lips.

"Both of you knock it off," Chris said.

"I'll be an agent in two months," she hissed.

"Still a probie," Beau said before they were both cut off by their boss's stern look.

As they approached Dr. Baang's front porch, the cop stepped aside, and the old woman turned to them, her face still white. Her creased eyes held the worry of a neighbor who was close to the victim. Before his boss could ask any questions, Vin said, "Officer Cranston, what are you doing forcing this lovely lady to stand out here in the middle of the night? You must be chilled to the bone, Mrs...."

"Ms. Childers and, yes, I am."

She relaxed as he'd expected. A comfortable witness gave information faster than a panicked one. Time was of the essence. He took her frail hand and led her into the house. She settled on the sofa. "Amber, can you get her a glass of water?" Amber nodded and went off into the kitchen. He turned back to the witness. "Can you tell us what you saw?"

With a grateful half smile, Ms. Childers said, "Four men, dressed in black and carrying what looked like—" she gulped, and her hand fluttered to her chest "—automatic weapons. One of them had poor Dr. Baang over his shoulder. I could tell because she has this unmistakable long, black hair and she's such a slender woman. Not more than five-four and she can't weigh more than a hundred and ten pounds."

Amber came back from the kitchen and handed Ms. Childers a glass of water. She took a long drink. "They put her into one of the two vehicles in front of her house and drove off."

"What were you doing up so late?"

"Couldn't sleep. I was doing needlepoint by the window, and I saw them come out of the house."

"So, you didn't see them go in?"

"No. They must have entered from the back. But I did notice the SUVs' sleek, dark color with tinted windows. They looked new. I thought maybe Dr. Baang had company. She works for the government, you know."

"The navy, actually. Did you get a license-plate number on either vehicle?"

"No. I had my reading glasses on to see with close-up work. By the time I got them off, they were gone."

"Thank you, Ms. Childers. The officer will escort you back home."

"That was smooth, Fitzgerald," Beau said. "She was on the verge of panic. I saw it, too."

"Back to the Yard," Chris, their boss, ordered. "Time is ticking."

When Vin arrived, he went straight to his desk as did the other three agents. He hoped this hunch he had panned out as he brought up the necessary website.

"Amber," Chris called out.

"On it," she said as she pushed a key on her computer and Dr. Skylar Baang's record popped onto the wide-screen monitor mounted in between Vin's and Amber's desks.

Vin glanced up and then did a double take.

Beau cut off Vin's view, but that face was burned into his brain. With an ooh la la shaking motion of his hand, he said, "Wow, hot *fille. Pas de bêtises.*"

Vin agreed. No joking. Dr. Skylar Baang stunned him. Almond-shaped eyes on an Asian woman were expected, but the brilliant blue color of the irises was not. Her gaze projected confidence and attitude, and her slightly raised chin clinched it. Her olive skin was flawless, her features decidedly a mix between Asian and American. Shaking his head out of his fascination with Skylar's face, he focused on the keyboard and continued working.

"She was born in the Philippines. Moved to China when she was four. Parents deceased. American mother in a car accident under suspicious circumstances and the Filipino father died in a Chinese prison just last year. Mechanical engineer accused of his wife's murder. She was raised by an aunt right here in D.C. She has a former name, Malaya Matapang. According to court records, it was changed to Skylar Baang when she was six. Baang is the last name of the aunt, first name, Audris. She's not the biological aunt, though. Looks like Dr. Baang was adopted by her legally when Dr. Baang was seven." Amber paused. "Wow, get this, guys. She was homeschooled by her aunt up to age seven and went straight to high school. She then entered college at ten."

"Bona fide genius, then?" Beau commented.

"I'd say. She earned her bachelor's degree in two years. While you were popping your zits, she was getting her master's."

Amber chuckled and shook her head, continuing. "Finished that in a year and had her Ph.D. in computer engineering by seventeen. From MIT, no less. Didn't you graduate from there, Vin?"

He nodded and she continued. "She went to work for the navy after a two-year stint in the private sector. She has a top secret clearance and is working on some heavy-duty stuff for the navy."

"Beau, get out to her aunt's house," Chris said.

Beau grabbed his things and exited just as the picture Vin was hoping for popped up on his screen. "Got you!" he said to the screen.

"What do you have, Vin?" Amber said, walking over to his computer.

"A nice clear picture of one of the SUVs all pretty-like with the license plate."

"The time looks right," Amber said. She studied the monitor, then added, "That's the corner of Connecticut and Porter. I hate that stoplight. Longest one on the planet."

He advanced the video and captured the second SUV.

"How can you be sure these are the right SUVs?" Chris asked.

"Like I said, the time is right," Amber responded.

"Run the plates," Chris said.

"Dammit, they're rentals from Savoy Car Rentals." Vin cursed.

"I'm sure they're closed," Amber said.

"Databases are never closed," Vin said, intertwining his fingers and stretching out his arms.

"What are you doing?" Chris asked.

"Ah...borrowing information," Vin replied. He was already through their first firewall. Piece of cake.

"Hacking."

"That's such an ugly word, boss, and illegal."

Chris shook his head. "I'm looking the other way."

"One is rented to a Mary Shelley and the other to Billie Holiday."

"Hmm..." Amber said. "One is a novelist and the other a singer. I suspect they're bogus."

Vin committed the addresses to memory. "We'll check first one, then the other. We'll report back."

"Whoa," Chris said, putting out a hand to stop him midstride. "If either of you discover her, call in for backup. No excuses."

Vin gave him a mock salute. "Yes, sir."

Sky maneuvered her hands under her butt, folding her upper body to get her bound hands underneath her legs and in front of her. Mobility wasn't good, but it was enough to pull the tape off her mouth. This was her one chance to flee. Using her teeth, the nylon rope smooth against her lips, she worked at the bonds. She had to get out of here.

As soon as her hands were free, she reached for the knot at her ankles. Swinging her feet to the floor, she lurched slightly, feeling the lingering effects from the drug they'd given her. She was still in the tank top and boy shorts she'd gone to bed in and her feet were bare, but she was free.

She crept to the door and opened it enough to see out. She was on the second floor of a two-story house. She crept through the hall and peered around the corner. She could see down the stairs and the room beyond.

She reared back, her heart jumping into her throat. The man with the shaved head who'd stabbed her with the hypodermic, or Death Head, as she thought of him, was on the phone, pacing back and forth near the front door. Two more were on the sofa, one with a ponytail and the other with a scar on his face. Her laptop! It sat on the coffee table between them. Hopefully they wouldn't be able to break the encryption on it. The fourth man was standing at the bottom of the stairs with his back to her. All she could make out was the automatic weapon slung casually across powerful shoulders.

Going this way wasn't an option. She wouldn't make it to the front door, and there were no back stairs.

She eased back down the hall and into the room, silently closing the door.

Fear welled like a deep, dark pool. Finding a way out was her only chance. Panicking wasn't going to help.

Taking a deep breath into her lungs and exhaling helped. The wind churned outside, sending those damn branches against the house. The branches. Trees. She cautiously tiptoed to the window, careful not to make any noise. It took a moment to unlock it and slide it up. A chilling October breeze caused gooseflesh to ripple her skin, and she shivered. Popping out the screen was also soundless.

The tree had long branches, but the trunk wasn't close enough for her to step onto it.

She would have to jump.

Just as she stepped up on the edge of the sill, the door opened. Death Head stood there with a shocked expression on his face before yelling out in Russian. She had no idea what he was saying, and she didn't care. Sky didn't hesitate. She pushed off with as much power as she could muster. She crashed into the tree and slid a few inches. She scrambled for a firm grip, her arms instinctively hugging the trunk. Branches scratched at her face, hands and body, but she ignored the stinging pain. Without hesitation, using her bare feet, she worked her way down the tree as fast as possible without breaking her neck. She heard shouting from the house. Her heart slammed against her chest, adrenaline buzzing her skin.

Death Head was running through the house shouting. It would be only a matter of minutes before they were after her. The urge to flee was overwhelming, but if she took a spill and hurt herself, she would find herself back under their control.

She hit the ground, vibrations from the impact tingling up her legs. She turned to run away from the voices and the noise of the men coming after her.

She hit a solid wall of human muscle. Lashing out, she had no intention of being caught again. She didn't know what these men wanted, but if they had her laptop, it had to have something to do with her classified navy work. She wasn't going to reveal that information easily. They would resort to torture. Death Head looked as if he would enjoy it.

She punched, kicked and used her knee to incapacitate her assailant. Then she was running again, adrenaline fueling her system like jet fuel.

Suddenly, like a linebacker, the solid wall hit her, and she went down hard.

Cold steel clamped around her wrists, and he hauled her up as easily as if she weighed no more than a child. With his rigid arm around her midriff, she couldn't see his face, but that didn't stop her from kicking out. He dragged her behind some hedges as she heard those all-too-familiar boots and that guttural language spewing words she was sure would singe the ears of sailors.

"Stop resisting," a resolute voice whispered in her ear. "Special Agent Vincent Fitzgerald, NCIS."

Relief crashed through her, leaving her wrung out and jittery. "Why the handcuffs?"

"You were fighting me. Now, shush. The cavalry is on the way."

Sirens wailed in the distance, and her rescuer, still clutching her against him so that she couldn't see his face, slipped out of the hedges, ducking around a fence. As he ran, her back bumped up against some impressive muscles, his biceps like a rock against her side.

It was easy to see he was running for a black car parked at the curb. His breath was harsh in her ears. A blonde woman was standing on the driver's side. "Vin, hurry up."

"I'm moving as fast as I can, Amber." Automatic gunfire cut across their path. Her rescuer dived for the ground, cushioning and covering her body with his.

They lay there trapped as the *rat-a-tat* sound of shots

caused dogs to bark and lights to go on in the houses around them. His weight bore into her, protecting her against the hot lead that whizzed around them. He dragged her, half crawling, half running, to a big oak. The blonde agent, Amber, courageously returned fire.

He still held her against his hard body as he pressed her to the tree to protect her from the flying bullets. Out of the corner of her eye, she saw his arm extended, and the snub nose of a pistol materialized. Vin opened fire, the retort of the weapon loud in her ears.

The sirens blasted closer, and the automatic gunfire ceased. She pressed her face to the rough bark of the tree at the sound of opening and closing doors. The SUVs. The Russians were on the run.

The breath whooshed out of her, a relief so profound, tears rushed to her eyes. He let her slide down the muscled length of his body, setting her gently on the ground.

Several vehicles raced by, presumably in pursuit of the kidnappers. The blonde woman went out to meet two other men, one tall and handsome, his body language unquestionably showing leadership. The other man was darkly attractive.

Finally, she turned around and looked up into the face of Special Agent Vin Fitzgerald. The man who had cuffed her, manhandled her and...saved her life in the process.

The words to thank him were on her lips until she got a load of him standing so confidently in front of her. For a moment it was as if she couldn't form words. The other two men were attractive, but he was more of a threat to her equilibrium and stole her breath. She stepped back and hit the rough bark of the tree.

"Whoa, steady there," he said, reaching out and cupping her elbow, sending goose bumps along her skin, hardening her nipples against the soft cotton of her tank top. Touching her like that did nothing whatsoever to steady her.

Reaching out her cuffed hands, she said, "Take these off me." She didn't have the social skills for this kind of interaction, especially with this man. And that was rude and blunt, after all that he'd just done for her. She bit her lip. Why did he make her feel so conscious of every breath she took, the half nakedness of her body, the tangle of her long hair, the dirt on her hands and knees? Most men weren't even a blip on her radar, but this guy was trouble.

His dark brows winged above his intense green eyes, and that power doubled as he took in her face, dropping down to her cuffed hands.

"Sorry about the cuffs, but you were fighting me, and this was the easiest way to subdue you and get you out of harm's way. You're Dr. Skylar Baang, correct?"

She nodded. "Yes. Those men kidnapped me, but since you're here, I suspect you know that already."

He reached into the pocket of his dark blue suit and produced a key. He stepped closer, invading her personal space, and she wanted to step back, but she needed to get the cuffs off. His hand slipped around her wrist; the warmth of it suddenly made her shiver. Bending his head, the wind tousled his dark sable hair, sending his enticing fresh scent toward her in an invisible assault on her senses.

Damn, he smelled good.

The cuffs released, and he clicked them shut and deposited them in a case at the small of his back.

He unzipped his coat and, without asking her permission, slipped it around her shoulders. The warmth was immediate, bringing with it that intoxicating scent.

Gratitude built in her chest, her stomach flipping over when he slipped his arm around her and helped her to the car. "Blast the heat, Amber," he said as he settled her in the backseat and climbed in beside her. "Dr. Baang, this is Special Agent Amber Dalton."

Amber nodded to her in the rearview mirror. "Good to see that you're safe and sound, Dr. Baang." She put the car in gear and pulled away from the curb.

"We're going to take you to the hospital to make sure everything is okay. Then back to the navy yard for the time being until we can figure some of this out."

Sky nodded. She hoped that it would be someone else who would be asking the questions. Even with a Ph.D., she was having a hard time forming words around this man.

"Did they…hurt you?"

She knew immediately what he was asking her, and she shook her head. "They drugged me and tied me up, but don't think any of them touched me while I was under. They just scared the living crap out of me."

Those tears threatened again, remembering the moment she'd seen her father's welcome face as he took her away from the men who'd taken her as a child. For a moment she wanted to lean into him, that same feeling warming her inside, as if drinking hot cider.

"After that I'll be able to go home, right?"

He met the female agent's eyes in the rearview mirror, and her dubious look made her anxious.

"Dr. Baang," he said gently, his voice as beautiful as his face, "we'll talk about that later."

"Oh, God, I forgot. They took my laptop." How she

had forgotten about the most important research in her life she could only attribute to the terror, the escape… and the rugged Special Agent Fitzgerald.

"One of our agents has already secured it. It'll be returned to you. Rest assured that we'll take good care of you."

She wasn't sure what scared her the most—interacting with this intriguing man who made her insides turn to liquid or facing the four kidnappers with automatic weapons.

Chapter 2

Vin stood in the examination room, not willing to let Dr. Baang out of his sight. He wanted to be in there and close to her, his protective instincts on high alert.

Amber was outside on the phone.

He'd never been in the presence of such an elegantly beautiful woman. Her straight black hair went to her waist; a swath of it had fallen over her shoulder on the nylon of his NCIS jacket. Her eyes slayed him every time he met them. He might be a geek, but he'd never had a difficult time with the ladies. But in this particular case, it was best that he not notice anything about her. She was his charge, and that nixed anything else.

"You're bleeding."

Her soft voice drew his gaze. "Your arm," she said, focusing on the sleeve of his white dress shirt. "You should have someone take a look at it."

She eyed his gun clipped to his side and his badge that was tucked in his waistband, and she noticed blood there, too. "You're hurt."

"We'll see to you first, Dr. Baang."

She bit her soft, full bottom lip and looked away from him. Her legs were quite bare, long and beautiful with slim ankles and delicate feet. In fact, she didn't have much on. The skimpy pink shorts left almost nothing to the imagination and showed off her slender hips; the tank top she wore revealed her nipples through the fabric as a reaction to the cold. It was a good thing that his coat covered up a lot. He'd have to get her something to wear back to NCIS. The perpetrators had literally snatched her straight out of her bed. It must have been a harrowing experience. He noticed her feet were very dirty.

He walked over to the sink they had in the room and wet some paper towels. Returning to her, he said, "May I?"

She nodded and bit her lip again as he slipped his hand over her warm, soft skin and started to scrub off the dirt. "Are you all right?" he asked.

"What do you mean?" she said, jerking slightly against his hand when he obviously hit a ticklish spot.

"Do you need to speak with someone about your kidnapping?" He moved to her other foot, once all the grime was cleaned from the first one.

"You mean a therapist?"

"Yes. We have one on staff at NCIS."

He cleaned the bottom of her foot, then dried both off. "No. I don't need a therapist. I'd really just like to go home."

He decided not to broach that subject here in the hospital. She wasn't going to like the answer he gave her.

A doctor and nurse came in. After looking her over and ministering to the cuts she'd gotten from the branches of the tree, they said she could leave.

When they saw the blood on his shirt, he rolled up his sleeve so they could clean and bandage the wound he must have gotten when he'd covered her from the hail of bullets. It stung a bit, and he caught her staring at him with a pensive expression before she looked away. He hadn't needed stitches, as it was more a scrape than a cut. But the one on his side, where a bullet had grazed him, hurt a lot worse and needed a few stitches.

Amber came in and said, "We ready to roll?"

"Just as soon as we can find her something to wear," he said and proceeded to talk to the nurse about it. They found her a pair of cotton scrubs in mint green and a pair of surgical bootees for her feet.

When she was dressed, he slipped his hands around her waist and helped her down from the examination table. She wobbled a little bit, and he steadied her, her face rising up, her lips trembling slightly, but then she got control of herself.

Her waist was tiny, and his hands had never felt so big.

"Did you know that Mount Everest is twenty-nine thousand and twenty-five feet?" she said, her voice a breathless hush.

The sounds of the hospital died away, and his attention focused on her. The ends of her long, dark hair brushed the top of his hand where it curved around her waist. With that delicate nose, her thickly lashed eyes wide with a slight tilt, she ignited a forbidden thought in him. His gaze drifted to her lips, a hot longing curling deep in his gut.

He smiled. Interesting the way she blurted out a random fact. She was a kindred spirit, a geekette. Not a stretch for a scientist who'd attended college at ten. He imagined that she'd never been given the opportunity to interact with her own peers in a normal manner. "Twenty-nine thousand and twenty-nine, actually."

She blinked those pretty eyes. And looked away. "Are you sure?"

"I've climbed it."

She breathed a sigh of admiration. "Have you? What was that like?"

"Exhilarating. Scary. The air at the top tasted like freedom."

She looked envious, and he wondered about her background and if she'd ever tasted freedom.

"You can let go of me now, Agent Fitzgerald. I think I'm quite steady."

She might be, but his knees were a bit wobbly and it had nothing to do with being shot at.

His hand slid away from her waist, and she looked down and tucked her hair behind her ear. He pushed the curtain aside, and they walked out of the examination room.

The temperature outside had dropped, and he smelled snow on the air. She shivered in his jacket. He needed to get her some warm clothes.

He opened the door for her, and she said a soft "Thank you" as she settled inside, and Amber got into the driver's seat.

He got in with her and they headed to the navy yard. It was still too risky to take her anywhere near her house.

"Amber, stop at Branson Station Mall. I'm guessing you don't shop high end, probably a mix between comfortable Gap and midincome stores."

She turned to look at him, her eyes wide. "Yes. How did you know that?"

Amber chuckled. "He's got observation skills like a freaking hawk," she said.

"I'd say you're a less-is-more girl and gravitate toward sleek and structured."

"That's a pretty good trick, Agent Fitzgerald."

He smiled. "It was easy."

"How?"

"You're a bit shorter than average, so women of your height often choose tailored clothes to maximize the fit. You're a scientist and you thrive on order and discipline. So, I'd say you were a minimalist. I'd guess your favorite designers work with raw and natural fibers."

Her jaw dropped open.

She met Amber's eyes in the rearview mirror. "He did that to me the first day on the job."

"Was he right?"

"To a T. It was his observation that actually found you in time to save you. It's just what he does."

Her gaze was direct when she met his eyes, assessing. He found her an interesting mix of bold and shy. Bold in her job. Confident, unbending and competent, but with people less so, more shy and wary. But a substantial backbone. It had taken a lot of guts to jump from that window to the tree. There was nothing he admired more than courage. On the battlefield, in performance of duty, in everyday life.

And there was something else. Some kind of shadow in her background. Something that terrified her. He'd seen it in her eyes when he'd caught her. That intrigued him, as well.

"Can I just go home?"

"Not yet," Amber said, shaking her head.

"The mall, Amber."

When Amber parked, he got out with Dr. Baang and followed close behind her into the store. He waited while she chose a couple of outfits, toiletries, her un-mentionables and footwear.

When he paid for the clothes, she promised to pay him back. He shrugged.

"I would really like to take a shower."

"We can take care of that at NCIS. There are employee showers where you can freshen up."

Back in the car, they headed to the navy yard located in Southeast D.C. bounded by I-395 to the north, South Capitol to the west and the Anacostia River to the south and east. Dr. Baang's work was not far from NCIS in a research building that was occupied by a government contractor, Coyne Industries. The owner, Russell Coyne, was Dr. Baang's boss.

Amber parked, and he kept close tabs on Dr. Baang as they went inside, signed her in at the lobby and went straight downstairs into the basement, where the showers were.

Amber went in with her while he waited outside. He paced, antsy. Protection detail hadn't been officially assigned, but he already knew he was going to ask Chris for the duty.

Just then his phone buzzed. "Fitzgerald," he said.

"Dr. Baang?" Chris said.

"She's showering right now with Amber watching over her. As soon as she is dressed, I was going to ask her some questions."

"Let me know when you're in the conference room, and send Amber back upstairs."

"Will do."

He opened the door to the showers and froze. Dr. Baang had just stepped out. She was wrapped in fluffy terry cloth, her shoulders glistening, rivulets of water running down her creamy skin, her dark, dark hair a wet ribbon of ink against the stark white of the towel.

She turned to look at him. With her hair slicked back, the stark beauty of her face hit him like a punch to the gut. Then he saw the dark circles under her eyes and her fatigue. She must be exhausted.

She took a breath, her slender throat working as if his eyes on her made her more…anxious. She grabbed her bags and scurried out of his sight.

He released a heated breath just as Amber spied him. "What?" she asked.

"Boss wants you back upstairs."

She turned to look toward the dressing room. "You got this?"

"Yes," he said. "I can take it from here."

He waited in the shower area for her to emerge. He heard the blow-dryer come on, then go off again after a few minutes. Finally she came out. She was wearing a pair of slim black pants. A short blue cardigan over a white cotton, long-sleeved T covered her torso, and a dark navy scarf curled around her neck. Her dark hair was pulled off her face in a low ponytail. She wore a pair of stylish, low-heeled black boots. His coat was neatly folded over her arm.

"How are you doing?" he asked.

She offered it to him and smiled. "Better, now that I'm clean, dressed and warm. Thank you for the use of your coat and taking me to the mall. That was thoughtful." She clutched the bags. "So, what happens now?"

"We're going to go upstairs, and I'm going to ask you some questions about what happened."

"And after that, I can go home?"

"Let's take it one step at a time."

She looked as if she was going to argue with him, but then walked out of the shower room to the elevator. He followed and pushed the button for the main floor.

"So, this is headquarters for NCIS?" she asked, getting out of the elevator a few moments later.

He ushered her to the right with his hand in the small of her back. "No, that's in Quantico, Virginia. This is the Major Case Unit."

"You're a special agent?" She turned to look at him as they walked close to where Beau and Amber sat working.

"That's right. He's special all right."

"Shut up, Beau," Vin said, passing by the desks on the way to the conference room. "Don't pay him any mind. He likes to pull my chain."

He looked over toward Chris's desk. "Let the boss know where we are when he gets back, would you, Amber?"

Once Dr. Baang was seated in the conference room, he asked, "Would you like something to drink or eat?"

"No, nothing to eat, but the coffee smells good."

"That could be deceptive, depending on who made it," Vin's boss said as he closed the door behind him. "Special Agent Chris Vargas."

"I remember. You were at the house a few hours ago." She gave him a look. "I'll risk the coffee. Black, please."

Vin stood and poured her a cup, brought it back to the table and set it down. She took a sip and smiled. "Must have been the good brewer."

"Beau."

"Not Amber?"

"No, I think she burns water."

Chris chuckled.

Vin sat down, and he intuitively knew Chris wanted him to take point. "Dr. Baang."

"Sky, please."

"Why don't you tell us everything that happened from the beginning?"

"I woke up when they were coming up the stairs." She trailed off and looked really spooked.

He reached out and covered her hand. "You're safe now."

She closed her eyes briefly. "They drugged me, and I woke up in that house. They had my laptop, but I'm not sure if they were able to breach my encryption. They asked me nothing because there was really no time. I escaped only minutes after I woke up."

"Our IT guys tell us that your encryption wasn't breached."

"That's a relief. Can I get my laptop back? My life is on there."

"Yes, I'll get it for you later." Her life? Really? For such a beautiful woman that made him sad. He remembered how hard his father had worked. He remembered how his father wanted him to take on corporate America and follow in his footsteps. But Vin hadn't been interested in that. He hadn't gone to Harvard or Princeton for business like his father had wanted. He'd gone to MIT and gotten a degree in computer engineering. When he was finished with his degree, he'd had to face his father again pressing him about joining him at the company and working his life away. That was when he'd told his dad that he didn't want to follow in his footsteps. But his father hadn't gotten it, so Vin had enlisted in the marine corps and took the decision into his own hands.

That single decision changed the course of his life.

He was doing work that mattered deeply to him. Protecting his country instead of making loads of money for sitting at a desk. As an agent at NCIS, he was challenged every day, involved in his job. It wasn't his life, but it was what he'd been looking for.

Chris's phone rang, and he excused himself and left the room.

"Did you get a good look at the men who took you?"

She shivered, and his hand tightened over hers. She pulled it out of his grip and wrapped her arms around her waist, her eyes going distant and scared.

"Yes, I remember the man who stuck me with a hypodermic. I only got brief looks at the other three. One of them had his back to me. I never saw his face. They were speaking Russian."

"Russian?" What the hell did the Russians want with a data-fusion scientist?

"Did you notice anything else that might help us track these men down?"

"No. I'm sorry, but I was unconscious for most of the time they held me."

"You're doing fine," he said and smiled, but that seemed to make her only withdraw more.

"I'd really just like to get this over with and then go home."

Vin captured her gaze. He knew what was going on here. She was in a state of fear, and fear made a person go for what they deemed was the safest place to them. Home. He took a breath and eased it out. "Dr. Baang, some unknown men broke into your home by bypassing your sophisticated alarm system and kidnapped you. Until we eliminate this threat to you, you won't be going home."

Her chin came up, and she stared at him, her eyes going mutinous.

"I want to go home."

"I understand that is what you want. But it's not safe. You are now under protective custody by NCIS. We're going to secure you at a safe house while we track down this threat to you and to national security."

She shifted and bolted up from her chair, her eyes a bit wild. "You cannot keep me here. You can't control me. I make my own decisions."

"You're not thinking rationally here," he said. Her emotions were running rampant. He understood that it was going to get worse before it got better. Maybe he could cut her off at the pass.

"They want your research."

"I'm sure that you're very good at your job, Agent Fitzgerald, but you couldn't possibly understand what I do."

"What? Data fusion? The process of integrating multiple data and knowledge representing the same real-world object into a consistent, accurate and useful representation? What you do is sensor fusion, specifically sensor-fusion algorithms. A way of classifying information with applications to traffic management, remote sensing, target classification and tracking, weather forecasting and, in your particular case, military and homeland security."

She stared at him for a moment, assessing, and then her lips tightened. "You're wasting your considerable talent at NCIS, Agent Fitzgerald."

He bristled. He'd heard that more than once, just recently from Brittany, his former girlfriend, who had pushed him to something bigger and better. She couldn't accept him for who he really was. She too didn't understand his commitment to what he did for a living. It had destroyed their relationship because she had no clue what made him tick. She didn't know him to his core, and, as far as he was concerned, there was no future there.

She headed for the door, and Vin went after her. Reaching for her shoulder, he tried to get her to see reason. "Dr. Baang, it's too dangerous…."

The minute his hand landed on her, she whirled around. "Don't touch me!" she seethed, holding her ground. "I don't want your help. I don't want to be in protective custody. I have a job to do, and I want to go home so that I can change and get to it."

"Dr. Baang," he said firmly, "you are not going home or to your job at this time. You are going to a safe house. You were kidnapped by unknown foreign enemies with a single purpose. To breach national security and compromise your research. Do you want that? Do you want to fall into the hands of these men again? They will not be gentle or persuasive. They will torture you, hurt you, anything to get at what they want. I am the man that's going to stand between them and you. Do you understand me?"

Her eyes were wide and so, so blue. She was breathing shallowly.

Without thinking, without analyzing or running any scenarios in his head, he reached out and pulled her into his arms. She remained rigid for a few minutes, and then she collapsed against him as if her bones just melted. Her arms went around his neck, and she buried her face into his throat, her breath still a little too fast, her arms clutching at him a little too tightly, but he was okay with that.

He would admit that ever since he'd laid eyes on her he'd wanted his arms around her, but not when she was freaking out from panic and terror. Her response was pure reaction to what she'd gone through, but he was sure there was something else there.

She clutched him and took a hitching breath. She was coming to terms with what she had to do. Understanding that she was now under his protection. Understanding that her life had been drastically changed, and there was no going back to it until he deemed it safe.

Until those men were caught and the threat to her neutralized.

Still, he couldn't help his response to her. It was unprofessional. Not strictly against the rules, but just not a smart practice. But that all went hazy when she was flush against him with full body contact.

The scent of her washed through him.

Intoxicating.

He found himself breathing deeper just to have more of her. Dumb. So, so *dumb*—the word went through his mind. He was a moron, trying to breathe her in, but damn, he loved the way she smelled. He wanted to erase that shadowed look in her eyes. He wanted her to know she was safe with him.

"This isn't the first time you've been kidnapped."

All the signs were there. The lack of trust, the need to return back to a normal routine, the irritability and the fear.

"No," she said, the word a puff of hot air against his skin.

She offered nothing else, and he didn't push her. He

would be patient and wait until she was comfortable. He wasn't her psychologist. He was her shield, her weapon. He would do what it took to keep her safe.

She pulled away, and he couldn't seem to step back, so luckily she did. She looked up at him. Raw fear stared back at him. A fear with depth, this fear had history. This was intimate fear, the kind that robbed a person of the ability to reason.

"They're going to have to go through me to get to you again."

Her eyes went glassy then, as if his concern for her undid something inside her. She nodded, then faltered. "I don't like putting myself in another person's hands. I—I've been determined that I would take care of myself."

"I know this is hard for you, but I'm nonnegotiable."

She bristled a little. "You are very high-handed, Agent Fitzgerald."

"When it comes to my duty, I'm an immovable object, Dr. Baang."

That caught at her, but she remained more defiant than pliant. "You will excuse me if I don't just skip down that path. I've had people who have told me it's for my own good, then manipulated me."

"I'm not interested in manipulating you. I'm interested in getting your cooperation so that I can protect you completely and fully. What I said about the danger, the men who kidnapped you—those are all hard facts. You're a scientist. You can appreciate that. Correct?"

"Now you're playing to my intellect."

"I'm not playing."

She sighed and sat down at the table. "I know you're

not. I know it's necessary. I guess I don't want to admit it because it scares me."

He sat down across from her and leaned forward. "Let us do our job. We'll find these guys, and then you'll be free to go home."

She nodded, looking at her hands.

"I'm going to get an artist for you, so that we can get a composite. You ready for that?"

"Yes."

"I know what you're going through."

She met his eyes. "How could you understand what I'm feeling?"

"I do. I was a marine. I know what it feels like to do everything you possibly can and still feel helpless to do what needs to be done. Maybe someday we can swap stories."

"Maybe." She lifted her chin and gave him a slight smile. He liked that most about her. She bounced back.

He left the room just as Chris finished his phone call. "Everything okay?"

"It is now. I'm going for the artist. In case it's not clear, I'm your guy for her detail—24/7."

"I can see that your mind is made up. Even though I'm the boss of this unit."

Vin straightened, taking in Chris's posture. He wasn't in the habit of challenging his superior, but in this case, there was no debate. He was going to be her guardian. "I'm the best man for the job," he said, knowing he didn't have to convince Chris that he was. "I'm one of your best agents, good both with weapons and hand-to-hand, and already have a rapport with her."

"I didn't say you weren't good, Vin. I'm just trying to decide if I can do without you."

"I can work from the safe house…or I could give up the detail for a morning on the job, if Amber or Beau took over."

"I need them both here working on this. I'll get someone to relieve you. She's the number one priority."

"The director?"

"He agrees. You've got the detail."

On his way back from the artist, Vin stopped off in forensics. "Math?"

"Yo!" a voice said from the left.

When Vin turned the corner, Justin Mathis, Math for short, was standing at his computer typing.

"I'm here for Dr. Baang's laptop. Are you done with it?"

Math left the computer and went to a metal table just behind the computer setup. Her laptop sat closed and powered down, its silver case reflecting the overhead lights. Math picked it up and handed it to Vin. "I checked it over thoroughly and found nothing out of the ordinary. It wasn't tampered with. From what I can tell, I don't think they even turned it on to try to access any of the sensitive data. Might not have been enough time, as you guys were on it so quickly. No fingerprints, either, except hers."

Vin accepted the lightweight machine. "Great, thanks. She'll be happy to have it back."

Math nodded, and with a shrewd expression, he said, "I heard she's pretty hot."

"She's stunning," Vin said, giving Math a knowing male look.

"You lucky dog," he said as he turned back to his computer. "Agents get all the chicks," he grumbled.

"Yeah, we're rock stars, if you don't mind getting shot at."

"Get back to work, rock star," Math said.

Vin chuckled as he left forensics and headed back up to the conference room. As he entered, the artist was just finishing up.

Math's words echoed in his head. She was hot, but there was more to this stunning woman than her looks. She looked up as the door opened, and her tense shoulders relaxed when she saw him. Something also eased in her eyes as if he was the one person she could depend on in a world gone mad. Her one and only guardian.

It gave him stupid ideas. He'd always been smart. Smart enough to take ahold of his life and mold it to his own goals and plans. Smart enough to do a job that required speed, skill and intellect. Clear cases, be detailed oriented. Well, he took in the details right now.

There were so many little things that added up to the big picture of her. The angles of her face delicately carved, the dusky cast to her skin that only enhanced her large almond-shaped eyes, the heartbreaking cobalt blue so striking in contrast to her ink-black hair. The cant of her chin when she was being brave. Especially that little detail. It gave him a window into the mettle of her. At first glance she looked a little on the nerdy side, awkward and unsure in social situations, but on the inside he suspected there was a core of steel.

And that genius brain had tried to take him down a peg with her intellect as a weapon. As if she was feeling the attraction and trying to fight it. Was she scared of him? Herself? Her reaction to him? He would admit he could be intense when he was interested in someone.

She had the most beautiful mouth he'd ever seen. The

curves, the hair, the eyes, the cheekbones—everything about her was gorgeous.

He let his gaze drift over her face, memorizing every curve. He held her dark-eyed gaze, and heat coiled low in his belly. When his attention settled on her mouth, she knew it. He saw her face soften, heard her slight intake of air. Whatever was going on between them, however tough she acted, she looked at him like a woman who wanted something more than protection.

He shifted and entered the room, his eyes never leaving hers. The artist was oblivious to the tension stretching out like a taut wire between them.

He was here to give her protection, and that was all. Temptation wasn't something that he'd ever had a hard time overcoming, but, in this case, he wasn't so sure. He was here to do a job.

He couldn't afford to get distracted by her kind of details.

Chapter 3

He couldn't have *stared* at her any harder. His green eyes always seemed to be intense, but moments ago she wasn't sure what had gone through his mind. All she knew was that he made her fidget and shiver.

He set her laptop down on the conference-room table as he headed toward the NCIS artist and the drawings he'd rendered from her description of the Russians who'd kidnapped her.

He'd looked at her mouth. Wait, that wasn't exactly looking. What he had done was more like consume her from a distance. He was solid, hard packed muscle. She'd leaned against all that strength when she'd been melting down into a puddle at his feet like some scared little kitten.

But she was scared. So, so scared.

And he was her lifeline. She wanted to hold on with both hands.

This was so strange. She was normally immune to men like him. Usually she just ignored the kind of man Special Agent Fitzgerald represented. Warrior. A dark and fierce warrior. And she knew them. She'd worked with the navy long enough to see them every day.

But her agent had something they didn't. Compassion and gentleness when he'd spoken to her. When he'd helped her down off the gurney at the hospital, when he'd had the forethought to let her get some dry warm clothes, when he'd held her as she broke down.

She was determined not to fall for her special-agent watchdog. She didn't have those kinds of thoughts. Relationships distracted her from her work, and she was too dedicated to make any time in her life for that kind of distraction.

She was special. She'd always been told so. It was up to her to make sure that she used her unique abilities to make a difference in the world. Sacrificing any kind of personal life was the price she had paid and would continue to pay. Both her parents had died trying to protect her, and she had to make their deaths mean something. Honor them.

So, no special-agent warrior for her.

No.

He walked up to the artist, keeping his eyes on her until the very last minute, when he addressed the guy who had coaxed the drawings out of her. As the face of the kidnapper she called Death Head materialized on paper, Sky got more and more agitated. Her thigh still throbbed from the hypodermic needle, a bruise that would darken in time until it was black-and-blue.

Fear twisted in her gut and made her limbs loose and watery. She licked her tingling lips and pushed away from the table, trying to distance herself from the drawings of the three men who had taken her from her home. She hadn't been able to describe the fourth man.

The dark memories assaulted her even as she tried to stop the images. The sound of her door creaking open, being snatched, light and shadow and men in uniforms.

Taken away from her parents as she cried. But it had done no good. They had taken her to an unfamiliar place, held her against her will, told her that she wasn't going to ever see her parents again. She'd been so little, but she remembered.

She remembered that they hadn't bothered to bring anything of hers, anything that would have made her feel more comfortable. All they'd done was told her to stop crying.

Even as she tried to clear the images from her mind, a heavy hand landed on her shoulder. She jumped and spun around, her chest heaving.

"Whoa. I'm sorry, Dr. Baang," Vin said, holding his hands up.

Trying to get her breathing under control, she closed her eyes, attempting to slow the effect of the adrenaline that had exploded into her system.

"I'm really sorry," he said, his voice low and comforting. So soothing she wanted to lean into him until she caught her breath.

"I'm just jumpy."

"It's been a rough day. How about we get you someplace safe so you can rest?"

She didn't want to, but she really had no choice. This time she couldn't call the shots because Agent Fitzgerald and NCIS were better equipped to handle her situation than she could ever hope to be. She couldn't fight off those men or protect her research, especially what was locked up in her head.

"Will you be there?" she asked, clutching his arm, cursing herself for her fear and panic. Wishing she could take the words back.

He smiled and covered her hand. It was so warm and

strong. His thickly lashed eyes focused on her, drawing her gaze to his. In the green depths was a promise. "Yes, I'll be watching over you."

Even though she was relieved, she let go of his arm. "Let me get these sketches to my teammates and we can go." He snagged her laptop and handed it to her, and she felt so relieved to have it back.

He picked up her bags as she followed him out of the conference room and back down the hall into the open area of desks. The dark-haired man, Beau, was busy studying a computer screen, and the female agent, Amber, was looking over his shoulder.

"Hey, guys. Here are the sketches. Could you run them through facial rec? I'm taking Dr. Baang to the safe house."

Beau nodded, and Amber smiled at her with reassurance. She felt some of that knot of fear subside.

These people were dedicated to helping her. Without another word, he took her arm and led her to the elevator and kept her close as they exited the building to his car. She clutched her laptop to her chest and got into the backseat of a dark sedan. After making sure she was situated and tucking the bags inside, he leaned down. His presence sent shivers over her skin.

Two men got into the car. "These are Special Agents Strong and Miller. They're going to drop you to the safe house and wait until I arrive. They're two very good agents. I'll be there shortly."

"But you said you were going to stay with me."

"I am, Dr. Baang. I just have something I need to do, and then I'll be there."

She turned around to watch him disappear as the agents drove out of the garage and out of the navy yard.

It wasn't long before they were on I-395, heading away from D.C.

"Where are we going?"

"Someplace in Baltimore."

"That's a big city."

The agent in the passenger seat nodded, but gave her no more information. She settled back in her seat. It was about an hour to Baltimore. Sky opened her laptop and checked it out. Everything seemed to be intact. They must not have had enough time to do anything to her computer. For that she was grateful. Her research on data fusion and sonar was highly classified. She was busy working on several algorithms.

She closed her eyes, and before she realized it, she'd fallen asleep. One of the agents was shaking her awake outside a brick building. She could hear gulls calling. It had started snowing. She guessed they must be close to Baltimore's Inner Harbor.

She exited the car, and the men took her into the building and to an elevator. Once they reached the top floor, they exited and moved toward one of the closed doors. Producing a key, they opened the door and ushered her inside.

Someone hit the light switch, and the door closed behind them. They locked the door, and she walked into an expansive loft, decorated in blues and greens. She went over to the big windows that overlooked the harbor with a breathtaking view.

"Are you hungry, Dr. Baang?" one of the agents asked. She thought he might be Miller.

"Yes, starving." Her stomach growled at the thought of food.

"I'll go get something. There's a sandwich shop in this building."

"A veggie on wheat, please."

"Will do."

She shrugged out of her coat, and Agent Miller took it and hung it up in the hall closet as she walked to the back of the loft, where the living room and the kitchen were located. She settled on the couch.

He turned on the TV to a local talk show. The snow continued to come down, but she'd heard on the radio that there wasn't going to be any significant accumulation.

As the sky darkened, Agent Miller came back with the food, and she ate. "Do you think that it will be possible for me to go to work tomorrow?"

The agents each looked at the other. "That will be up to Special Agent Fitzgerald, ma'am."

That sent a frisson of anger sparking in her gut. She had worked so hard to get out from under being handled, but now circumstances were dragging her right back into it. It was getting late, and she was tired. "Could you show me where my room is?"

Agent Miller rose and grabbed her bags for her and took her down the hall. "This is the master bedroom. The bathroom is right in through there. Call us if you need anything."

As she came out of the bathroom, there was a knock at her door. She walked over and opened it.

Agent Fitzgerald stood there with a couple of green suitcases. She recognized them. They looked like… hers. "What's all this?"

"Some of your things," he said. "I thought they would make you feel more at home."

Her heart pulsed in her chest and melted a bit. She just stared at him, unable to form any words. His lips curved just a little, but his gaze remained serious. "May I come in?" he asked. She stepped back. He dragged the bags past her and set them on the bed. His tie was askew, and he looked dog tired, his sexy green eyes heavy-lidded. A dark stubble coated his square jaw. She realized that he'd been up longer than she had.

She opened one bag and bit her lip. Her pillow and a throw from her bed were tucked inside. The familiar smell of her things loosened something up inside her. When she found the meditation and relaxation CDs, her heart caught again. The name of the company was printed in bold red letters across the front: Espiritu.

Her company.

"I thought they might help you to relax," he said, rolling his shoulders and rubbing at his temple.

"This was very thoughtful of you." He was close to her, too close. All six feet of pure masculinity, the hawk-like gaze and chiseled cheekbones and those breath-stealing eyes. He smelled good.

"Figured you did that yoga stuff and probably needed them."

She tried not to smile, tried to think distance. "Yeah, I like to do that yoga stuff," she said wryly. She didn't allow herself to think on it often because it was something that she'd love to do, but she fantasized about opening up a yoga studio and teaching.

She swayed toward him, and he reached out and set his hand against her waist, reacting immediately to steady her, just as he'd done so many times since she'd met him. She felt a strong magnetic pull like nothing ever before. With his closeness it made it hard to think clearly. She was too aware of his warm clasp at her waist. Thoroughly inside her personal space. Right where she wanted him most and least needed him to be.

"Sorry, if I seem a little off. I'm tired," he said, not removing his hand. "I'm not my charming self, and while I'm at it, I have to warn you that I riffled through your underwear drawer, just so you know."

That made her blush, thinking this virile man had been touching her silk and lace, those strong hands roving over her bras. It made her think about his hands roaming over her.

He flashed her a grin when his eyes wandered over her face, no doubt reacting to the deep rose tint to her cheeks.

She laughed. She was in awe that he could make her do that in the circumstances she was facing. This would be easier if he'd stayed an enigmatic hard-ass.

"I grabbed clothes, but I can't guarantee they will go together."

"I'll make do," she said.

"And your girlie stuff in the bathroom, including your blow-dryer." He reached in and smiled as he showed her the light blue machine in the bag; his hand climbed up her waist to brush her rib cage. So aware of his touch, she could barely concentrate on what he was saying.

"I'm sure every woman needs one of those. Even on the run and in hiding," he said, that smile flirting at the corners of his mouth—a beautifully sculpted mouth.

A mouth she had no business looking at.

She may be totally nerdy and truthfully had very little contact with men, but the way he was looking at her left no doubt in her mind that he was interested in kissing her. Pressing those firm, soft-looking lips against hers. Her body should be stiffening instead of feeling like liquid. Those tingles should be stopped right away, and her mind…yes…her reason… He lowered his head… Her reason should be…be…

His mouth brushed hers, his fingers tightening in the fabric of her T-shirt where his hand still rested. The hand that she hadn't even bothered to push away.

Instead, her traitorous body moved closer to him. Her hands slid up the length of his arms, her fingers digging into his solid shoulders before she cupped and caressed the back of his neck, making him gasp into her mouth. He slid his hand around to the middle of her back, gently splaying his fingers until everywhere he touched her skin, it responded with waves of warmth and tingles. He urged her against him, against his wide, hard chest. She drew her palm along his dark, stubbled jaw, the roughness there sending more sizzle through her bloodstream. The hand on her back slipped up into her hair, curling around her scalp. His other hand moved across her lower back and then his arm banded around her waist, holding her immobile.

He deepened the kiss, more pressure, more softness. His mouth moist and a little less gentle. Her breasts flattened against his chest, and she wrapped both arms around his neck.

She forgot everything, her oath, where she was, that she was being hunted, her terrible ordeal last night. She was getting lost in Special Agent Vincent Fitzgerald when she had yet to even call him by his first name or get him to call her by hers.

It was seductive on a primal level—this man was a stranger, but not quite a stranger. When he'd declared that he would be standing between her and danger, well, she couldn't stop her heart from melting into a pool in her chest. It was the first time anyone had declared they were going to protect her. Of course, her parents had tried, but they'd both lost their lives. That thought sent a shiver down her spine. Just the thought that anything would happen to him made her chest ache.

"Damn," he whispered against her lips, his breathing as ragged as hers.

His lips slid along her jaw, pressing slow, heated, breath-stealing kisses as he went. He kept her hard against him as if he was going to spend the rest of the night just breathing her in.

She buried her face in the hair at his temple, like silk against her face, then her mouth as she kissed him. As he bent to slide his lips down into the hollow of her throat, her mouth moved against his ear, and he swore low and soft when she breathed heavily, his hands tightening.

He spread his legs, bracing her against the full hard length of his body, his muscled thigh supporting her now wobbly legs.

She wanted to move against him. Wanted to give herself over to abandon, but she just couldn't seem to let go that far. She wanted it, though. His mouth on her, the hard length of him between her legs, inside her.

She was all but coming apart at the seams as he continued to drive her wild. She dragged his mouth back to her lips. He pressed his hips against her and groaned against her mouth. Then his ravenous mouth captured hers, robbing her of breath. His hot, silky tongue slipped inside. Unable to stop herself, she groaned, sucking on his tongue. He pulled away and stared down into her eyes.

She had no idea what to say as the reality of what she was doing started to crash back in. Breathless, her mouth tingling, she whispered, "Vincent—"

"Shh," he instructed, taking her mouth again, only this time in a kiss so gentle, it seduced her all over again.

She was powerless against this, against him. It was too good, and he was impossible to push away. Especially when she didn't really want the contact to end. She shut out thoughts of what would happen next and tried hard, very hard, to just enjoy this for what it was.

She kissed him back, her fingers still in his hair, toying with the thick waves as he continued. She'd stop him. At some point. Just not quite yet.

He slowed the kiss, then finally ended it. But rather than having an awkward moment when he lifted his head and looked into her eyes again, he smiled. And she was so charmed, she smiled back. He made it somehow normal, and natural, with a little hint of naughtiness in his twinkling eyes.

From the living room, someone yelled, "Fitzgerald?"

He stared at her as if he was trying to figure her out. As if she was a puzzle he needed to solve. "Okay. I'll be right there."

He lowered his voice. "That wasn't something I planned to do, Dr. Baang," he said, his voice filled with remorse.

"You should probably call me Sky."

He closed his eyes and dipped his head, letting out a hard breath. "I should actually stick with Dr. Baang. It'd be easier to keep my hands off you, which is what I should be doing instead of…this. But Sky it is when we're alone. But when we're not, it's Dr. Baang." He brushed the backs of his fingers against her cheek. "You call me Vin. Only my mom calls me Vincent."

He hadn't wanted to kiss her? Of course, this was a bad setup for both of them. He was her watchdog, and she was nothing more than a woman who needed to be looked after. She really should keep everything in perspective. But the way he'd kissed her…he'd let his guard down. Was he now sorry about that, or was he just trying to manipulate her in some way? She was much too tired for this.

"Sleep well, Sky," he said softly. "We'll be watching over you."

When he parted from her and slipped out the door, closing it with a click as he left, she could hear muttering in the hall.

She touched her tingling lips. She'd been so sheltered when she was young, never experiencing normal interaction between her peers since she entered college at ten. But now she was twenty-two and had tried sex once. It had been awkward and uncomfortable. The guy had been all over her, barely giving her a chance to breathe, let alone acclimate to being intimate. Maybe if she'd experienced the normal interaction between males and females, it wouldn't have ended in such a disaster.

He'd also been more interested in her work than he was in her. He'd tried to steal her ideas. After that terrible experience two years ago, she'd thought it best to sacrifice any personal life for her achievements. Especially after her father died in that terrible prison. She pushed back the hot rush of emotion that always pressed against the backs of her eyes when she thought about him.

So she had no business kissing Vin or enjoying any

of it. But she had. He wasn't fast or overwhelming. He'd kissed her as if it was she he was enjoying, not in a rush to get to the next thing.

That made her hot and cold all over.

She grabbed the bag of toiletries, went into the bathroom and finished getting ready for bed. After settling down to sleep, she snuggled into the mattress, her head against her own pillow, and she relaxed knowing that Vin was between her and those kidnappers.

So accustomed to waking at six to do yoga, she didn't change her routine, thankful that Vin had brought her CDs. If she wasn't doing work that could protect and serve the United States, she would choose to be a yoga instructor. She quickly pushed those thoughts out of her head. Yoga was exercise and a frivolous pursuit, not a career.

Her destiny had been set on a different path beginning when she was six years old.

After showering and dressing in the garments that Vin had brought her, she left her bedroom, trying to tamp down her eagerness to see him. But when she came out into the living room, Miller and Strong were sitting there.

"Where's Agent Fitzgerald?"

"He's at NCIS. Left about forty-five minutes ago."

Her stomach dropped. He had said he would be here for her and the thought that maybe he was saying those things just so she'd be easier to handle not only brought distrust, but anger. She knew all about manipulations and was only disgusted with herself for falling for it. She hated being *handled*. She was unschooled concerning men, especially when it came to Vin. He was confident and smooth. She had been so burned in the past. It was best she forget about holding on to him as a life-line. She should go right back to relying on herself. That lapse in her judgment needed to be chalked up to her inexperience.

"Fitzgerald."

"She's at it again, man. She's on the rampage about going to work. Insists that she be allowed."

He was actually happy to get away from Dr. Baang. He needed breathing room after last night. What had he been thinking? He hadn't been. He'd been tired, and she was so damned enticing, smelling so good, standing there staring up at him as if she knew he wanted nothing more than to kiss her damn sexy mouth.

He'd just been riffling through her unmentionables drawer, his hands all over lace and silk that had been against her body. Tiny bits of frilly, feminine lingerie that had cupped those full breasts. For a woman who dressed so simply, he had expected white everything, but no. There had been red, leopard print, blue, delicate pink and sinful black, and he felt like a freaking perv for touching it all.

And he'd lost the battle with temptation. Now in the light of day he realized that it had been a bad move, but it didn't stop him from getting sidetracked here and there thinking about her soft mouth, the way she'd breathed into his ear. Damn, he'd gotten as hard as a rock after that.

But he couldn't seem to get that comment she'd made out of his mind. That he was wasting his talent at NCIS. It could have been that she was angry and it was an off-the-cuff comment, but it brought back all the emotions from dealing with his former girlfriend and, to a more intense degree, his family.

Not to mention the impact it could have in his professional life. Getting involved with her wasn't strictly against NCIS's rules, but it was splitting hairs. She was vulnerable because she was scared, and that was something he should keep in mind. Although kissing her yesterday had nothing whatsoever to do with taking advantage of the situation. It was all about his deep attraction to her.

Vin cringed when he heard her strident voice in the background. He had been summoned here early by Chris to help Amber and Beau track down the kidnappers. But they seemed to have disappeared into thin air. Facial rec had come up with nothing.

"Really, Miller? You can't handle a five-foot-four little slip of a woman. She probably doesn't even weight a hundred and ten pounds soaking wet."

"She's tough as nails and relentless. She's been at us since you left. For three hours, man."

With derision in his voice, he interrupted. "I know. You've been calling me and interrupting me for three hours with your complaints."

Sounding completely harried, Miller said, "I'm just telling you like it is."

He sighed. "I'll come back and take care of it. Sit tight." He rose from his desk and approached Chris. "I'm going back to the safe house, and I think it's best if I stick with her from now on."

"What's up?"

He rolled his eyes. "She's giving your two agents a hard time. She wants to go to work."

Chris shook his head. "That's out of the question."

"Is it? It's a restricted area with heavy security. It might take her mind off the danger she's in."

"Are you sure about this?" One of Chris's eyebrows arched upward. "We still don't know why those guys kidnapped her or even who they are."

"I can handle her. Keep her in line. Besides, Beau is damn good and so is Amber. We work as a team. I'll take my laptop and work when I can."

With a quick flick of his wrist, Chris gestured with his thumb. "Okay, you shepherd her. I'll have Miller and Strong come back tonight to back you up."

"Hooyah." He grabbed his laptop case and shoved the machine inside and grabbed his gear. The hour drive went by quickly, and he was soon pulling into the garage. He told himself that he would have to keep himself in check. Getting in any deeper with her wouldn't be smart. He gave a quick look around as he went inside. Vigilant on the ride over, he'd seen nothing out of the ordinary.

He could hear her through the door when he got close enough. With a grin on his face for her tenacity, he knocked.

"Who's there?"

"Your relief."

"About time," Miller grumbled, opening the door looking browbeaten and sheepish.

"*Dr.* Baang, if you could just lower your voice and calm down, you'll see reason." Strong was backed against the kitchen counter, and Sky was in his face. His hands were raised as if to ward off a thug. Vin chuckled softly.

Sky's voice sliced through the air like a knife. "You are the one being *unreasonable, Agent* Strong. I've been working on important research, and keeping me holed up in this loft isn't getting the job done. My facility is so secure a gnat couldn't get past it."

Vin rubbed a hand across his mouth to hide his smile. She was a spitfire—no two ways about it. He couldn't help but admire her resolve. She had no shortage of strength or courage, even though he was sure she would disagree. "Are these guys giving you a hard time, Dr. Baang?" Miller gave him a murderous look, and Strong narrowed his eyes and tightened his lips.

She wheeled on him, her eyes blazing. "What would you know about it? You weren't here."

Miller chuckled, and Strong patted him on the back as they both hightailed it out of the apartment. "Good luck, smart-ass."

"Oh, believe me, I heard about it. I'm here now."

She folded her arms over her chest and glared at him. "I want to go to work. Why is that so—"

"Okay, I'm here to take you." He shrugged.

That snapped her mouth shut. She was more than ready to lay into him.

"You're very good at handling people. Aren't you, Agent Fitzgerald?"

"I'm here to do a job, Dr. Baang. Protecting you is my assignment," he said with a hard cast to his words. Yes, he needed that reminder. The moment he saw her, everything in him wanted to just walk up to her and... He pushed those thoughts away. "What's gotten you so upset?"

She looked him up and down. "Nothing, it seems."

Confused, he studied her face. Something was wrong. Somewhere between last night and this morning, he'd lost her. Which was actually a good thing. It was the distance he needed. But he needed her to be cooperative, too. This was going to be like walking a tight wire with no net.

He leaned against the counter and rubbed at his eyes. He really needed to get some sleep. He met Sky's gaze and tried to read what she was thinking. She didn't flinch, didn't blink, didn't smile. There were delicate purple shadows beneath her cobalt-blue eyes. But she didn't give him anything—except the impression that he'd disappointed her somehow, and she was too proud to bend beneath the weight of it.

But her disappointment in him only made him sigh. He knew about disappointing his former girlfriend Brittany and bitterly disappointing his family. "What's wrong, Sky?"

"Absolutely nothing, Vin," she said. "Except I hate being handled," she muttered under her breath, but he heard her. She better get used to it. Until this was over, he was going to be handling every aspect of her protection. She marched across to the closet and pulled out her coat and shrugged into it.

He had the stray thought of what she was wearing underneath the black trousers and the cream silk shirt with a blue raw-silk sweater over it. Most guys wouldn't even know what raw silk was, but Vin was a detail guy, and he didn't miss anything. Every nuance about this woman added up to one interesting, sexy package.

"I'm ready," she said.

He preceded her, making sure the coast was clear before they descended to the parking-garage level. The air was cold, and when he glanced back at her, he could see her breath fogging the air. She was mad. At him. Damned if he knew why and damned if he asked her again what was wrong. This was better...for both of them.

She sat in silence in the passenger seat as he made sure they weren't followed or watched. There was no one in the street. No suspicious cars, no suspicious people. Nothing to alarm him, yet there was a sense of danger that prickled on the back of his neck and twisted in his gut.

Just because he couldn't see anything out of the ordinary didn't mean there wasn't something out of the ordinary. He could chalk it up to lack of sleep. Something that he was used to not only as a marine, but also as an NCIS agent. There were times when the leads were so hot that he, Beau and Amber hadn't slept.

It was the nature of the job. Even as he turned the corner, he was studying everything around him. Looking for that one detail out of place, that one distinctive sign that would point to something amiss. But there was nothing.

Maybe he was paranoid.

He rolled his shoulders to ease that sixth-sense feeling and glanced at Sky. "I'm sorry."

She sniffed and just kept her eyes forward. "For what?"

"For whatever has upset you. I'm sorry."

She turned to look at him, her eyes softening just a tad. Then they hardened. "I just want my life back. Could you work a little harder at that?"

Okay, all her barriers were in place, tighter than they were yesterday after he'd rescued her from those bastards. Something had ticked her off. He wanted to find out what it was, but it was best that she stay mad at him. This assignment wasn't going to get any easier. Sky was an ache that settled in his gut. He couldn't give in to the temptation again. But, even though she was giving him attitude, all he wanted to do was kiss her again.

Chapter 4

He caught himself staring at Dr. Baang without even realizing he was doing it. *Not again.* He'd lost count of the times he'd looked up from his notes. He tried to force his gaze back to them but failed. He might as well forget about getting anything done; it was almost lunchtime anyway.

It was chilly outside and downright frosty in her lab. She was giving him the cold shoulder. He should be thankful. Kissing her hadn't really been a genius move. And he was a smart, dedicated agent. But she was distracting, and he couldn't seem to help it. Every time he looked at her. She didn't seem to have the same problem. She focused on her work, but he noticed that she glanced at him every so often as if she'd almost forgotten he was there. When she looked at him, her mouth tightened. He must have reminded her that she wasn't free to do as she pleased.

He had to wonder about that. She'd said her work was her life. Was that something she'd actually chosen? Or was it ingrained in her from the time that she'd been a little girl? He couldn't imagine what it must have been like to grow up in a world full of people who were older, but not smarter than her.

He liked Sky and was definitely intrigued by her. It was clear to him that she didn't really know how to interact with a man who was deeply interested in her. She was good at what she did. That was clear from the way she was immersed in her research. But she didn't seem wholly at ease in her own skin. She didn't play on her femininity like other women did, which made her only more sensual and attractive. She was so different from Brittany. Blonde, blue eyes, she was a stunning woman, and they'd been together for two years. But she hadn't understood him, not to his core. He got the gut feeling that Sky had the same kind of philosophy, which made her all wrong for him and someone he shouldn't even be looking at, let alone wanting. But there was something about her, something he couldn't seem to let go of.

The thought had tugged on his thoughts through the morning and right up until the lunch hour.

"You ready to get something to eat?" he asked.

She either didn't hear him, or she was ignoring him. He walked up to her and touched her shoulder. She jumped away and turned toward him. "Are you trying to scare the crap out of me?"

"Ah, no. I asked you a question."

"What is it you asked me?"

"Whether you were ready to get something to eat. Take a break." She looked at him as if he'd just spouted gibberish. "You do eat, don't you?"

"What kind of question is that? Of course I eat. I sometimes get caught up in my research and forget."

He decided to just let it go. She turned to her computer and secured it, and then she walked toward the door. He followed her out and to the cafeteria.

"How is the investigation going?" she asked as she chose a salad, water and some broccoli soup. He picked up a roast-beef sandwich and grabbed a soda.

"We're rerunning the sketches through facial rec. We didn't get a hit on any of those guys."

They settled at a table. "Does that mean they just aren't criminal types or wanted by the international community?"

"Doubtful. I think running them again can't hurt. Not sure if they're mercenaries or not, but from the looks of them and the way they executed your kidnapping, that would be my guess."

She picked up her fork and toyed with her salad. Her face told him she was trying to remain calm, but her fork kept moving. "What do you think they want?"

He took his eyes off her fidgety fork. "If it was your research, they would have stolen your laptop and been gone, but that's not it. They wanted you. So, it's something locked in your head."

"You don't think it's ransom or something like that?"

Now she looked agitated, and he so wanted to still her hand with his own, but touching her again wasn't a good idea. Touching led to kissing. "No. They didn't make any demands."

"Maybe there wasn't time for that," she said, looking hopeful.

If it was a money thing, maybe they wouldn't try again, and the threat would go away. She was scared. That was a given. Anyone would be scared when there were unknown foreign men trying to capture you. He wanted nothing more than to neutralize this threat to her, but he also didn't want to sugarcoat the danger she was in, either. She was just too smart for that, and talking down to Sky wasn't an effective way to get her co-operation. "There's a very slight possibility that they were after money, but I don't buy it."

"Then what do you think?"

He leaned forward, capturing her gaze and lowering his voice. "This is just my theory, and I haven't proved anything concrete right now. I'd like to get my hands on one of the men who took you to get a confirmation, but I think that they kidnapped you for a singular purpose."

"Linked to my research, then, if not the actual research?"

"Not necessarily. It could be related to your background of knowledge." There was no way he was going to drop the ball on this case. One way or the other, he was going to get to the bottom of this. He'd examine later why it suddenly meant a hell of a lot more to him than a normal case would. "Kidnappings are, for the most part, the result of a long and carefully orchestrated process. They don't happen in a vacuum. There are almost always some indications or warnings that the process is in motion prior to the actual abduction. Do you remember anything out of the ordinary?"

"I have to confess that I'm pretty vigilant," she said and took a forkful of her salad, chewing. "I have reason to be. Not only because of my sensitive and classified research."

The torment in her eyes made his heart jump a bit. "You've been abducted before."

She hauled in a tight, unsteady breath for a memory that had to be pretty terrifying.

Her gaze didn't waver, though, and he admired her for that. She was direct and intent. "Yes, when I was six after I entered kindergarten. The Chinese authorities got wind of my ability. Without my parents' knowledge, they tested my IQ. They then showed up one day out of the blue and took me right off the sidewalk in front of my house to a place that looked like a barracks. It was a special program." She had dropped her fork, her face scored by the same deep torment.

His gut twisted for her, understanding a little bit more about her life. Kidnapped at six, isolated, thrust into an adult world as a child, too smart to not understand and know that she had the potential to be exploited. No wonder she hated being controlled. "How did your parents get you back?" He clenched his fists, thinking about her being taken and used like a human computer. Bent and twisted for the Chinese government's use.

"Amnesty International. They made a huge stink. My father was Filipino and my mother was American and a lawyer. She fought it hard and there was quite a bit of fallout. The Chinese government relented and let me go home. Six months later, my mother was killed in a car accident. My father was charged with the murder. He ran, and through some family channels in the Philippines, he smuggled me out to a good friend in D.C., and they changed my name. But my father was caught, arrested and convicted. He died last year still in prison. I wanted to get him released, but he insisted that I was to go on with my life."

He should stay detached. Step away from the raw emotions churning in him, but he couldn't. Even though he'd had so much practice at it while serving in the marines. Snipers didn't have emotions. They were blank. The mission was it. That was all it boiled down to, and it was a hard-and-fast, never-take-your-eyes-off-the-ball rule. He reached out, curled his fingers around her hand and squeezed. "That must have been very difficult for you."

She stilled against his touch. "Being exploited…it's something sure to set me off." She worked her hand free and sat back as if his touch was way too distracting. "Anyway, my father's friend took me in and home-schooled me. She watched me like a hawk. I grew up always looking over my shoulder."

There was more there in her eyes, a complex emotion that tugged at his heart. He wanted her to feel comfortable enough with him to talk about it. "You saw no signs that you were being watched or followed?"

"Nothing that looked out of the ordinary to me."

"As we have noted several times in past analyses, one of the secrets of countersurveillance is that most criminals are not very good at conducting surveillance. The primary reason they succeed is that no one is looking for them. But that wasn't the case here. We're dealing with pros."

"They were very organized. In and out of my house very fast. I hid in the attic, but that Death Head leader of them heard me make a creaking noise, and he…he came up the stairs. I was trapped. I tried to fight, but he was too strong…."

"The hypodermic…" He trailed off and fell silent, getting angry all over again at the thought of anyone hurting her. "In deliberate, as opposed to opportunistic kidnappings based on financial or political motives, the kidnappers generally follow a process that is very similar to what we call the 'terrorist-attack cycle'— target selection, planning, deployment, attack, escape and exploitation."

She nodded, biting her lip. "We know they had a particular purpose. We just don't know what it is."

"I bet they were beyond pissed when you jumped out that window."

A small smile curved her lips, her eyes flashing. "He was shouting his head off and probably called me a bitch."

He chuckled. "That took guts, lady. You were quite fierce."

"Yes, I was. You had to cuff me."

He smiled again, and they shared that moment of triumph when he'd rescued her right out from under them.

She looked thoughtful, as if the wheels were turning in her head. "Kidnappers, like other criminals, look for patterns and vulnerabilities that they can exploit. Their chances for success increase greatly if they are allowed to conduct surveillance at will and are given the opportunity to thoroughly assess the security measures employed by the target," she said. "They had to have been watching me. I never saw them."

She was a fast study.

"For a high-level target like me and their apparent skill, they *must* have been a team of specialists."

He nodded. "These guys must have been good if you didn't see them. Military good. I'm still betting on mercenaries."

"That is downright terrifying to think such elite men are after me. I wouldn't have a chance against them. I know I've been contrary, Vin, but I'm glad you're here." She looked at her watch. "I should get back."

He'd finished all his lunch, but she'd left most of her salad and all of her soup.

"How about you eat a little more? The world isn't

going to crumble in the next fifteen minutes if you take the time to eat."

"You managing me again, Vin?"

"What if I was?"

"I'd tell you that I'm capable of taking care of myself better than you could imagine."

"But you're going to eat anyway, right?"

"Did you go to charm school to learn that?"

He couldn't help the smile that spread across his face at the slight give in her voice. "Yes, ma'am, I was at the top of my class."

She laughed and shook her head. "I bet you were."

At the end of the day when they got back to the loft, Miller and Strong were already there, ready to relieve him so he could sleep.

After taking care of their stomachs, she retreated to her room with her laptop in tow. He watched TV with the two agents and then turned in himself while they watched over them both.

He wasn't sure what woke him up. But the moment he was awake, fully awake, a trick he'd learned as a sniper, something didn't feel right. Something was wrong.

He pushed himself out of the bed soundlessly and slipped on his clothes. Reaching for his firearm was automatic—a SIG Sauer DAK with a reset trigger that required very little pressure to fire. Racking the slide and chambering a round was deliberate, something he usually did before he fell asleep. Marines were always prepared, even ex-marines.

But he'd been thinking about Sky and her unmentionables. On her, off her, which he'd hoped to hell wasn't indicative of the way things were going to be, that he'd be so preoccupied he wouldn't be able to think straight. When he was guarding someone, he did not fall asleep without his gun cocked, locked, loaded and less than an arm's length away.

He started toward her bedroom door when he saw Miller's body sprawled in the hall, his throat open and blood still spreading away into a pool around his head.

Adrenaline instantly drop-loaded into his veins, switching on every survival and protective instinct he had. He tightened his hold on the SIG, bringing it up, wrapping his right hand around his left on the gun's grip, his gaze raking the area.

He went into sniper mode. He couldn't think about Miller's pretty wife or his two kids, who would have to grow up without their father. He released everything except his senses, his reflexes honed to a razor edge.

The hall was clear and Skylar's door was closed. He ran his gaze over Miller again and caught a glimpse of a polished shoe just jutting out from the edge of the wall. *They got Strong, too,* he realized.

He listened for a breath, for a step, for any little snick of sound that would tell him where the killers were, where Sky was, hopefully still *here*.

Damn. If she'd been taken from the loft, the odds of him finding her this time were small. They would have made sure of it.

Then he heard it, the sound of keys on a keyboard being pressed, and relief flooded through him.

Vin saw a shadow slide across the window in the living room, and he moved to intercept, silently, quickly, across the open wooden floor. He was waiting for the bastard, his knife now in his hand, when the guy came around the wall.

Shooting him with the SIG would have done the job, but the gun was loud. The noise would alert any other kidnappers who were in the loft or outside.

The loft was big, took up a lot of floor space with many closed doors.

The five-inch deadly KA-BAR blade was just as efficient and far quieter, but there was always the possibility that the guy would fight back. Which he did, instantly countering Vin's attack.

Vin could feel the man's desperation as he struggled, but Vin had no sympathy and no remorse. The son of a bitch was fighting for his life, just like Vin would have. But this guy had killed Miller and Strong in cold blood.

The kidnapper got in a good hit with his elbow, catching Vin right in the damned bullet graze on his side. White-hot pain flashed over him like a brand. Stars sparkled in front of his eyes, but he didn't make a sound, didn't let go and didn't let up. The guy bucked and struggled, until Vin body-slammed him hard into the doorjamb and stunned him enough to wrestle him to the floor. He got in one deep cut to the guy's gut and jerked the blade upward—hard.

As added insurance, Vin grasped the kidnapper's head and twisted, hard and fast, breaking the guy's neck. The sound was clearly identifiable. He heard the snap loud and clear.

So did Sky.

Her gasp brought his head around.

She was standing in the ambient light from her open bedroom door, staring right at him, frozen in shock. The look of horror on her face did absolutely nothing to ease the rush of adrenaline coursing through him, jacking him up. He knew he looked fiercely violent, kneeling on a guy he'd just brutally killed. The guy had gone down, and except for whatever screwup had tipped the guy off and the resulting grappling around, Vin had taken him down almost without a sound. If there were other gunmen in the loft, they didn't know he was on the hunt.

But they would have heard her soft cry. It was quite audible, and when he saw a shadow materialize behind her, he drew his SIG, his knee still firmly in the dead kidnapper's back.

Sky's eyes widened, the blood draining from her face. He would have to make the time to explain to her that when a man pointed a gun at her, that was her cue to run, duck, drop down and grab some real estate. The deer-in-the-headlight stare would only freeze her in place for a kill shot. But it was all over before she could have moved. The kidnapper brought up his own automatic weapon, but Vin was already squeezing the hair trigger twice on his weapon, rapid-fire—precise heart shots. The guy dropped like a stone behind her.

Well, that would do it. He'd just alerted anyone in the vicinity that someone was discharging a firearm. More likely any backup baddies waiting for their buddies to capture Sky and haul her out of there.

Aiming at the unmoving guy's head, he rose to his feet and, standing between the man and Sky, fired off another bullet. He wasn't taking any chances.

In the next split second, he grabbed her arm, rushing her down the hall and away from the light before she could get her mouth closed. Holding her close, he shielded her off to his right side, and, as he passed, he squeezed off another head shot into the first kidnapper he'd killed. Neither of the bastards was ever getting up again.

Turning her around, he hustled her toward the front door. He took a few precious minutes grabbing their coats. Jamming his feet into his shoes, he urged her toward hers.

Shrugging into his coat, his hand on the knob, he waited until she had her boots on, then her coat. He pulled her out into the hall and raced toward the elevator, but stopped dead when it dinged, her small body slamming into his back. Reinforcements?

He wasn't going to wait to find out. He headed toward the stairwell, but when he started to go down, he heard voices. They had effectively blocked all paths out of the building. There was only one way to go. Up.

He switched directions, and she stumbled with a soft cry. The voices got more agitated, and it was easy to make out the Russian clearly.

Clasping her hand tightly in his, he gave Sky a quick glance. She was still in shock, her face white, her expression dazed.

He was moving too fast for conversation, which was just as well. The past few minutes had been pretty intense. He was in full-out battle mode, and all his survival instincts were kicking in. In the back of his mind he was aware this situation was completely outside her realm of experience. But there was no time for questions, emotions, fear or her shock right now. It was time to move and keep moving until he had her safe. If they were caught... Well, he didn't want to think about that.

When he hit the door to the roof, he pulled her behind him and waited, listening and trying damned hard to hear anything beyond her breathing. Sky was hyperventilating. There wasn't anything he could do about that now, except say under his breath, "Try to calm your breathing."

She started and made an effort. He heard nothing behind the roof door or anything that indicated they'd placed someone on the roof.

It really didn't matter. He had no choice—he was going through.

He'd cased this whole area from top to bottom. He knew where the ladder to the fire escape was from the roof. He knew there was a renovation of the second half of the building going on, and that building butted up against this one.

He could only hope they didn't have the roof covered. If he was planning this job, he would have made sure there was no way for his quarry to get away. That meant a sniper.

He pulled the door open just a crack and swore. It was snowing—no, dammit, that was freezing rain, the soft whoosh of the tiny ice balls loud in the night. The roof looked icy. A gust of frigid wind blew into the hallway and froze him to the bone.

He reached into his pocket and pulled out a black knit hat. He slid it over her head and cupped her face gently. "We're going out. Hold on to me."

She nodded, terror in her eyes, but he felt the courage in her fingers as she grabbed his forearm and squeezed, nodding.

He couldn't hesitate. They were right behind them. He grabbed her hand and stepped out onto the roof, slamming the door behind them. Hitting it three times with the butt of his pistol, he tried to jam the lock. His eyes on the fire-escape ladder, he took off at a run, hoping like hell they didn't go careening off the roof, or this would be over very quickly.

The cold went through her, knocking her backward a little as she stood on her feet. She gulped in a great lungful of frozen air, and the pain of it almost dropped her to her knees.

The roof was slick with ice, and she felt almost sick with the sudden, awful cold, but he wouldn't let her slow down for an instant to catch her breath.

Lungs burning, heart pounding, she held tight to his hand. He wasn't even breathing hard, and she could hardly breathe at all. He still had the gun in his hand. Hadn't once let down his guard and was aware of everything. She trembled, her stomach roiling after what she'd just seen.

Then she heard a ping above the sound of the rush of sleet. When he grunted, something wet and warm splashed onto her face.

Someone was shooting at them! Vin was hit!

He dragged her behind him, turning in one fluid motion, and the gun in his hand recoiled three times. There was a cry, and then he was running again as if his blood didn't decorate her face.

She was trying with all her might to keep her terror at bay, but he never hesitated; everything he did was calm, collected and precise.

Sure-footed, he raced across the roof, through a maze of air conditioners, ventilation equipment and a blinding, swirling mess of sleet, keeping her firmly in tow as she lost traction several times, but he steadied her. She had to keep her feet under her, or they would be caught. She didn't want to think what would happen to Vin.

A banging came from behind them and then a crash as the sound of the door thumping open had him making a sudden, lightning-quick change of direction. Her boots slid again, and she slipped, landing against him with enough force to send them both tumbling.

"Hold on!" he ground out through clenched teeth, falling into a slide and taking her with him, his arm coming around her.

Sky went down on top of him, and the two of them careened across the roof, heading for the edge, her heart in her throat. He scrambled to try to slow their momentum as they slid out of control. A low wall kept them from going over, but he couldn't stop their slide, and they ended up jammed behind a ventilation unit in a tangled heap of arms and legs.

In the middle of scrambling to his feet, he suddenly froze, still on his knees, and pulled her tight against him with his gun hand, his other hand going over her mouth.

She heard it, too, the sound of someone approaching, footsteps crunching through the ice, slip-sliding every few steps.

He caught her gaze, his warning clear. *Don't move, not a muscle.*

She gave a short nod and saw that the shoulder of his coat was torn, and blood, wet and slick, soaked the leather.

The second time he'd gotten shot for her.

She shivered with the awful thought that something would happen to him. This vibrant man who had done unspeakable things to keep her safe. This man's skill and cunning was all that stood between him and certain death. They wanted her alive, but they would surely kill him in a blink of an eye.

Something inside her would die if that happened.

She stayed kneeling with him, facing him as he slowly and silently lifted his arm from around her waist and, with a one-handed grip, pointed the gun toward the opening they'd slid through. If anyone rounded the ventilation unit, they were going to be looking straight down the gun's barrel.

She shivered with the aching cold. It had to be close to zero, the sleet changing over to snow falling in endless, white waves from the sky, as the Russians came closer.

Another shiver racked her. Her feet felt frozen in her boots, and she didn't even want to think about her knees. Her ears were so cold they burned. Her teeth started to chatter.

Without a word, Vin removed his hand from her mouth and reached down to open his coat. In seconds, she was wrapped inside, his body heat soothing her skin.

He was so, so warm. She looked up at him, but his eyes were on that crucial opening, his muscles taut and ready. Her heart slipped and plummeted straight down to her toes. Something she'd never felt in all her life ached inside her. She looked up at him and knew courage, determination. She'd never be able to look at him again and not think this man was a hero.

A warrior.

Steadfast, tough and true.

She shivered, but this time the cold had nothing to do with it.

He put his mouth close to her ear, his warm breath sending sparks into her blood, and whispered. "I want you to stay here. Whatever you hear, whatever you do, do not move. Are we clear?" His voice was hard and unwavering.

She nodded.

He rose in one fluid movement, and his heat was gone. He moved to the end of the ventilation shaft, gave a quick glance around it, then looked back at her. There was that fierce look again, the one he'd had on his face when he'd killed the first kidnapper with his knife. He reached into his pocket and pulled that knife out and opened it.

He crouched and disappeared into the shadows and the blowing snow. Her heart felt crushed as she knelt in the frigid weather and didn't move a muscle.

Sky stayed on her knees, stayed exactly as he'd told her to. He would come back for her. He would.

It was what she'd believed when she'd been snatched from her parents. They had come back for her.

But she'd still lost them.

Chapter 5

He stepped around the ventilation shaft. The lingering feel of Sky wrapped around him, her shivering, her being in danger spurred him on. He had to get her off this roof, out of the cold and someplace safe.

There were three of them with those snub-nosed machine guns. Three semiautos to his one handgun. One of them peeled off, and that left two hanging around the ladder. Their only escape. He let the third man do his searching and flushing, the snow helping to give him some much-needed cover, the night black. It looked as if the power had been knocked out. No streetlights, either.

When he and Sky had first burst through the door to the roof, he'd assessed in seconds the best place for that damn sniper they'd put on the roof as an insurance policy to take out anyone with Sky. It was just a matter of taking a bullet to the shoulder. But that had given him the guy's location, and his dead-eye aim and the SIG had done the rest.

He'd been the best shot in his marksman class at Quantico. Best in the corps. He was very glad about that tonight as he'd held her trembling body.

Vin still needed to up the odds more in his favor.

He also had a feeling there was another man lurking

around, using the snow as cover just as Vin was using it. Even though he couldn't see him, he could feel it in his bones.

His shoulder throbbed, but luckily there was no bullet lodged in there. It hadn't quite grazed him, though. It was more of a through and through on the fleshy part of his shoulder, missing both the bone and the joint, thank God. He moved his arm and absorbed the pain. He wouldn't let the agony impede him while Sky's freedom was on the line.

Vin crept forward, crawling on the frigid roof to get as close as he could to the sniper. He would lose the cover of the snow, but by then he would be close enough to do lethal damage.

When he was only a foot away from the first guy, he rose up off the roof, grabbed him around the neck and dragged the knife across his throat.

The second man jerked around and brought up the semi, but Vin was already squeezing off two shots right to the guy's heart.

The fourth man materialized out of the snow, and he had Sky. His arm was around her throat, and he was dragging her, her feet sliding along the roof. His first instinct was to charge at the man who had her, but he knew they weren't going to hurt her. They wanted her alive. He tamped down his impulse to maim. He needed a cool head to get them out of this.

He squared his shoulders as the third man came running, but that wasn't a good idea, as Sky and he had found out only minutes ago.

The kidnapper lost his footing. Going down hard, his body hurtled toward the fourth kidnapper and Sky. Sky was taken down as her legs went out from under her, and she hit the roof with a jarring thump. The move distracted the fourth guy as Vin took his own running start, and when that semi came up, he went to the deck, folding his leg under him. As he was propelled forward, sliding on his knee and shin, bullets whizzing over his head, he depressed the trigger rapid-fire. The guy dropped to the roof and lay still. Vin used one hand as a fulcrum to whip around, and even as the third guy was scrambling to get up on the slippery ice, he put three into him: two to the heart and one in the head.

Ejecting his magazine, he reached into his coat pocket, pulled out another one and jammed it into the gun. He waited a couple of seconds to make sure these were the only guys around, but when there was no activity, he exploded into motion.

Certainly there were more around, and the shots would bring them.

Rushing over to Sky, his heart pounding with more adrenaline, concern that she wasn't moving with each rapid beat, he reached down to her, but she was unresponsive. She must have hit her head. He couldn't hang out until she woke up.

He crouched and lifted her into his arms, then slung her over his shoulder, capturing her legs with his arm and completely ignoring the searing pain that shot into his chest from his wounded shoulder. Behind him, he heard voices.

Taking off at a careful run, he headed for the north side of the building and the ladder rail he'd seen curving over the edge. There was no way to the street from the roof other than this access. And the building next door would provide him with plenty of places to hide.

Now all he had to do was get down the ladder while

carrying her without dropping her or losing his grip or footing.

After all he'd been through tonight, that sounded like the easiest part so far.

Sky woke slowly. There was a pressure in her middle she didn't understand, and she was swaying. When she opened her eyes, she found herself upside down and hanging from...Vin's shoulder. She looked down and wished that she hadn't. It was so, so dark and empty, her stomach twisted.

To top it off, he didn't have his hands on her—anywhere. He was balancing her as he descended the ice-slick ladder.

She latched on to the back of his coat, and he wobbled a bit. "Whoa, there," he said. "Slow movements, sweetheart. Nice and slow."

Her frozen fingers gripped his coat with every ounce of strength she had left, which wasn't much.

Her head pounded, and she remembered abruptly that she'd been caught and dragged out to where Vin was, but he'd already taken down two of the kidnappers. Then she'd been...knocked down. That last image she remembered was Vin, sliding on the ice and pumping the man who had been holding her with lead.

Okay, she might just have to reassess the whole hero thing.

More like superhero.

"Can you put me down?"

"Not yet. We're still not out of the woods. They're going to be coming down this ladder after us. They're not going to give up. We've got to get the hell out of here."

He slipped on a rung, and her heart, which was already lodged in her throat, stopped for a long, painful second until he steadied himself.

It was a long, cold drop. Even squinting against the snow, she couldn't see the end. He just kept moving at a quick pace.

She started to tremble deep down inside, her body shaking, and a strong arm immediately went around her legs—which meant he had only one hand left on the ladder. That made her stomach plunge.

"I'm not going to let you fall," he said, his voice brusque but composed. She didn't feel at all composed. She felt scraped and frozen and raw. Fifteen minutes ago she'd been calm and warm, gratefully tapping away on her laptop.

Shit! Her laptop had been left behind.

He stepped down off the ladder onto solid footing, and relief flooded through her. She hadn't died...yet.

But nothing else was right. Nothing. The night had spiraled out of control—and the only thing that could keep her free of those men was staying reasonable and smart.

He bent his knees and gently pulled her off his shoulder, grimacing and groaning softly in pain. But he didn't let her go. He supported her with his arms around her until she steadied. Her head was really hurting right at the temple.

"Can you walk?"

"I think so."

"Can you run?"

"Now you're pushing it."

Before she could say a word, he picked her up in his arms, clenching his jaw hard against what had to be more pain from his shoulder wound. He started moving into the half-finished building, taking the stairs, still not even breathing hard. She was still trying to catch her breath. She was so, so cold.

When he hit the street level, he paused and looked around.

There was the sound of sirens in the distance coming from different directions. The police. That gave her a measure of relief. Vin didn't seem to care. He set her down, slipped his arm around her waist and pulled his gun again. Keeping it to his side, he started moving with her slowly, his eyes darting everywhere.

As he approached the parking garage, he slowed and pressed them back against the wall until he had a moment to check everything out. Cautiously, he moved forward, and as they sprinted toward the car, she was finally going to breathe a sigh of relief. There would be warmth and safety.

Then out of nowhere Death Head slammed into Vin and tore him away from her as she went spinning toward one of the parked cars. Her hip exploded with pain, and she gasped, trying to regain her balance.

She understood why he hadn't used his gun. She and Vin had been way too close together. He must have been lying in wait here for them.

Vin brought the gun up, but the Russian delivered a stunning blow to his wounded shoulder, and Vin cried out and doubled over. Death Head knocked Vin's gun away, and it went skittering under a car. He punched Vin in the face, and he flew back and hit the concrete pavement hard, the air exploding out of him in an audible rush. Death Head didn't hesitate. He straddled

Vin and grabbed him by the throat with both hands and started to squeeze.

Vin fought hard, going for the guy's eyes and trying to break his hold. Still dizzy from getting her head slammed into a hard surface, she frantically looked around for something, anything, to save him.

She saw a chunk of rock that had broken away from one of the parking barriers. She half shambled, half ran for it. Grasping it in her hand, she turned and rushed to him. Clasping the concrete in a tight knuckled hold, she slammed the rock into his head.

He slumped forward onto Vin, who then pushed him off, gasping for breath.

Sirens blared, but Vin was up and grabbing her hand. He paused to reach for his gun, and then he was tugging her along to the car. Once inside, he started it and pulled out of the parking space. He drove for the exit, passing a cruiser coming in the opposite direction.

Gasping for breath, reeling from the sudden adrenaline and shivering from the cold, she reached for the heat with numb fingers. As he went around a corner, she saw the sign for the interstate out of Baltimore.

He drove through the wind-driven snow strafing the windshield as the car warmed and her skin tingled and burned with returning feeling. She was starting to feel every bump and bruise.

She looked over at Vin, but he was focusing once again, looking tough and fierce as he drove, the bruises from Death Head's hands discoloring the skin of his throat, the blood on his coat looking dark, almost black, against the brown leather.

The heat didn't seem to reach her or even begin to thaw the core of her, even though it blasted across her face. She was numb with panic. *Terror* was really too mild a word to describe the emotion that had taken hold of her heart.

"Wha-t-t-t are we-e-e going to-o-o do now?" She shivered uncontrollably.

"Run like hell."

As soon as he saw the Walmart, he pulled into the parking lot and cut the engine. He closed his eyes for a moment and leaned his forehead against the wheel. His throat hurt; his jaw and his shoulder hurt. The adrenaline rush was over, and that left a heavy, lethargic fatigue that ripped at him.

He needed patching up and sleep. A lot of sleep, but that wasn't going to be possible for some time, so the next best thing would be caffeine. He knew exactly where they were going to go and no one would know about it but the two of them.

The safe house had been compromised. How, he couldn't know. But his only thought was it had to have been insider information. Now there wasn't anyone he could really trust with the information of their whereabouts. Not even his boss.

That left only one thing to do. Run like hell, just as he'd told Sky.

Run and disappear.

When Vin raised his head and looked at her, she was staring at him, and two things registered in his tired brain. She was scared, so, so scared, and she was a lovely mess, her hair damp with snowflakes glistening and melting in the inky black, her cheeks pale, mascara smudged beneath her eyes—but still so beautiful it was all he could do to drag his gaze away from her.

Then as he stared at her something soft came into her eyes, and for a moment their gazes locked and the windows in the car fogged. He dragged his attention away.

Not good, he thought, taking in a deep breath that was full of pain, to his heart, his neck, his shoulder. The look in her eyes made his heart tremble and roll over. It could be that she was just grateful for what he'd done for her tonight. It could be that. He wanted it to be that so he wouldn't have to think about what that look said to him. Because resisting her was getting tougher. He knew it was the right thing to do. But he'd made a tactical error, a rookie mistake. He'd already kissed her. He already knew what she felt like, tasted like. He was already a goner. The big, bad ex-marine was a fucking goner. "Give me your phone."

He wasn't going to kiss her again, no matter what she looked like, how she looked at him, no matter how poleaxed he felt. Hell, he could hardly breathe, and kissing her wasn't what this was all about. She was a target. A designated target. She needed protection, and that was his mission, his assignment. Protect and serve. For his duty was all about the navy's best interest, a life put in his care.

A precious, brilliant life.

"What?" she said, snapping out of that dazed look.

"Your phone."

She looked at him but pulled it out of her pocket, setting it into his hand. His gut twisted with the depth of her trust. He pulled his out of his pocket and dialed.

He pushed the speaker. "Vin! Are you all right? Dr. Baang?"

"We're both still alive, but a bit banged up."

"You left more than enough bodies in your wake."

"I did what I had to do." His throat tightened, and pressure built on the backs of his eyes. He massaged them with his thumb and forefinger. "Chris, I'm sorry about Miller and Strong. They were good men."

"They were good. But you all did your job and protected Dr. Baang. They gave their lives for her safety."

Sky gasped softly, and he glanced at her. Her eyes glistened, and she covered her mouth, her face crumpling.

"Where the hell are you?" he said.

"Getting her out of Baltimore. Away," he growled, his voice thick.

"What? Bring her in to NCIS. We'll get her to another safe—"

Anger streaked through him, settling into his gut. "No way, Chris! Someone gave away her position. Someone had to. There were only a handful of people who knew where she was. You need to get someone on that!"

"Don't you argue with me, Special Agent Fitzgerald! Get your ass back here!"

His boss was reminding him who was in charge, but the marines and NCIS had taught him that sometimes disobeying an order was the right course of action. The navy was all about freethinkers, and he was freaking freethinking right now. "I'm ditching the phones," he said with finality, and Chris swore again. "I'll contact you when we're safe."

"Agent Fitz—"

He cut his boss off, quickly disassembling the phone and tucking the SIM card into his coat pocket. He did the same with her phone.

"You stay put. I'll be right back." He gritted his teeth as he shrugged out of his ruined coat, excruciating pain radiating out from the bullet wound down his arm, across his chest and into his back. Throwing it into the backseat, he grabbed his NCIS jacket. They would track the phones here anyway, so broadcasting that he was an agent wasn't going to compromise anything. Tucking the gun into the holster at the small of his back, he exited the car and headed for the Walmart. Once inside, he dumped both phones and batteries into the trash. He bought prepaid phones, caffeinated drinks, water and gauze bandages. He headed back out to the car, the blowing snow icy against his exposed skin.

Getting back into the car, he handed her the bag, which she set at her feet, and then he stripped off his coat, his sweatshirt and the T-shirt beneath. "There's a roll of gauze in the bag. Could you give me a quick field dressing?"

While she made fast work of wrapping his shoulder, he popped the top of one of the cans and sucked the liquid down, then another one. After she was done, he put his clothes back on and handed her the water. "Drink something. We'll get food when we get to where we're going."

She took the water and pulled off a bottle. "Where are we going?"

He turned to look at her, determination like a promise. "Somewhere safe."

She didn't say anything. Another sign that she trusted him.

She raised the bottle to her lips and took a long swig.

He downed another can of energy drink and put the car in gear.

When the phone went dead in his ear, Chris swore low and viciously beneath his breath. Vin was going to do this his way. He looked down at the bodies of Tom Miller and Mike Strong. Two good men. This whole thing was a disaster. Then he looked at the two men who were sprawled in the hallway where Vin had left them. There were four more up on the roof being brought down and another one over on an adjacent roof.

That one had astounded him. A fifteen-foot shot in the dark of night with a handgun.

Vin was a deadly son of a bitch.

Chris had been a navy pilot. He had been trained in hand-to-hand, but let's face it, he rarely had used that in the air. It wasn't until he got into NCIS that he'd honed that part of his training, but what Vin had done to those two kidnappers... His shots were so precise. The guy with the slugs in him had been tapped right in the heart. The M.E. said his heart was gone. Exploded. But he'd followed up with head shots.

Thorough.

He'd picked the right agent to cover Dr. Baang. Had Vin been right? Had someone from NCIS leaked the location? Vin's account of that was accurate. But still, he hadn't liked that he'd gone rogue. He'd better call in and update him, or Chris was going to have his lethal ass in a sling.

He walked down the hall, stepping over the dead kidnapper, and went into Dr. Baang's room. Her laptop was sitting on top of her bed. He reached down and picked it up. It was interesting that the kidnappers hadn't snagged it.

He tucked it under his arm and headed out of the loft and back to NCIS. Once those bodies arrived, his forensic M.E. would be mighty busy.

DNA, tattoos, dental records—maybe they could get at least one hit on one of these guys and see what they were up against.

What Vin was up against.

Alexander Andreyev wanted to kill someone with his bare hands as the black SUV pulled up to one of their safe houses in D.C. He exited the vehicle, fuming. That NCIS bastard! He wanted a name to go with the agent. He wanted to know who he was up against.

"Dmitry, find out who that agent is."

"Da," Dmitry said, turning to his computer.

The agent had taken out seven of his guys, and now he was going to have to get more over here to finish this job. The people who'd hired him wouldn't pay a dime if they didn't deliver the woman alive. But finding her was an iffy ploy. He could only hope that she was as predictable as his employer thought she was.

Or this job was over and he'd have to cut his losses.

Snarling, he kicked over the coffee table and closed his eyes against the pain in his head. "Get me something for a headache and some ice," he growled at one of the men poring over a map on the dining-room table.

Looking at a map wasn't going to help them find the female scientist.

This mission had taken months of planning, and the execution had gone like clockwork. He himself had found her hiding in the attic and drugged her.

But she had been resourceful, and he'd underestimated her. And in the parking garage when he'd had her protector beneath his hands choking the life from him, she'd blindsided him. He wouldn't underestimate her again.

He looked at his watch. They had a deadline, and time was running out.

Vin drove through the heavy snow, his shoulder throbbing and a weakness stealing over him. Probably from the blood loss. When the caffeine hit his system, it was like a surge of jet fuel in his bloodstream and it pumped him up. But he knew it was an artificial high from the drinks and the receding adrenaline. By the time the snow let up after about an hour out of Baltimore, his shoulder was on fire. "We're going to a fishing cabin near Newport, Pennsylvania, on the Juniata River," he said to reassure her and distract himself from the shooting pain in his shoulder.

"So we're going to rough it?"

"Not quite. I've packed a bag for both of us, got a thousand in cash. Marines call it a 'battle pack.' We'll be fine for a bit. Until we can get a lead on these bastards."

Staying on I-83, he made Harrisburg, starting to feel light-headed a bit, his shoulder now in agony because of the damaged nerve endings. Crossing over the Susquehanna River, navigating through the maze of the I-81 interchange and ending up on Route 322, he skirted the Susquehanna. They crossed over it again as it split into one of its tributaries—the Juniata River.

After a two-hour trip, he turned off onto a heavily wooded road and ended up at a cedar-and-glass cabin.

By then, his wound was burning, sending prickling pain with each beat of his heart, each movement.

He was moving slowly as he exited the vehicle,

meaning to go to the trunk and get their battle packs out, but his knees buckled.

Sky rushed around the car and caught him as he clasped the door for support. "The bags," he managed to say.

"Forget them for now. Let's get you inside."

"The med kit is in mine."

"Inside first, Vin. Then we'll get you taken care of. Stop being a hero for just a few minutes."

He grimaced and met her concerned gaze.

She supported him as they headed to the porch, and his hand trembled as he fitted his key in the lock. He pressed his hand against the doorjamb as she pushed the door open.

"Wow. This is gorgeous. There's no roughing it here."

"Belongs to a buddy," he managed. "He's deployed and lets me use it anytime I want."

She helped him inside, and she headed straight to the bathroom and deposited him onto the commode. "I'll be right back."

"I don't like you going back outside without me to cover you."

"What's going to attack me out here? The squirrels?"

He leaned his head back against the wall and laughed, feeling as if he was losing it a bit, but unable to let down his guard.

When he opened his eyes, she was gone, and he tried to stand but clutched at his shoulder as he collapsed back against the tank.

He closed his eyes again, for just a minute. The soft touch of the backs of her fingers against his face made his eyes pop open. Had he fallen asleep? He couldn't have. He couldn't leave her unprotected. He went to rise, but she kept him in place with just the soft touch on his skin.

"It's okay," she said softly. How did she do that, make him breathless? He'd run up stairs today, across an icy rooftop, took out six dangerous men toting semiautos, and here he was, trying to catch his breath.

Her exotic eyes were assessing him, her expression a bit tight, but not quite so strained as it had been in the loft or on the roof, as if she knew that, for a while, everything was going to be all right.

Watching her, his eyes went over her face, slowly, settling on her mouth.

He wasn't going to kiss her.

He was so glad he got that straight in his head. So little was straight in his head right now. He was so tired. But they were safe here, and he could rest.

The sound of water intruded into his thoughts. He turned his head. The water was running from the sink faucet. She had the med kit open.

She filled a glass that she must have brought from the kitchen and shook out several white tablets from the bottle of painkillers.

"Take these," she said softly, a slight tremor in her voice.

"Yes, ma'am," he said, falling to his military training as he sank deeper into a dazed kind of sensation, feeling disconnected. Was he crashing or was it her?

After dutifully swallowing the pills, he closed his eyes again to try to clear his head.

The feel of the terry washcloth was warm against his skin as she gently cleaned off the blood around a particularly nasty gash. As he opened his eyes, she was close, her eyes so blue, her fingers against his chin, tilting his head so she could get to the blood on the side of his face, right at the curve of his jaw. Her touch was as warm and as her blue eyes. With every breath she took, an irrepressible longing was building inside him, making his chest tight.

There was a bloody smear at her waist, but he knew she wasn't hurt. He'd gotten the blood on her. There were several times he'd gotten blood on his hands and then grabbed her. She had blood on her shoulder, too. A handprint—his.

"You okay?" he asked. He was a seasoned agent and an ex-marine. He had been a scout sniper, saw heavy and unrelenting battle where death stalked him and had seen many men die at his hands. He'd learned how to handle battle fatigue, stress and soul-deep fear and knew how to put all that he had seen into perspective so that it didn't mess with his head. Even with all of that, he'd been scared down to the bone tonight. But Dr. Skylar Baang was a sheltered, naive and cerebral innocent.

She blinked several times and gave him a wry look, dabbing antiseptic ointment on each cut, then setting butterfly bandages carefully to minimize his pain. "I'm not the one who's been shot twice, punched out and strangled," she said. Her thumb slid across his jaw in a slow, deliberate caress. Did she even know that she was doing that as if she couldn't seem to help herself?

"I'm not talking about physically." Why did he have to get himself on that train of thought? He needed to derail it, but it was too late and the fight was draining out of him.

He had to wonder what she was wearing underneath that conservative plain white button-down. The hint of blue strap flashed as she moved. That turquoise number, edged in white and lime-green lace, with a matching set of panties and that little lime-green bow centered right in the middle.

"I'm okay for now," she said, hooking her thumb over the hinge of his jaw and tipping his head back. Setting the washcloth down, she reached into the med kit and picked up a tube of liniment. Squeezing out a generous amount onto her fingers, she rubbed it against the tender bruises of his neck in slow, soft caresses.

"My head hurts a little at the temple where I fell. But I'll take something for it as soon as you are...ah... handled."

"Ha!" He laughed. "Funny, Doctor." He let his breath go in a heated rush. He shouldn't have thought about her in a physical way. Damn him.

Now that they were safe and he was getting tended by her, his thoughts went where he didn't want them to go. Everything was falling into place in a little bit different order, stacking up to one undeniable truth: he wanted her.

Chapter 6

She was in his sights in a way that was impossible to ignore, deep down in his gut, visceral. When he'd opened his coat and invited her inside, it was because she was freezing—all part and parcel of the whole badass-protector thing. Keep her safe in every way. But she'd looked up at him, and he'd suddenly noticed everything about her—the thickness of her lashes and the softness of her breath, the paleness of her skin and the racing of her heart, and he'd wanted her.

She was off-limits for so many reasons. But he couldn't seem to bring any of them to the forefront of his mind right now.

She had shown a lot of courage tonight, and she had saved his life. That bravery and quick-thinking action was the reason he was here right now. His charge had become his guardian angel. That tied him up in knots. Just watching her breathe made his skin hot.

He was supposed to guard her, not touch her, getting his mouth and hands on her, getting inside her.

Oh, yeah. Inside her, that was the picture hardwired in his brain all the way down to his groin, short-circuiting his common sense.

"We need to get your shirt off," she said, and his

heart stalled in his chest. But she was focused on the bloody mess of a wound on his shoulder.

"I'm going to need some help," he said. His shoulder wound was still radiating pain while he was mobile; raising his arm over his head wasn't happening, and doing it one-handed would only cause him to struggle.

She reached down to his waist, and the brush of her fingertips tightened him up in good and bad ways.

Instead of grabbing the Henley at the edge, she slipped her hand under the material and ran the palm of her hand up over his stomach and chest to his shoulder. He sucked in a surprised breath as everything went hot inside him. Around the pleasure of her touching his skin, he saw what she was doing. She was going to help him out of the sleeve. Less movement.

He closed his eyes and took a hard breath, partly in pleasure and partly in pain. It was a helluva way to feel.

"Pull your arm out," she instructed, leaning over him, smelling so damn good and only adding to his arousal. He wanted to bury his face in her hair.

She met his eyes, suddenly aware that he was turned on. She swallowed, her delicate throat working.

"Vin...your arm."

He pulled at the same time she held the sleeve immobile so that he could extricate his arm. Reaching down with her free hand, she grasped the edge of the shirt and pulled it over his head. When the material moved over his wound, he twisted his head and swore softly, his breathing going ragged. His stomach heaved with the piercing pain. He inhaled deeply through the worst of it.

She was upset. It was written all over her face, but instead of moving or taking the next step, she was staring. At him. At his chest. Her eyes going over him as if she couldn't believe this was what he looked like without his shirt.

He willed her to stop looking at him with that shell-shocked expression on her face.

"Sweetheart," he said softly.

Her eyes met his and she blushed. She couldn't hide her appreciative gaze, what the sight of his nakedness did to her. He was a red-blooded American male, and he was so okay with that. But trying to hold on to his sanity was getting so damn hard.

She dropped the shirt and turned away, fumbling with the med kit, and he couldn't help the grin that spread across his face. He loved that he flustered her enough to make her clumsy. How would she react when she saw the rest of him?

He wanted to see that.

She turned back to him and noticed the grin. Her lips tightened as if she thought he was making fun of her. When she bent to his injury, her hair flowed over her shoulder and brushed against the exposed skin of his chest. Even as she probed the wound, he focused on the feel of her warm silky hair instead of the sting.

He gritted his teeth against both.

His head went back, and he groaned against the agony when she tugged something out of the bullet hole. His vision went gray, and he started to slide.

"Vin!" she croaked, catching him against her.

He grabbed the edge of the tank and pulled himself back up. "I'm okay," he said, the dullness receding.

"Are you sure?" she asked, her eyes moist.

He nodded, reaching out and squeezing her arm. "Go ahead and finish."

"I need you to stand over the sink so I can wash it

out with peroxide. I'm afraid it's going to hurt, and I'm so sorry about that." Her voice trembled. Pushing himself up, he did as she asked.

"Ready," she said, biting her lip.

"Go ahead." Before she poured, she set her arm around his waist. It was a good thing she did. When the liquid hit his open skin, his knees buckled, and he gritted his teeth so hard his jaw ached. His hands shook as he hung on to the edge of the sink.

She helped him to sit back down. Then dabbed at both sides of the through-and-through. She pulled out the needle and the topical anesthesia and applied it, stitched up the front bullet hole, then the back one. She was aware that the topical couldn't totally alleviate the pain from the needle, but Vin had stoically endured the procedure.

"Almost there," she said, rubbing in antiseptic ointment. "Hold this," she instructed as she placed a gauze pad against the front part of the wound, then grabbed another to place at the back. Then she wrapped a gauze bandage around his upper chest and his shoulder, covering and binding the two pads against the bullet holes, securing it with medical tape.

He leaned back, catching his breath.

"Vin," she said softly, "are you okay? Did you pass out?"

"No. I'm still conscious," he said and opened his eyes.

"Good. Can I have that nervous breakdown now?" she said, her voice cracking and tears welling to overflowing. Covering her face, she burst into tears.

He came up off the commode and dragged her into his arms without hesitation. He wasn't one of those guys who went all stupid when a woman cried. He'd had a buddy tell him once that a guy didn't have much to offer in this kind of situation. Vin disagreed wholeheartedly. He had two strong arms, even though one of them was throbbing. Comfort. That was all a woman wanted at a time like this.

Okay, she wasn't technically crying. She was sobbing, which was so much worse. But he was an ex-marine. Uncle Sam had trained him for anything. He could handle it.

She shifted and wrapped her arms around his neck, choking on her tears, and he wanted to soothe her, help her get control.

"It's okay, sweetheart. You did real good. Real good," he murmured. Carefully, he moved her over to the sink and wet a washcloth with one hand, as she sniffed and made those soft, little distressed sounds. He stepped back and carefully smoothed the cloth down one of her cheeks and over her bottom lip.

Her gaze lifted to his, and he thought, *How could I have gotten so lost, so fast? I barely know her.*

He pulled her closer. She took a hard, shaky breath, and he felt her tears slide down his chest as her hand cupped his nape.

Closer to all her soft, warm skin. Closer to her body. Closer to her mouth.

He leaned in, kissed her temple, and her hand tightened, sliding into his hair. He trailed his mouth down her face to her mouth, brushing his mouth against her lips. "So, so good," he whispered and wasn't sure if he was talking about the sensation of her skin beneath his lips or her toughness. He lowered his mouth to hers and gave himself up to the second biggest mistake in his career and in his life.

"I was so scared for you…Vin."

He nodded. He gently moved his mouth over hers, breathing her in—and she sighed in his mouth.

Hooyah. That was it. He cupped the side of her face with his hand and tilted her face up while opening his mouth over hers and pressing her back against the wall.

Her breasts pushed against his bare chest, the cloth a thin barrier between what he knew lay underneath. He was aware of what she might have on because he'd touched her lacy things, and it only jacked him up more. Her hips settled into the cradle of his hips, one of her hands sliding down over his good shoulder, pulling him closer. He loved the hot sweetness of it, the way she softened against him.

He slid his tongue into her mouth and felt the sharp need of desire take hold, the taste of her, the delicacy of her tongue sliding against his, teasing him.

Yeah, this was good. Damn good. Really good.

Her palm was soft and hot against him, sliding over him and pulling him even closer.

Closer and closer. He felt the edge of her desperation, could taste her tears, the salty dampness of them where they flowed over her luscious mouth.

He should stop.

But he was powerless.

He needed a guardian angel to save him.

But his guardian angel was the one turning him on, ratcheting him up and taking him down.

There was no rescue coming.

Oh, God. Oh, dear God. She was drowning. He was… so beautiful, so courageous, so badly hurt. He scared her at the same time he thrilled her beyond any man she'd ever met. It was the hottest thing she'd ever done—to sink into his kiss, to hold him close. She'd wanted to touch him so many times since he'd gotten her off that roof. The smell of him was like a balm to her soul, soft skin over hard-packed muscle. He was ripped beneath his shirt. She'd had no idea he was hiding that body beneath his suit.

She pulled him close, loving the hard-ridged feel of him, the life of him.

She needed it, even as she chastised herself for letting go. Just a taste, she vowed. But a taste had a way of leading to devouring, consuming.

How was she supposed to come to her senses when he just simply blew them away? She'd never considered herself particularly sensual or sexual. She was used to men who were cerebral, not hot and toned. She worked in a sterile, cold environment with men who were more interested in research than in getting it on. As focused as she'd been. Her personal life was barren, closed and solitary. Just as she had striven to make it. Not full of heat and color, touch and taste.

He was doing it again like he'd done at the loft, just inhaling her and enjoying kissing. She wasn't sure about males, but what she was certain of was that something came after the kissing. She'd had that miserable, embarrassing, messed-up "wham bam, thank you, Dr. Baang" sex. It had been awful.

But this…what he was doing with his mouth…was heavenly. What would it be like with him? She shouldn't want to find out, but she did. She so wanted to see what it would be like to be with him. She had an inkling it wouldn't be awful.

So new, so forbidden.

He scared her more than anything on this planet, even the kidnappers.

But he was sagging against her now, and her concern for him won out over the sensual torment of his mouth.

She broke the kiss, and he leaned his forehead against hers. Now that she wasn't buffeted by his sensual assault, she felt that familiar guilt spread out until she squirmed against the shame of easily giving in to him. Her work should be her focus, and she wanted nothing more than to get back to it, back to that sterile environment.

She closed her eyes. Trying to forget the color and the warmth. "Is that your way of kissing it all better?"

"Um, is it better?" he said, his words slurring a bit.

"Yes. Thank you, Vin. For…"

He sent his thumb over her mouth, effectively shushing her. "I keep telling myself this is such a bad idea."

"I agree."

"Yet you still participate. And you're welcome. I was doing my…"

This time it was her turn to cover his mouth. "Don't say 'job' because I know that's not all you were doing out there."

His lips curved beneath her fingers, his eyes lighting up.

"Did you mention there was some food in this place?" Sky asked.

"Yes, food. Good idea. I'll get some wood and get the fire going."

"Oh, no, you won't. You're going to sit down and rest. I'll get the wood and make the food," she ordered.

She dipped down and pulled out a long-sleeved cotton T-shirt. "Let me help you into this." She slipped the sleeve of the shirt up his arm and carefully over the bandage, over his head. He put his arm into the other sleeve.

She curled her arm around his waist, trying to tamp down her feelings for Vin. Feelings that would only cause both of them heartbreak. This was not going to go anywhere. It was a temporary thing. A crazy, out-of-control, temporary thing.

She settled him on the couch and turned away. Keeping busy would help. Wood and food. It gave her something to focus on.

Even as her mouth tingled and her hands ached for the touch of his skin, she turned away and headed out into the cold.

He looked like a battle-scarred and dangerous warrior with the white bandage against his shoulder. Fresh from the fight and hurt, vulnerable. Her heart just melted. She trembled inside, trying to look at him all at once. Breathe him in like the most delicious scent.

The way he had held her when she'd broken down humanized him from that untouchable warrior to the hot, tantalizing male sprawled out on the bed.

The dark stubble on his face, the way he looked down into her eyes with that open compassion was fixed in her brain.

She was sitting in a chair close to the bed. He'd felt a bit warm when she'd insisted he get some sleep after she'd fed him vegetable soup and a PB&J. She was eating and he was sleeping. He needed it so badly.

She was worried with the way he seemed restless. An infection would be a complication. She wouldn't hesitate to get him the needed medical help if that was the case, but the bullet wound would mean she'd have to explain and get NCIS involved. Vin wouldn't want that, but she wasn't going to jeopardize his life if it came down to that.

He rolled slightly onto his stomach, with one of his legs drawn up, and he was so beautiful that even though she was hungry, she found herself forgetting to eat.

He was particularly gorgeous, more powerfully built under his clothes than she would have guessed. He carried himself with such fluid, unconscious grace. The way he had moved across that roof, so sure-footed... If she hadn't lost her balance and fallen, he wouldn't have even slipped.

His shirt had ridden up, revealing the rippled muscles of his abdomen, and a sigh lifted her chest.

She finished eating and walked over to the bed. It was a king and had plenty of space. She didn't think she could rest if she wasn't close, to be there if he needed her. He had been there for her last night, and she wasn't going to let her guilt keep her from offering him help if he needed it.

She put her knee on the bed and crawled up next to him and lay down.

Holy God.

Everything came rushing back, and she wondered if it was some way for her brain to make sense of the night's events. She couldn't believe what she had seen, what he'd done. Her heart had stopped when he'd pulled his gun and pointed it straight at her, right after her heart had damn near jumped out of her chest when he'd...

Vin, his knee planted in the man's back, the fierce, violent twist that had broken the man's neck. Vin drawing his gun. The booming dual blasts. Vin using the dead man's shirt to clean the bloody knife, folding it back and slipping it into his pocket even as he rose to his feet, his other hand still holding the gun steady and aimed.

The complete and total focus of Vin's gaze, every move precise, everything fluid, a lethal dance.

They had somehow found her in spite of NCIS taking such precautions with three agents guarding her. Miller and Strong... Oh, God, she was going to hyperventilate if she thought about them. She'd been in her room and she'd wanted some coffee. She was going to ask if one of them wouldn't mind running down to the coffee shop to get her a cup. As soon as she'd opened the door, Vin had been in the shadowed hall, slamming an automatic-gun-toting kidnapper against the wall and...

Vin, attacking hard and fast, sinking his knife in the man's stomach, wrenching the blade upward.

Blood everywhere.

She had no idea. Not really. Sure, she'd experienced kidnapping terror when she'd been young, but she'd been shielded from the savagery of the world. Shielded from everything, it seemed. It was part of her sacrifice. It didn't just isolate her from relationships and a normal, balanced life, but it shielded her from the ugliness, too.

She'd been touched by it. It had marked her and not just from the blood on her clothes. There was no going back to that complete isolation. She wasn't even sure if she could manage it. Especially after the way Vin had kissed her.

God help her, she wanted more.

She got up and slipped her CD into the player on the dresser. As rain and intermittent gong reverberations filled the room, she lay back down. The peaceful sounds calmed her.

He twitched in his sleep and turned over so that he was facing her. She reached out and felt his forehead. He was warm, but not overly so. She stared at his face until her eyes drifted closed.

She felt safe.

So safe.

Beau stood in front of Chris's desk, and there was a look on his face that made him sit up straighter.

"We got a hit on one of those dead Russians."

"I haven't got all damn day, Beau."

"He's part of The Red Sickle."

Alarm rang in every nerve ending of Chris's body. The Red Sickle was a band of mercs linked with political kidnappings, assassination and small wars across Europe. They were brutal, notorious and relentless. NCIS had them at the top of their Most Wanted list.

Vin was up against a band of international killers: Out there somewhere on his own.

"Find them," Chris said softly and then pushed back from his desk. He headed to the director's office.

He had to report what he'd learned to his boss.

This was an all-out manhunt.

NCIS had to get to those mercs before they got to Vin and Dr. Baang.

Chapter 7

Sky's cry jerked him out of a deep sleep. She was next to him flailing, and when she hit his shoulder, he doubled over.

"Sky. Sky." He grabbed her hands and pulled her close, trying to keep any more damage to a minimum. She was wild-eyed, her body stiff and unyielding. "Sky, shh. It's okay."

"Vin." Her breathing was ragged, and she sent her hands over him to make sure he was here and whole.

"Oh, God. It was just a nightmare." She breathed out a sigh, and before he could open his arms to let her go, she snuggled against him.

Now he was in even more trouble. He was on a bed, warm and too damn cozy with Sky after just telling himself he wanted her. Hot, wet and naked. On top of him, underneath him, all over him. Yeah. Damn.

"Do you want to talk about it?"

She took a long, shaky breath. That must have been some nightmare.

She was silent for a moment. "It was about you."

"It was?"

"Yes. You were shielding me and…" Her voice caught. "Death Head killed you."

"It was just a nightmare," he said softly. "Death Head?"

"That's what I call the guy who was strangling you. He was the one who found me in the attic and stabbed me with that drug. He looks like a Death Head."

"I bet it felt doubly good, then, when you clocked that bastard."

"Damn good, actually."

"Therapeutic even?"

"Very."

"You saved my life. So, thank you for that."

She moved closer to him, and he really liked the way her body was snuggled up to him. He felt her head move against his shoulder as she nodded.

"I'm going to make it as damn near impossible for him to find you as I can."

She tightened her arms around him. "This is all so awful. I keep seeing Agent Miller...."

"Don't torture yourself with that, Sky."

"What were their first names?" she asked, her voice thick.

He didn't say anything, not sure if this was good or bad for her. His chest got tight thinking about the two agents. But if she wanted to know. "Miller's first name was Tom and Strong's was Mike."

"Do you know anything about them?"

"Yeah." He cleared his throat. "Are you sure you want to do this?"

"Yes. I owe them that much."

"Tom loved basketball. We would play pickup games. He was really good, and I always wanted him on my team. We played really well off each other. Neither one of us was a ball hog—okay, I was a ball hog, a little."

She buried her face in his neck, and he damn near

groaned from the pleasure of her warm breath against his skin and that she inhaled deliberately as if she was breathing him in.

"His…personal life? Was he…married? I thought I saw a ring."

"Sky…"

"Please, Vin. I want to know. It's hard on you. I understand that. But I need to know. He sacrificed his life for me. Please."

"Yes, he was married to a sweet, gorgeous schoolteacher. He has…two girls. Lexi and Miranda. Randy for short, and she's a pistol."

"Oh…God." She pressed harder against him, and he sent his hands through her hair. "Go on. Mike Strong."

"Mike was a practical joker, and when I first came to NCIS, I worked with him briefly before I was assigned to my present team. He loved to laugh, was a die-hard D.C. sport fan. Went to any and all games he could and often dragged me along. He was engaged to be married next year to a researcher for the FDA."

After that she was quiet, and it wasn't long before he heard her deep breathing. She'd fallen asleep in his arms. It was another sure sign of trust, and it rocked through him.

Trouble. God, he was in trouble here, and it had nothing to do with being hunted by some very determined and brutal Russians.

Before he'd met Dr. Skylar Baang, self-control was his middle name. He wouldn't have kissed a charge or gone rogue. But damn, she'd done a number on him. She stirred against him, all that softness, and her hand trailed up his neck to his jaw and lingered there as if she was half in, half out of sleep. Was she dreaming about him this time instead of having a nightmare? He liked that better. Dying anytime soon wasn't an option. She moved her hand up to his forehead and pressed it there. Apparently she was happy with his temperature, because she fell asleep again with her hand still on his face. Trying not to move too much because he was afraid of what he might do, he thought briefly of extricating himself from her sweet grip, and while he was at it, he should try to find his brains.

But he was still exhausted, so he drifted and drifted some more, and then he slept. His rise up from the sweet oblivion of sleep was a lazy meandering of his mind, the limp relaxation of his body, the comforting sensation of Sky against him.

His eyes fluttered open, his every cell coming fully awake and the full extent of his current situation hitting him all at once. He'd turned in his sleep, and his body was completely against hers, from her breasts plastered to his chest all the way down to their thighs. The ease with which a man obtained an erection upon waking up only added to the sudden tension. His dick was hard, and now that he was aware of her, getting harder. She moved, and he gritted his teeth at the pressure on his groin.

He was debating his best move when her eyes fluttered open, her face all but touching his, her hand resting on his temple and cheek.

Her eyes widened, and she went to pull her hand away, but he caught it. "Don't you need to check to make sure I'm okay?" he said.

She met his gaze directly. "You feel hot to me. Are you always this hot?"

He was hot for her, but he didn't think that was prudent to say right now. "I don't have a fever, Sky. This is my normal temperature."

She felt his forehead, "I guess you don't have a fever, then." She went to move away from him, but he tightened his arms.

"I thought this was a mistake," she whispered. "Me here."

"It is. But I'd be lying if I said I didn't want you here…or want more. I'd be a huge freaking liar."

"By more, do you mean…sex?"

He couldn't really deny it and evade that question. Honesty was better. "Yes, Sky. I'm talking about sex."

To his surprise, she didn't pull away; her gaze just got more direct, and she said, "That's not a surprise to me. The scientific findings are that men think about sex more than women do. Men have more intrusive thoughts, too—it's harder for them to ignore thoughts about sex." Then she closed her eyes as if she couldn't quite believe she'd just said that.

Well, there was some truth in that clinical description, but it also gave him a bit of insight into the woman in his arms. Inexperienced came to mind or…maybe even a virgin? Did she talk about sex in clinical terms as a way to keep it clinical? Was it about avoidance? If she was avoiding it or not receptive to his advances, he could understand that. But that wasn't the case. She was wrapped around him right now. She'd melted into him each and every time he'd kissed her. So that wasn't in question. What was in question was should he pursue this when it was such a bad idea.

He still wanted her.

"I'm going to go take a shower." He went into the bathroom, slammed the door and leaned against it, giving himself a few moments to get under control. Being professional and smart was getting harder and harder. She was an enticing woman and he was finding it increasingly more difficult to keep his hands off her— his hands, his mouth, every part of his body. He pushed away from the door and ran the water. He was okay to shower with the bandages on. That wasn't going to be an issue. He unbuckled his belt and undid his pants, letting them drop to the floor. Using one hand to push off his boxer briefs, he kicked them away. He stepped into the shower, trying to ignore the pain. His shoulder joint was tight from keeping it immobile and the wound stiff and sore, hurting like a bitch. He should have taken some more painkillers.

He was crazy to make himself crazy over this woman. She didn't understand, just like Brittany didn't understand. Of course, Brittany was all about lifestyle and status. He didn't believe that was what motivated Sky. Her guard was in place and would probably be even harder to crack. After trauma, people tended to withdraw into themselves.

He washed himself awkwardly with one hand. After he stepped out of the shower, he realized that it was going to be hard to wipe his back and set the towel around his waist.

To top it off, he hadn't brought any clothes in here with him. He groaned softly at his lack of forethought. She really scrambled his brain. He didn't want to ask her for help, but at this point he didn't really have a choice. Better to ask than cause his wound to start to bleed again or ruin her careful stitching.

He walked to the door and cracked it a little, and the sounds of rain and gongs filtered through the opening.

She was on the floor, bent into a pretzel, staring at the bathroom door. She looked away quickly.

"Sky?"

"Yes," she replied.

"I need your help."

"To change your bandage?"

"Um…no. A little more than that." He sounded distressed and looked even more annoyed.

"What, then?" she said, her voice concerned. "Are you okay?"

"I can't dry off very well, and I can't really get the towel around my waist."

She unbent herself and sat there for a second or two, letting his words sink in. Had he just said he was wet and naked and he needed her to help him? Her eyes widened and she swallowed. She hadn't seen a naked man. Not really. And, to top it off, Vin was…well, he was irresistible. She was having a very hard time keeping her thoughts on why she shouldn't get involved with him. He intrigued her and it was hard to focus when she was talking to him. How the heck was she supposed to… function while he was stark naked?

She wanted to know all about him. Something that was foreign to her. She dismissed people, deliberately didn't ask questions or try to find out too much. She didn't have time for friendships or relationships.

But she wanted him to understand her, which surprised the heck out of her. Deep down, she wanted that. That someone special to get her, even all her nerdy quirks. It would open her up, this sharing of herself, but she felt compelled to take a chance and reveal more of herself to him.

"Sky? It's not brain surgery. I'm just a naked guy." Now he was exasperated.

"But I've never seen a naked man," she blurted out and then covered her face. "Oh, shit." She felt the heat from her blush scorch her face. The "act" had happened so fast, and it had been so strained and awkward, the guy had gotten dressed in the dark and left so quickly. It had been mortifying. Now she had another mortifying incident to go right with it. "Could I be any more nerdy?"

"Probably," he said.

She moaned softly. Gah, she'd said that out loud.

"Look, I'll turn my back," he said, his voice low and raspy, sending shivers over her. It was hard enough yesterday to see him without his shirt. She had gotten all flustered, especially when she saw that he realized it. When she didn't move, he said with a sigh, "I'll manage."

"No. I'll do it." She got up off the floor and approached the bathroom door, her stomach twisting with anxiety and something that made her tingle all over.

He kept the door cracked and handed out a towel to her. "When I open the door, just quickly wrap it and tuck it in front. Okay?"

"Okay," she said, her lungs feeling compressed.

She was ready. It was a simple, easy task—a monkey could do it. But when he opened the door, Sky froze. The magnificence of him struck her dumb. His dark hair was wet and plastered to the back of his strong neck, and her eyes took over with a mind of their own. Her gaze moved from the back of his neck to his oh-so-broad and heavily muscled shoulders and triceps. Thick, solid shoulders that did the trick when a girl needed one to cry on. His upper back was rippled with muscle, ropy and solid down either side of his spine. His lower back was as smooth as his magnificent backside.

"Sky?" he said, his voice strangled.

He'd turned his head and was looking at her over his shoulder. Staring at her. But her eyes had no intention of jerking up to his face. Instead, they decided to take a second look. She leisurely slid her gaze back up until, with a start, her eyes climbed over the stubble coating his handsome face. When she met his eyes, they were hot, very green and scared her in a really good way, making her stomach tighten. Desire. That was what she saw there. Hard, intense desire.

"Sky," he said again, a little sharper.

She stepped forward after snapping out of her brain freeze and wrapped the towel around his waist. Oh, God, his skin was so hot, soft and moist, his waist rock hard. She had to lean into his amazing ass to get the towel properly tucked. Moving up against him was the only way. He sucked in a breath and stood very still. She pressed her face into his back. Damn, he smelled so good, so clean and male. She'd had no idea that men could be such a feast for the senses.

It took a couple of tries for her to get it done, her hands rubbing up against that ridged abdomen she couldn't see, but damn, did she ever want to.

She wanted to see all of him.

Even after she'd tucked the towel, neither one of them moved. She wanted to kiss all that wet skin beneath her cheek, press her lips there and take them on a joy ride over all that muscle.

"I'm drowning here," he confessed, his voice a rough, suppressed kind of growl. "I want you to touch me."

He was real, flesh and blood, not some sculpture, and she'd been so forward, sliding her hands over him, even if it had been in the name of lending a hand. He could have both of them all over his body. Yeah, she was a freaking Good Samaritan.

"But…" He took a deep breath and let it out slowly. She wanted to glide along his body and get a good view of his front. If the front of him looked as good as the back…whoa.

He was gorgeous, not just his face with his rather elegant nose, chiseled cheekbones and that mouth, which she so wanted to kiss again and again. He'd put himself in the line of fire. He took care of her. He'd taken bullets for her. He was dedicated to protecting her, and he had the kind of wit she needed in a man. The kind that could challenge her.

She wanted to touch him, nuzzle his neck, lick his skin—get into him, get onto him—and she was at a loss in knowing how to make that happen or in judging how dangerous giving in to those desires might be.

"But what?" she whispered.

"It's a step into madness," he said. "I'm not sure we're compatible. I don't want to take advantage of the situation. It's definitely not professional."

She was taken aback. "You want to get to know me better?"

"Is that a crime?" he managed.

"I guess I thought you were like any other man when presented with a willing woman. Take what you want."

"Make no mistake. I want you. That's not the issue. But we're under a traumatic situation here. I've saved your life and am the only thing that stands between you and a bunch of determined, brutal Russians who are willing to kill to get you back. Let's just…not do this right now. I don't even know if you've ever been… intimate."

She took a breath and nodded against his skin. "Yes, I have, but it was so miserable and uncomfortable and so embarrassing."

"It won't be with me. I promise you that. If you're with me."

"What if I want you, too?" That admission made her skin heat and sizzle with the heightened tension that poured off his too close, tantalizing body.

He swore softly under his breath. "I'm not willing to take that step right now. I don't want you to rush into anything, then maybe regret it."

He had good points, but right now she couldn't seem to care. There was no maybe about wanting him. She wouldn't regret it. She knew all about pheromones, hormones and chemistry. She knew all the scientific terms and all the science behind it. But Vin made her want to experience something more than science. She wanted the magic. Something she'd denied herself for so long. Then she came to her senses, realizing that she was compromising her vow. Gotten lost in the physical sensations and the emotional attachment she was developing for this man.

She stepped back, and Vin breathed a sigh. Her hands shook, and she grabbed a towel to keep them from trembling. She drew the terry over his back, finding that she couldn't seem to help her movements as they were slow and deliberate caresses. She felt terribly guilty for wanting what she shouldn't, but she couldn't seem to help herself. She knelt down and dried his calves, shins and feet, before rising and walking around to face him.

When she met his glittering eyes, a soft, deep flash of heat exploded under her skin and washed through her entire body. She reached up with the towel and dried off his face and jaw, being gentle around his cuts. Then his strong throat where his pulse beat just as erratically as hers.

It was a small consolation that he was as affected as she was.

"Bend down and I'll towel dry your hair."

He did as she asked, and she ruffled his hair until she got the majority of the water out of it.

When he straightened, his hair a tousled mess around his face, she dragged the towel down his chest, soaking up the rivulets of water that slid over his pectoral muscles. When she touched his stomach, trailing the terry over those ridged muscles, he sucked in a breath.

"I want to kiss you," he said very softly. "Just kiss you."

"Do you dare?" she countered, her eyes roving over his face.

"No," he said. "Not right now."

That made her smile, and she was sure it went all the way to her eyes because his mouth curved up. He reached out and ran his hands through her hair, then brushed the backs of his fingers against her cheek.

"I suppose it doesn't help that I want you to kiss me?"

"No," he said. "Not right now."

She laughed. She didn't think she'd laughed this much in forever. There was one more quality about him that simply melted her heart. He made her laugh.

"I don't know how to resist."

He shook his head, settling some of the spikes into

place. "I guess it's up to me." He smiled and her heart dissolved into goo.

"That isn't helping, mister."

He closed his eyes and took a breath. Easing away from her, he sat down on the commode. She sighed, just a bit disappointed at his formidable control. "Are we going to dance around this subject, then?"

"I'm trying to stay sane here. Bandage time."

"Oh, all right," she said, sighing.

She hung the towel over the rack and grabbed the med kit. Pulling out surgical scissors, she cut away the sodden bandage wrapped around his chest. Then pulled away the gauze pads. The bullet wound was red and ragged, but her stitches were pretty good, considering she wasn't a doctor.

Then it struck her hard. They were still in danger. It hadn't felt so, being in his arms while she slept and then laughing with him, then pissing him off. But he could still get seriously hurt or even killed. Her stomach lurched so hard she covered it with her hand.

"Are you going to get sick?"

"No," she said. "I'm fine."

But he looked skeptical.

She was scared. She'd be a fool to get attached to him, open her heart to him, because he could break it into a thousand pieces, and she wasn't sure if she had the strength to survive that. He was the closest she'd come to having a friend—a romantic partner—ever. She kept people at a distance, but the circumstances of their situation made it impossible not to feel, care. She had never sought love. It hurt. A lot. She still missed her father and mother. They'd left a gaping hole in her heart.

Of course, in her cynical, scientific, totally logical

mind, love was easily avoided. She might have to refine or rethink that hypothesis.

She was a creator; she built and constructed. Her whole life had been about using her talents to the fullest. She'd promised. Guilt assaulted her again. She'd promised her mother and father. Could she be falling for a man who was a force of destruction, had already destroyed to keep her safe?

Even as she stood there, grabbing gauze pads so that he wouldn't see her turmoil, she wanted to just throw all her worries, cautions, hang-ups to the wind and take her chances at just a taste of life before those kidnappers came back and tried to take away her choices and her freedom, maybe even her life.

And could she say that she had even lived?

After gently cleaning the wound, she repeated the bandaging process that she'd used last night, securing the edges with tape.

He watched her with heavy-lidded eyes, and she noticed how the towel tented over his genitals. *Genitals.* Really, she thought. She hoped to God she never said that out loud.

Without really thinking about what she was doing, she leaned down, placing her hands on either side of him and bracing them against the tank. She had no earthly idea how to seduce a man. But from her experience, they responded so well to stimulus and she so wanted to put her mouth on him. She was about to put it into practice and experiment. She'd never been so eager for research.

He did nothing, just continued to look at her with those burning hot eyes. Maybe he was convinced that she didn't have it in her. That spurred her on. She moved closer.

"Sky," he said softly, and she got what she wanted, that strangled sound, his voice a hard rasp. Her hair flowed forward, over her shoulders, hitting his chest like the spill of black ink. He reached out with his good arm and bunched the silky strands in his hand.

But he didn't drag her forward. The steam from his shower and the heady smell of his clean skin made her feel dizzy. Tension, thick in the air, ratcheted up as he parted his sensual lips. She groaned softly, brushing hers along his. Her tongue came out, and she licked them, took his bottom lip into her mouth and sucked. Then she bit him, ever so lightly, then harder.

He groaned, *"Sky."* Only this time, his chest heaved, and his breathing increased. All good biological signs that she was making headway. Experimentation had never been this fun, this good. His hand tightened in her hair, tugging ever so slightly against her scalp. She leaned into his lips harder, pressed her mouth more fully against him.

His hand still in her hair, he cupped the back of her neck, his mouth going ravenous, devouring her.

His hand abruptly slid down as he released her hair and snaked around her waist. He dragged her against him until she was straddling his lap. Against the heated strength of his chest, she braced herself on his powerful thighs. The hard, hot length of him burned through the terry cloth and her flimsy shorts, his erection fitting between her legs and pressing hard against her wet center. She pulled her mouth away, both of them breathing hard.

She traced his lips with her fingers, and he rested his

head back against the wall. She rubbed her face against his stubble, her fingers still on his mouth.

She leaned forward and kissed his neck, ran her mouth down, then up his throat, tasting the male tang of him against her tingling tongue. She scored him with her teeth, down and back up, sucking on the pulse point at his throat.

His sexy lifeblood thrumming in her mouth, the life of him beat in rhythm with her own heart.

He twisted his head, thrusting his hips up against her core, and it was her turn to groan. Her hips moved, sensually, wildly, and so naturally, she was floored by how good it felt.

She trailed her hand down his chest, over those muscles her eyes had caressed. This was so much better. He was like tempered steel beneath her hand. She ran her palm over his skin, just taking in the sensation of not only touching him, but turning him on. She rubbed over his hard nipple and got fascinated with his reaction when she went over it again, making it bead up even more. Dipping her head, she flicked her tongue over him. He sucked in a breath and jerked his hips.

"Your mouth," he whispered. "Use your mouth on me."

Her stomach a mass of trembling, electric butterflies, she closed her mouth over him, sucking and licking. He arched his back, the long line of his rib cage the perfect place for her to explore next. He twisted his head again when she dragged her nails across the ridges of his abdomen, loving the feel of his muscle.

"Damn!" he said under his breath, a heated whisper into the thick passion-soaked air. With the flat of her tongue, she laved him, her hand coming up and tracing

the line of his pectoral muscles, teasing his other nipple with her fingers, then pinching him hard.

He groaned low and deep in his throat, arching his back again. She raised her head and watched him unravel for her, and it was the most powerful feeling she'd ever had. Vin coming undone. Controlled, calm and collected Special Agent Vincent Fitzgerald. His face was stark with his desire, his mouth slightly open, his eyes glazed and unfocused.

She cupped his jaw, loving the roughness of his dark stubble against her hand. She slid her hand up and into his damp, silky hair, clenching her fingers in it and gently tugging his mouth to hers.

Capturing his lips, she kissed him over and over again.

He made a low growl in his throat and rose, groaning softly in pain.

"No, Vin, your shoulder." But he either didn't hear her, was too far gone or didn't give a damn.

He carried her out of the bathroom to the bed, where he gently let her slide down the length of his body.

Chapter 8

He was in so much trouble right now. He should get control of himself, take this slow—slow it down.

He should be stopping.

But Sky had a different agenda. She hooked her fingers into his towel and looked up at him. "I want to see you. I've never really... Do you mind?"

What the hell? Was she seriously asking if he cared if she looked at him? Was she out of her mind? He wanted her to look, touch, participate.

"Sky..." he said, truly not sure what was going to come out of his mouth, but saying no to her was simply beyond his capability. "Take it off." She tugged at the towel, and it dropped off him, slid and fell around his feet.

She caught her breath and stared. Her eyes not just roving over him, but caressing him with so much fire, he could feel the heat down the length of his body. Her appreciative gaze slid over his abdomen and down to his dick. It was hard, jutting out from his body. She lingered there as if she was studying him for a test.

Slowly she raised her head and met his eyes.

Yeah, he was fucked.

"Can I touch you there?"

He took a heated breath and gave her an incredulous look.

She dropped her head. "Please, Vin. I can feel that you're worried about us being together intimately, but I want to know what it's like to be with a man I truly care about." She took a deep breath. "And I do care about you. This has only been bearable because of you. What you did to save me from those Russians… I'm so thankful.

"I've never been very good with the opposite sex. I'm very aware that I'm sexually appealing to men. I see the way they look at me. I'm so nerdy. I figure you can help. That is, let me explore and experience you."

He leaned forward. "You are hot. You don't have to ask permission to touch me."

"It's your body. I just thought… Was that stupid?"

"No, you can touch me only for about a million years. Then you'll have to stop."

"What?" Her head popped up, and when she saw his face, she smiled. "Oh, you're being funny."

Her hand moved over his lower stomach around to the small of his back. Then she cupped him and pressed on his butt, driving his balls into her hand. He could barely breathe. He watched her, and the look on her face only revved him up more.

He closed his eyes when her hand slid over him, her touch tentative at first. There was nothing funny about this.

She leaned against him, her hand sliding up around his erection, then sliding back down.

"Looser," he rasped, and her grip relaxed slightly, perfectly, so freaking good at the same time she palmed the head. He moaned, arching his back. His knees almost buckled as he reached out, bending forward at the exquisite feel of her, and set his hands against her shoulders. She trailed soft, slow kisses against his chest, passing over one of his nipples and sucking on him again.

He had no idea how much he enjoyed that until her mouth and tongue were driving him wild.

He snagged her wrist and pulled her away from him. She made a soft noise of protest, but he couldn't take any more. "I don't want to come in your hand, sweetheart."

She pressed her face against his chest, her breathing erratic. It turned him on that she was so aroused from touching him.

"Condoms," he said as he moved back and headed to the medicine cabinet, praying there were some in there. Opening the door, he jerked when her arms slipped around him. She was completely naked. He could feel it against his hot skin.

She rubbed her face against his back, curling her hands around him and caressing his chest, then flowing down over his ribs, stomach and hips.

"Did you find them?"

Lost in the sensation, he said stupidly, "What?"

"The condoms?"

"Oh, damn, that's right." He used everything he had to focus his attention on locating them, breathing a sigh of relief when he found a full box.

She chuckled against his back, and he smiled like a fool. "It's your fault. You distracted me."

"Did I?"

"Yes, a naked woman kinda does that to a man." He turned around, clasping the condoms in his hand. "*You* do that to me," he whispered. She gazed up at him, looking so striking in the warm light from the late-afternoon sun. He had no sense of time, was lost in her eyes, drowning in the bottomless blue depths.

For a split second he had doubts about this, but she wrapped her arms around him and pressed her body against his. "You are making this something I won't easily forget. You're so wonderful, Vin. Do you know that?"

"I'm a friggin' saint," he said wryly, taking her hand and drawing her over toward the fireplace. "You're going to get the chance to take control, sweetheart. I can't put pressure on my injured shoulder. You'll have to get on top."

She pulled back against his hand, looking spooked. "But I've never."

He couldn't stop his eyes from roaming over her, taking in her creamy shoulders, her delicate collarbones, flowing over her high, pink-tipped breasts, down the smooth expanse of her flat stomach, touching on her slender hips to the thatch of hair between her sleek thighs. He tugged her forward right up against him. "It's okay," he said gruffly. "I'll be here every step of the way. How's your head feeling?" he asked.

Her eyes went over his body. "Just a headache. I'm not thinking about it right now."

Everything in him tightened. He lay down in front of the fire; the thick, warm, soft rug beneath him was so comfortable, but the pressure against his shoulder was painful.

She folded down next to him on the rug, looking awkward and unsure. Without saying anything, he grabbed her by the waist with his good arm and dragged her across his lap and promptly forgot about his shoulder.

"Do what feels natural, Sky. Chances are I'm going to like it a whole lot."

She smiled and dipped down, pressing her mouth to his, whispering, "How will I know?"

"Oh, believe me, you'll know."

She pressed her mouth to his at the same time that she slid along his rock-hard erection. He groaned at the pleasure she gave him.

She raised her head. "Oh, like that?"

His breathing ragged, he said, "Exactly like that."

"More?"

"Yes, ma'am, please."

Her slick heat closed over him, and he wanted to get inside her, but he was going to have to settle for letting her control the situation this time. If he was in control—ah, when was he ever with this woman—he would probably have gone too fast for her, and that was what he wanted to avoid. He didn't know who the guy was who had been so insensitive to her needs, but he was missing out big-time.

He grasped her hips and dragged her across his chest, to his mouth. She made a soft sound in her throat, and he breathed deep of her heady, feminine scent. "Lower yourself to my mouth."

Her hips jerked against his hands, and she complied as he clamped his lips over her lush core and sucked.

She cried out and arched her back, so hot and wet against his tongue. He used the tip to stroke, quick flicks with soft suction, then a slow languorous slide of his tongue against her. She rode his mouth, her hips undulating; her pleasure-filled voice only made him want more.

"Vin," she breathed right before she pulsated against his mouth as she released a long, drawn-out sobbing cry.

"Condom," he ground out when she moved off him.

"But…I want…"

"Next time," he rasped out. He couldn't wait any longer. "Put the condom on me."

She reached over and snagged one out of the box and opened the foil packet. "Damn," he said between gritted teeth as she slowly rolled it over him. As soon as it was on him, he pulled her forward and groaned. "Lean toward me," he instructed, and she braced her hands against the floor. Slipping inside her, he thrust at the same time that he pressed on her hips. But he didn't have to help her along any more. She made a heated sound in the back of her throat and met his thrust. Then, before he could catch the breath that was eluding him, she rode him hard and fast.

He captured the back of her head and drew her mouth down to his, and she kissed him, her mouth ravenous, her breathing erratic. "Sky…" He pumped against her with every deep thrust wanting, wanting, getting so strung out, his mouth all over her—endless minute after endless minute, until she gave him everything he wanted, her body going stiff above him. He groaned softly as the pleasure built and built inside him. Her head went back on a cry, and her back arched. He'd never seen anything so beautiful, never felt anything more exquisite than the cascade of her contractions tightening around him, and it undid him. His breath caught. His release so fierce and hot, his hips came up off the rug, his back arching, crying out against her mouth.

She collapsed against him, and he wrapped his good arm around her, breathing hard.

She stayed on him, and he was okay with that as he absorbed the feel of her against him. Finally she moved and slid off him. He rose, went to the bathroom and took care of the condom.

Back on the rug, he reached out for her, but she didn't go far, snagging the throw blanket off the couch. Covering them both up, she slid down and settled her head against his good shoulder and buried her face into his throat, where she pressed soft, heated kisses.

He rubbed his hand against her scalp. Her hair was thick and soft beneath his hand. He drew her face up and pressed his mouth over hers, needing the feel of her lips.

"Thank you," she murmured against his mouth. "That was—"

"Fantastic?"

She slid her arms around his neck and tugged him closer. "Oh, yes, but that's not what I was thanking you for, although I appreciate it."

He kissed his way along the soft line of her jaw. "What were you going to say?"

She sighed and relaxed more fully into him, tipping her chin to allow him access to that tender spot beneath her ear. "That was much different than what I have ever experienced. I appreciate your patience."

He kissed the spot where her pulse throbbed, eliciting the tiniest of moans. It was enough to make him hard all over again, aching to the point of pain. And he wanted desperately to hear her do that again. "This is the bottom line, sweetheart. That guy was a complete selfish jerk."

She flinched at that, and her expression went uncomfortable. "I'm beginning to understand that."

"It'll be better when I can fully participate."

"Better—" She broke off on a short moan when he cupped her breast, rubbing his thumb over her hard nipple. "Are you kidding?" she managed.

She pushed him back and dropped a set of fast, hot kisses against his neck, her hand slipping down his body to score his rib cage with her nails that had his body twitching hard with a grunt deep in his chest. "No. I'm not."

"Wow," she said, her voice soft and husky.

Then she took his mouth this time, but she slowed it down, gentled the assault, which perversely turned him on even more. She teased; he taunted; they slipped their tongues more sinuously along the other, tasting, touching. Soft sighs filled the warm room. His, hers, he'd lost track. He was drowning, and he didn't want to be saved. Reality would intrude soon enough. It always did. He wasn't going to hurry it along any faster.

This time he rolled her to her side and reached for a condom. Ripping the foil open, he rolled it on one-handed, and then his head bent down to her breast. He covered her nipple with his mouth, laving it with his tongue. He sucked on her, and she buried her hands in his hair, holding him to her.

"That feels so good," she breathed.

"You taste so good," he growled, moving to her other breast and her sweet, hard nipple.

"Vin," she moaned. "Oh, God, Vin!"

He shifted them both to their sides, paused there for a moment to absorb the pain in his shoulder, kissed her, then moved the rest of the way, sinking deeply into her as she lifted up and wrapped her leg around his hip.

He held her gaze in between long, slow kisses, moving inside of her, feeling her match his steady rhythm as easily as if they'd done this forever. He finally slid his arm around her hips and tilted them just slightly, instinctively searching for the sweet spot that every woman had. She gasped and tightened around him almost convulsively. The one he knew would take them both over the edge. But he held her there, for that one moment out of time, and looked into her eyes. "Sky..."

And her eyes glazed over at her name whispered with that hoarse cast to his voice. He shuddered at the connection and the trust. There wouldn't be anything he wouldn't do for her to keep her safe. He thrust into her, the pain in his shoulder mingling with the pleasure and making it bearable. His hips sped up, and she met each hard push with one of her own until they were both groaning raggedly as they dropped off the edge together.

Exhausted, they fell asleep as the fire crackled and the snow thickened outside the window.

His throbbing shoulder woke him. Extricating himself from her, he went to the med kit in the bathroom and took some painkillers. He turned sideways and looked in the mirror. There was no blood on the bandages. That was at least something. He rubbed his face. The day had slipped into night, and he really should check in, but he decided that he'd do that tomorrow.

"Vin?"

He turned to find her standing in the bathroom doorway, the ambient light from the fireplace illuminating her. She was dressed in one of his black NCIS T-shirts.

Her long hair was a dark tousled mess. He'd never seen a sexier woman; his heart twisted at the sight of her.

She came into the small space, and he liked feeling crowded by her. "Are you all right?"

He turned toward her, and she reached up to feel his forehead, then fluffed his bangs.

"Shoulder is hurting like a bitch."

"Come back and lie down. You should get more sleep. Exhaustion and stress aren't going to help heal that wound. I'll play one of my CDs. Great for relaxation."

"If you try to get me to start chanting om, it's not going to happen, honey."

"*Om* is not just a sound or vibration. It is not just a symbol. It's a communion and a way to connect to your own being and the universe, whatever we can see, touch, hear and feel. It is a phonemic representation bridging to our spirituality."

"You are quite serious about om."

"Oh, I see. You were teasing me?"

He walked the short distance between them. "Yes, I was teasing you, but I'm intrigued. How does a hard-fact scientist buy into the cosmos through spiritualism?"

"You forget my culture. One of our most fundamental mental challenges is to reconcile our scientific understanding of the world with our spiritual experiences and beliefs. There must be a unity at a higher level of reality, despite the outer appearances to the contrary."

"Ah, that's what led you to your master's degree in sound and then to the yoga stuff."

She blinked and didn't say anything for a moment. "Yes. You are certainly good at observation and a very clever man. You have a sexy brain." She reached up and curled her hand against his nape. "Yes, exactly. How are you with the Theory of Everything?"

"The Theory of Everything is all about combining the idea that there are many parts to the universe and there is one thing that links them all."

"Smarty pants. So this links to om. It's not exactly a tangible thing. Not like hard science but the idea that it's just as powerful."

"I like it, sweetheart."

"I have really underestimated your intelligence, Vin." She moved closer to him. "Great in bed and can keep up with metaphysical conversations. I'm getting hot."

"Okay, who's teasing who now?" he said, sending his hand through the tangled strands of her hair. "I like focusing on the material universe, especially your material universe. It's my...big Baang theory?"

She laughed and settled her head against his chest, wrapping her arms around his waist and squeezing. "I can almost forget we're not in terrible danger."

She tensed, and it tugged at his heart. She did that a lot, that heart-tugging thing, mostly without even trying. He didn't want to intensify her worries, especially when it was his job to worry. This was a much-needed break from the running-for-their-lives thing. The balance to the bad stuff.

"So what now?" she said, sounding contemplative. With her brilliance, glossing over their predicament didn't have a chance of fooling her.

"What do you mean?"

"What are we going to do now that we're hidden and relatively safe?"

"Lie low until I have a chance to figure this out and get healed," he murmured, squeezing her tighter.

"Mmm," she hummed, kissing his chin, then rubbing her cheek on his stubble. "You hung up on your boss." She sighed a little, then gave him a worried, solemn look. "Are you going to lose your job because of me?"

He held her gaze for a long minute, then sighed a little himself. "I don't know. I don't care at this point. What I told him is sound. They found us, and I want to know how before I'll feel confident in taking you back to NCIS or anywhere near D.C. Your life is more important."

Her eyes widened. "You really mean that, don't you?"

"I say what I mean, Sky."

She rose up on her tiptoes. Her face softened, and his gut twisted at the look there. She cupped his face and ran her thumb over his cheekbone. "I'm so scared. It would really help if I could get my laptop. I need to work."

"I know you're scared and you want to work to keep your mind off it, but we need to stay off the radar for a bit. I'd like to know what they want you for. This guessing game is getting old. I wish I could have interrogated one of those bastards."

"But you were forced to kill them all."

He drew her to the bed, and they settled under the blankets, snuggling up against each other. "I'm sorry you had to see that…brutality." He'd been trained as a warrior, had seen more than his share of combat and had carried the scars of all those battles on his body in one place or another. He was honed, and, after the military, it just was natural for him to continue to keep that edge. NCIS was not just about chasing down murderers. He'd had run-ins with rogue CIA assassins, terrorists and had been in Afghanistan and other parts of the Middle East that were extremely dangerous. All his combat experience had been a factor in each of those assignments. He knew how to conduct himself out in the field. Did he still think of himself as Uncle Sam's weapon, even though he was in a civil organization? Maybe that was how he'd kept his edge, and with this woman, this beautiful woman in his arms safe from harm, he was grateful he had.

She rose on her elbow. She was looking him over pretty good, her blue-eyed gaze focused on his, taking his measure, which was damned unnerving. What did she see when she remembered how vicious he'd been? "You said you were in the marines. Is that where you learned…?"

"How to kill so efficiently?" He hesitated, not sure he wanted her to know anything about this. "Yes. They trained me as a scout sniper. It's all about stealth, and a knife makes no noise. I made damn sure I was good with a knife."

"What is a 'scout sniper'?"

She distracted him as she ran her fingers into his hair at his temple. He closed his eyes, trying to concentrate. "Shooter and spotter in teams of two. One scouts. One takes the shots. Both of us are trained."

When he opened his eyes, she was looking down at him with a thoughtful expression on her face. "What are you thinking so hard about?"

"What? Oh, nothing. Go on."

"What did you want to know?"

"Everything. All of it."

"After boot camp and service, becoming a sniper is elite training."

"What was that like, boot camp?"

"Hot, sweaty, intense, exhausting. A lot of running, physical conditioning, martial arts and classes. Thirteen weeks of intensity and almost zero personal time. Every moment you're expected to do something. The cliché, I'm afraid. The marines did make a man out of me. I had no idea what exactly I was made of until I went to Parris Island, South Carolina."

She was quiet for a moment. Then her hand slipped down to his chest for more distracting caressing. He loved the feel of her hand on him. He raised himself up on his elbow, and she took a breath watching him.

"What? Why do you keep looking at me like that? Tell me I didn't scare you. That seeing me…that…savage…"

Her eyes widened, and she covered his mouth. "No, Vin. Seeing you in combat didn't scare me. The total opposite. I'm awed by the lengths you went to protect me. I feel like you have lived, and I have just…well, existed."

He leaned forward and nuzzled her neck. She smelled like heaven. "Why is that? Why the isolation?"

"The work. It's consuming…." She trailed off, lifted a shoulder.

They both collapsed to the mattress, settling against each other. He grazed her jaw with his teeth, and she trembled. A shuddering sigh left her, and her hips rose against him, the smallest movement. "Ah, now you're ducking my question."

She let out a shaky breath when he reached her ear.

When she didn't say anything, he stayed silent and let it go. They were both tired. The air was almost still, and the smell from the fireplace lent a cozy sense of safety Vin knew was a lie.

There was something special about Sky, something inherently innocent in this woman. He could only wish she had a little more defense against him. He still wasn't convinced they were compatible. Her comment about him wasting his time had been shunted aside by his desire and their passion, but it was still there. He and Brittany hadn't worked because she couldn't accept who he was. He couldn't remember her asking anything about the marines. Maybe it was his failing that he couldn't get past that disappointment in her. It was much too familiar.

Right now was about getting through each day. If there was one thing that he was sure about, it was that problems had a way of showing themselves eventually.

He always had to be true to himself.

Always.

That was what drove him.

He tightened his arms around her.

He wasn't sure where this would all lead.

But what he was sure about was that he was her shield.

They would have to go through him to get to her.

Chapter 9

Alexander Andreyev bit into the chicken, pulling the meat violently off the bone, seething. It was probably not good for his digestion. It was late afternoon of the next day after he'd lost the navy scientist. His name was shit with his employer after having lost her once and missing her this time. They were adamant. She needed to be in their hands in two days or everything they had done would be all for nothing. They assured him that meant he would not get paid.

He hated not getting paid.

He turned to look at Dmitry, who approached cautiously. He had a terrible temper, and his men knew it. They often gave him a wide berth when things didn't go his way.

"Alex," Dmitry said, crouching down so that Alex didn't have to look up.

"What is it?"

"I have information on the agent as you instructed."

"Talk," he said, taking another bite of the succulent meat.

"Special Agent Vincent Fitzgerald has been with NCIS for three years."

"He doesn't conduct himself like a wet-behind-the-ears recruit."

"He isn't. He was a marine before he joined NCIS."

Alex swore softly under his breath. "What kind of marine?"

"Scout sniper."

He swore again. "That is how he was able to take our guy on the roof so easily. He is obviously a very good marksman. Dangerous. Anything we can use?"

"Nothing that I could find out from the information I was able to get. He doesn't own any property, rents an apartment. I could not find anything about his family. That was wrapped up tight. We've already been to the apartment. He and the woman are not there. He didn't return to NCIS in D.C. I believe he is off the grid."

"He's gone dark."

"Looks like it."

"Can you hack his email account?"

"I can try, but the security at NCIS is formidable. It might not be possible."

"No, not his work account. His personal account. See if he's got any friends he corresponds with or family. I need to find out where he's gone to ground."

"But we have the microdot...."

"That is not an ace in the hole, Dmitry. I want the advantage to be solely on our side." He grabbed the younger man behind the back of the neck and squeezed. "Don't let me down. Earn that high cut I give you."

"Yes, sir."

She couldn't seem to help watching him out the window as he hiked around the cabin. He studied the area, storing information, looking for the best escape route, she was sure, looking for a weakness in their defense.

When she'd awakened, he was already up and dressed, stocking wood, saying that his shoulder was better, but she wasn't so sure he wasn't just enduring the pain.

By midafternoon, he'd gone outside and started to walk around the perimeter, doing what she could only call reconnaissance. She suspected that was ingrained in him from his military training.

She'd slept with him. Had sex with him, and she couldn't regret a moment of it. Still the guilt was there, buried beneath the surface. She should be open and clear with him. This was a time out of time. She wasn't looking for a long-term relationship. She had her work. That was enough. Would have to be enough.

Now it was getting dark as he disappeared from view, she craned her neck as she started dinner. He was dressed in jeans that hugged his lower body, a white turtleneck and a red sweater with a zipper at the throat. On his feet were sturdy work boots that traversed through the mud and snow. She could see the river from the window and a dock with a boathouse attached to it. The water flowed past, not yet to the freezing point in Pennsylvania.

He came in through the back door, stamping the snow and mud onto the rug. "I'm going to run into town and pick up some supplies. Did you make a list?"

She nodded and walked across the kitchen to where he was standing and handed him the list. Her skin tingled as she got closer to him.

"Dinner should be ready by the time you get back."

"Lock the door and don't let anyone in while I'm gone. I'll be quick." He left, and she went back to the preparation.

Fifteen minutes later, it was getting dark. She heard the car before seeing the headlights. Holding her breath, ready to move like he'd instructed, she kept her eyes on the driveway. When she saw the car and him behind the wheel, she let her breath go slowly.

She forced herself to glance at him with nothing more than a quick smile from the pot of chili she was stirring. "Hey. Get everything?"

His eyes never left hers as he shrugged out of the leather coat that had been hanging on the hook by the door. She wondered if it belonged to his buddy. It looked good on him.

Her whole body thrummed in reaction to him coming toward her. Not that it was any surprise. He'd done some pretty wonderful things to her body earlier; of course it was going to react a little. Okay, a lot. But she should be worried about more important things than where she would sleep tonight. Was it bad that it was all she could think about while she made dinner?

She'd have to chastise herself later; she was more intent on how he fitted himself against her backside as if they had been doing this wonderful interaction for months instead of one night, his breath fanning the back of her neck, fitting into her personal space as easily as breathing. Her instant response was to rest her back against him.

"Did you find everything on the list?"

He leaned in and brushed his lips just below her ear, inhaling deeply. "You smell good."

"Probably dinner."

He sniffed again. "Nope. That's all you, sweetheart."

She couldn't help it; she was impossibly charmed with the way he so effortlessly made her light up inside. Dipping her chin to hide her besotted expression, she continued to stir the blend of beans and hamburger meat. "I'm sure you're hungry."

"Mmm," he murmured. "Starving."

Her body went from buzzing to shuddering, and it took formidable self-control to keep from turning into his arms, maybe even pushing him down on the small kitchen table and having her way with him.

"How is your shoulder?" she said, the warmth of his breath against her skin tantalizing.

"Better. Still hurts, but usable."

"You should have let me change the bandage this morning."

"I didn't want to get…distracted."

Her pulse dipped, immediately getting his meaning. Maybe she was getting less nerdy and more worldly? "Don't you think we can behave long enough to tend to you medically?" She turned to look at him over her shoulder, and her insides sizzled at the hot green of his eyes. Okay, maybe not.

"I can only speak for myself and go by the experiences of yesterday. So, that would be a no for me. How about you? Do you have this…this thing we're doing under control? Any scientific theories?"

"Newton's Law of Motion fits. When one body exerts a force on a second body, the second body simultaneously exerts a force equal in magnitude and opposite in direction to that of the first body."

"Now you're teasing me in nerd-speak. That's making me hot."

She giggled. Actually giggled. "We should be focusing on other things. That might help."

He tightened his arms around her. "Like what?"

"Dinner, for one."

"It smells great." He nudged her hips and shifted her around to face him.

She lifted the spoon to offer him a taste but suspected it wasn't chili he wanted to savor. "We also need to talk about...other stuff."

He cupped her hand and drew the spoon to his mouth, where he slowly licked the chili sauce off, while watching her with twinkling eyes. "Mmm-hmm," he agreed.

Her knees became unsteady, and she knew she should be ashamed at how easily he could seduce her into shirking her promise, but damn the man, he made it really hard to concentrate. And it wasn't as if there was anything they could do right now to figure out what was going on. That was the whole point of lying low. But she wanted to know if NCIS had found out anything. When she could go home and leave this dreamy time with Vin and this terrible uncertainty of the threat of kidnapping.

"I'm not kidding, Vin," she told him, the warning directed more at herself than him. But if she'd been hoping to solicit some of his help to remain cool, she was fooling herself. Except being cool was far from what she was feeling when his eyes went dark and he removed the spoon from her hand and set it on the counter, covering the pot and turning the burner right to simmer.

Simmer was right.

"You started it with the sexy nerd-speak and all that body talk. I got a feeling you don't know you make me crazy?" he murmured as she backed up. He walked toward her as she playfully backed away from him with a smile. His eyes lit all the way from the kitchen to the bedroom, without laying a hand on her, but remaining so fully in her personal space, she felt thoroughly joined to him on a deep level.

She'd never felt this safe before, this close to a man, and yet she couldn't seem to open up. Was she fooling herself? It was probably some sane form of self-preservation. She needed to hold on to her sanity here. This was a temporary situation probably brought about by adrenaline, fear and dependency on this man who was smiling like a rogue. A warrior rogue.

"Did you figure out a good escape route while you were outside?" she asked him, hearing the thread of need in her voice, even as she tried to fend off his charming magic. He wouldn't be around long, and she was fighting with the need to indulge herself while she could and maintain some semblance of control to stop herself from wanting too much, want what she couldn't really have. Certainly more than she was ever going to get to keep, as that was going to be exactly nothing. It wasn't about her. It was about what she'd promised.

"I'm always prepared for escape," he said, as she slipped into the bathroom.

Was that the sniper in him? The hit-and-run kind of mentality. Surely he was referring to them escaping, but she couldn't be sure about anything. She didn't really know him that well. It was for the better, she told herself.

"That's exactly what I want to hear from the guy who's supposed to be protecting me," she said, although the words weren't much more than a hushed whisper as she came to a halt up against the sink.

Maybe she just needed to take him and keep taking him until they both burned their need for each other out of their systems. Apparently they hadn't come close to reaching that point yet. Not if the flames of desire presently raging between them in the small confines of the bathroom was any sign.

"As it should be. Can you change my bandage now?" he asked, keeping his eyes on hers.

"This couldn't wait until after dinner? After all, you waited this long."

"I was busy doing my job and keeping you safe. You wouldn't want me to get an infection, would you?" He kept his eyes pinned on hers as she reached out to unzip the sweater to his breastbone, the knit warm beneath her fingers.

"Oh, no. We shouldn't chance that," she said, reacting to the amused smile turning up the corners of his delectable mouth. "That would be too dangerous."

She slipped her hand under both the sweater and the turtleneck, helping him work the garments off.

This was dangerous. Just as dangerous as the men chasing them.

Pulling the clothes over his head revealed his broad chest and wide shoulders. He leaned down and tried to kiss her. She smirked as she put her hand into the center of his chest and pushed him onto the commode. "We shouldn't waste a minute. Look at that. You feel overly warm."

He smiled, full out, and her heart stalled. It transformed his somewhat austere face into something boyish and appealing, as if he wasn't already appealing enough.

"I don't think my temperature rising has anything to do with infection," he said softly, "but everything to do with…fever."

He placed his hands on her waist, sliding them beneath her shirt to the bare skin of her abdomen, his head tipped up to hers, that smile still in place.

She shamelessly enjoyed how his hands felt as they brushed against her skin. "You wouldn't be seducing me in order to keep me from more geek-speak, would you?"

Pushing her shirt up, he looked up at her, then down at her exposed midriff. He grinned. "Would it work?"

She shook her head.

"Then I guess the answer is no." He leaned in closer, tugging on the waistband of her jeans, the smile disappearing from his face as it went intense and sexy-serious, as if her stomach was something to be investigated fully.

He was an *experience.* Everything about him was so rich and flavored. Vin wanted her. Passionately, his hands sliding around her waist and drawing her toward him, his breathing ragged. He settled his mouth against the skin of her stomach, his lips warm, reverent and soft. The feel of him was intoxicating, dizzying. He set her on fire with his kiss, made her gasp, and every inch of her wanted more.

Her hands tingled, and she thought about that so embarrassing moment when she'd asked him if she could touch him. The warmth of his face, heavy breathing sending shivers over her skin, and the prickle of his stubble all added to the desire to fondle him.

Her hand went into his so soft hair, kneading his scalp and tugging at the inky strands, her palms absorbing the deep sensual feel of Vin.

They were in the middle of nowhere. No rules and no one in control. No one knew where they were. She couldn't even *hear* the traffic on the highway. Was that because she was so caught up in watching him? Feeling him?

The realization added a dark thrill to the whole heart-stopping experience of having Vin make love to her with his mouth.

It was crazy. Crazy and hot and utterly sexual in a way she'd thought she would never know except in her fantasies where men didn't roughly take her when she hadn't been prepared and have it over before she could even say good-night.

Ah, damn, now she thought about how Vin could take her roughly. She was more than ready for him, and now she realized the difference between that terrible past experience and her joining with Vin. He'd taken it slow, and it had almost been as if she was experiencing it for the first time. The other incident was fading away, becoming nothing but background noise.

The experience with Vin was ongoing, even when they weren't touching. Just looking at each other, like back in the kitchen. The kiss was already in his eyes, and that was just as unexpected as finding out Vin could keep up with her intelligence; doubly unexpected was the way he was so comfortable with it. "I thought you said that my Newton geek-speak was getting you hot," she said, torn between a laugh at how freeing it was to be with him and a soft moan on how deliciously good the things he was doing with his tongue made her feel. The soft moan won as he continued kissing her.

"I said your teasing was getting me hot, although your clever sexual innuendo was pretty damn good."

She bent over and kissed the top of his head, sliding her hand to his nape, and then her gaze snagged on the bandage. Damn, she was supposed to be changing it. She'd been so caught up in him.

"Wait," she said, pulling away, and he raised his head with a quizzical expression on his face.

"Your bandage. We need to change it."

He rose, sliding against her, pressing against her breasts, his hands working on pulling up her sweater.

She grabbed his wrists and looked into his hot green eyes. Of course he was stronger, but Sky knew without a doubt he would never use his strength against her.

"You're going to insist," he said.

"I am. We've already waited too long."

"You're right. Better to be safe. If I get sick, I won't be able to function."

She nodded.

"Afterwards, can you stop teasing me and let me kiss you?"

She stared up at him with his sexy stubble, his eyes going soft and tender, the beautiful form of his mouth. "Oh, just shut up and kiss me." She lifted up on her tiptoes and pressed her mouth to his, wrapping her arms around his neck. The kiss she gave him was something more than just sexual. Her mouth fused to his, softening and responding to the heat and feel of him. Regardless of the physical attraction, she couldn't hide that she had real affection for him.

Oh, damn. She'd been spontaneous without thinking. That made her stomach tie up in knots right away. She had to really think hard about the last person she felt this way about. She came up with no one. Sure, she'd had affection for teachers and classmates, but this feeling for Vin... It was different.

When she pulled away and pressed against his chest to get him to sit, he took a breath as if he'd just had the same kind of revelation she'd had.

"You should tell me to shut the hell up more often," he said, dropping down onto the commode.

Getting involved with Vin would be a mistake. She wasn't going to be a long-term prospect for him. But then she realized that he was probably thinking the same thing. It was understandable that she would have feelings for the man who had gone to such courageous lengths to protect her from danger.

It was just infatuation.

She had to put all this into perspective.

She was so sure Vin would.

"You are full of surprises," he said as she got to work on the bandage at his shoulder, avoiding his eyes and pretending to study his wound.

What was that saying? It was like closing the barn door after the horse had escaped. Yes, that was the vernacular. That horse had definitely escaped. She busied herself with changing the bandage. The night he'd taken this bullet came back to her like a wrecking ball. She squeezed her eyes tightly closed, exhaling a whisper-soft, distressed sound. Then her heart twisted in her chest, and before she realized what she was going to do, she leaned forward and kissed the freshly bandaged wound.

He took a quick breath, his face swinging around to meet her eyes, and she couldn't seem to hide what she was thinking. She trembled at the new emotions and sensations this man evoked in her. And she knew she was just kidding herself, even as she mourned the lost distance.

"Sky," he said softly and took her hand, drawing it to his mouth. "Aw, sweetheart…" His voice trailed off. When his lips touched her skin, she felt it all the way to her heart, because his eyes were luminous in the bright light of the room. He didn't say anything, just kissed her skin and gazed up at her under those thick, black lashes that veiled not only the green of his eyes, but the heartbreaking look that she didn't want to see there. She didn't want it.

It was her next breath—that look.

And the fear that lurked in her heart at the same time.

How was she supposed to handle this?

She had no experience.

He turned her hand over and placed a hot kiss on her wrist, sliding his mouth along her skin, his breath warm. When he reached the tender spot where her forearm met her elbow, he slipped his hand around her waist and urged her forward against him.

She was stunned, charmed. He gathered her closer, settling her against him as if she was his next breath. The full length of him pressed against her, the soft places yielding against his hard body. She sank against him, wanting to never leave and feeling the terrible pressure to run. The warmth of him relaxed her in a way her meditation CDs never could.

Her intellect wasn't helping her here. Her high IQ wasn't giving her any answers, and Vin was tougher than any math equation she'd ever tried to figure out.

He rested his chin on her head, and she released the pressure of those deep emotions that had built in her chest. She buried her face in his chest and tried to breathe through the tightness in her throat.

Keeping their gazes disconnected a little while longer, she didn't want to risk him seeing anything else in her gaze, especially when she hadn't sorted it all out herself just yet.

When the silence continued and reality began to creep in, he pressed a kiss to her hair and said, "Dinner is probably getting overcooked."

Grateful that he was getting them back onto such an ordinary plane, she gave him a little shove with her shoulder, smiling in spite of herself.

She shifted in his arms, felt that strange bubbling inside her. He made her feel...happy? Was that the word she was looking for? She dug into his ribs this time with her fingers, and he let out a huffing sound and gulped in air while laughter erupted. He made a grab for her hands, but she backed up.

"No fair, attacking a wounded guy."

"I'm the dirty, street-fighting kind of scientist."

He smirked, his eyes twinkling.

"Right. Let's see if you can take it as well as you can dish it out." He broadcast his intention. She tensed to run, but moving faster than she thought possible, he lunged forward. He snagged her around the waist with his good arm, and his strong fingers went right for her rib cage.

She giggled and struggled against him. "Stop it," she ordered breathlessly as he held her.

He laughed, swinging her around, pulling her back against him, placing a kiss where her neck met her shoulder, and she couldn't seem to think. She sighed and leaned into him, knowing her walls had crumbled so swiftly that there was sure to be a big, ugly reckoning coming her way later. But she was happy now, and it was something so new, so unexpected, she decided to worry later about the eventuality of dealing with whatever was going to come.

"Come on, street fighter," he said, lifting her hair

and kissing her nape, sending a delicious tingling sensation skittering over her skin. "You can show me your deadly moves later."

He was teasing her and she liked it a lot. Her skin heated just thinking about what moves she wanted to show him. She bit her lip as she tried to fight off the inevitable reality check. It would be nice if this time with Vin could be about them and not about safeguarding her from danger. She wasn't naive. He was her protector and they had been through something intense together. It was natural to want to celebrate life. "I bet you want to see my moves, too."

"I do," he growled in her ear as he nudged her forward and slapped her backside. She turned around, met his eyes and wished she'd just exited the bathroom and left it alone. Her heart bumped against her chest, and she immediately spun around and started out.

"Whoa, there," he said, catching her by the shoulder and spinning her. He captured her chin and turned her face up to his. Obviously she wasn't as good as she hoped she was in hiding her anxiety about anything right now.

"We'll refuel. Talk. Get to know each other a little better. Strategize. It'll all be good." He got close and tilted his head and smiled, giving her such a cute boyish look she couldn't help smiling back at his appeal.

"Strategize? Plan A and plan B."

"Maybe even—" he took up a stance and put his hands out, and his face got serious "—a plan C." He leaned forward and kissed her.

For some unexplained reason, it was that quick, soft kiss, so natural and so damn sweet, that did her in. Tears welled in her eyes, horrifying her, but there didn't seem to be any stopping them.

"I don't want to lose myself to those…terrible men." *And I don't want to lose you.* This was really the whole reason for the tears welling up. That thought sucker punched her out of nowhere. But he didn't have to know how she felt, could never know that. Not after she'd been the one to seduce him into taking their relationship to a place he was trying to avoid. Yes, he had wanted it to go the way it had, but he was better at fighting the temptation than she had been.

"I'm here to prevent that." He tipped up her chin. "Hey, where's my tough street fighter?"

She gave him a wan smile, and he chucked her under the chin and said, "Come on. That chili smells delicious."

She preceded him out of the bathroom, but stopped short outside the door. "Um, you go ahead. I just need a moment."

He nodded and slid past her. "Don't think too hard about it, Sky," he said, disappearing out of the bedroom door.

She swiped at her eyes, wondering when she'd lost her mind.

That was simple. The instant she'd stopped taking care of herself and let herself lean on somebody. Maybe he'd had the right idea all along. Letting themselves want each other, giving in to that want, led to allowing themselves to depend on each other. To needing things that they shouldn't be needing…and wanting things they couldn't have.

Right now she needed a little privacy, a chance to

regroup, to figure out what she wanted—no, what she *needed* to do next. She knew what she wanted.

She leaned back against the closed bathroom door and let out a long, contented sigh now that Vin couldn't see her. Yeah, the thought of him taking her roughly was back. She squeezed her eyes shut. It only made the images in her mind stronger. The sensations, how he filled her when he'd been thrusting inside of her, made her thighs clench together as her muscles jumped at the thought of him.

She turned suddenly away and rubbed vigorously at her face, catching her reflection in the mirror as she did so. It stunned her that she looked no different, completely unchanged, same long, dark hair, same delicate arched brows, her full mouth and plump lips and the same cobalt-blue eyes. She looked closer, meeting her gaze headlong in the mirror. No, she'd been wrong. The blue was the same, but that depth was new. Something that hadn't been there before she'd gone through this ordeal. Before she'd met a very special agent. Confusion was new to her, though. Usually her head was quite clear. Her gaze landed right on the bed. How likely was it that they wouldn't end up back there? Not long from now. She took a long, deep breath as her body made it clear that it was enthusiastically on board. So much for regrouping.

She jumped when his voice came sailing in through the open bedroom door. "If you don't get your butt out here, Sky, I'm going to carry you over my shoulder, then force-feed you with *choo-choo* whistle sounds."

She snorted. She was a goner. How was she supposed

to shore up her defenses, resume her steely-eyed distance from a guy who'd brought her through hell, taken her to heaven, then made her laugh?

Chapter 10

Chris paced while the news played in the background. He could hear Sia laughing as she bathed their son, Raphael.

Why the hell hadn't Fitzgerald checked in? He was already skating on thin ice with the director for disappearing with Dr. Baang.

His cell rang, and he snatched it off the coffee table. "Vargas."

"Boss, it's me."

"Beau, what are you still doing at work?"

"I couldn't relax, knowing that there are tangos out there dogging Vin. I found some hacking activity on our database. Not much of a breach, but they got something on Vin."

"What the hell!"

"The guy was good, but not good enough to get deeper into our database. IT is on it."

"They damn well better be. Where's Vin's family?"

"Boston."

"Call the field office and get some agents over to his family's residence. Tell them to use caution, and, for the love of God, don't freak out the family. If he doesn't call in soon, he's going to be in even hotter water."

"He's doing his job, boss. Protecting Dr. Baang. I don't know how the safe house was compromised unless there was an internal leak. It seems to me he's justified."

"We have protocol for a reason, Beau. Do you have any idea where he could have gone?"

"No, but I can dig around and see if I can come up with something. I'll call you back if I find out anything."

"I'm worried about him, too. See what you can do. Is Amber there, too?"

"Um…would you believe me if I said no?"

"No."

Chris hung up, but then his cell phone chimed again. He answered.

"Special Agent Vargas, this is Dr. Russell Coyne," the man on the other line said. "I was wondering if Dr. Baang is all right. I've tried her cell numerous times and she's not answering."

"There was an incident at the safe house. She's been moved."

"I really need to speak with her. I have a presentation at the end of the week, and I need the results of a test she recently ran. It's imperative."

"I'll see what I can do to help, but her safety is much more important than data, Dr. Coyne."

"Of course it is. I'm as concerned about her welfare as you are. If you could ask her to call me as soon as she can, I would very much appreciate it."

"I'll relay the message when I can."

"Thank you. Good night."

Chris disconnected the call and swore softly under his breath. He got up and walked into the bathroom. "Sia, sweetheart, I have to go back to the office."

"Is Vin still off the radar?"

"Yes, and if he doesn't call in soon, I'm going to have to put him on administrative leave and pull him off this detail."

"Really, even though he's trying to save this woman. Chris, can't you stall? You know Vin and how good he is. I've never known his observation skills to be off."

"I agree." He cupped her cheek. "I may be home late or out all night."

"You do what you have to. We'll be here when you get home. Be careful." He kissed her and headed out the door. He wasn't going to sleep while his team was working hard. One more head might help.

"That looks really good," Sky said as she settled across the table from him. "Look at you. You set the table and everything."

"I have skills," he said, watching her without trying to watch her. He was completely screwed. He knew it deep in his gut. Sky was trying to hide her anxiety, and really he didn't even know her story. He was sure she had one, especially after she'd dropped that bomb about him wasting his time at NCIS when he'd first met her. The woman drove him crazy with the wanting of not just her body, but of that agile and brilliant mind. She was clever and funny, but what was putting that anxiety in her eyes? It wasn't tied to the kidnapping. He was sure it was tied to him.

He was the root of the problem, but he was very observant, could read people just like he'd read what kind of clothes she would prefer. It was all about that *knowing* he'd always possessed.

She wasn't even doing anything particularly remarkable or cute at the moment. She was just digging into her food, sipping at her iced tea from a bottle. He'd guessed correctly that she didn't drink soda. She was dressed in faded jeans now, along with a light green T-shirt and an oversize sweater that refused to stay on both shoulders at the same time. Her hair was loose, spilling over her shoulders in a long, inky fall, no makeup on her face, her cheeks a little flushed from their encounter in the bathroom.

He took a spoonful of the chili, trying not to think about what he'd wanted to do just a few moments ago in the bathroom.

The mere thought brought his body leaping to life. He'd stayed away from her all day on purpose, trying to get his head around what exactly he was doing. This compromised him. Compromised his professionalism. He wasn't proud of that. But was it just skin deep? Was it about the physical and sex? She was a beautiful woman. That was evident just from looking at her. But the complications and the complexity of her intrigued him more.

He drew his eyes away so that she wouldn't catch him staring at her with a sappy look on his face.

It was getting close to her that had triggered it. He could overcome it.

Exactly after he'd had her, like, maybe, a hundred more times.

Yeah, maybe.

She reached up and tucked her hair behind her ear. "Oh, I made garlic bread. I'll get it." She pushed away from the table, and he watched her graceful moves as she grabbed a napkin-covered basket off the counter.

"That sounds good."

"It's nothing to get excited about. Might be a little cold. Do you want me to warm them up?"

"It's all good," he said as she offered him the basket. He reached out and snagged a piece of garlic bread. "I appreciate you taking the time to make it." If she was aware how she turned him on, she'd run and keep running the hell away from him.

It was both relaxed and amazingly awkward between them. He was pretty sure he knew why; they weren't sure where things stood between them or where they wanted them to stand. At least he wasn't, anyway. They both dug into the food, neither speaking for several long moments. "It looks like the snow is finally letting up. More wet than anything else. I won't even have to shovel the driveway."

Taking a sip of her tea, she said, "How long do you think we'll have to stay here?"

"Until we find out if there's a leak at NCIS or we catch the Russians, neutralize the threat to you."

"Do you think it would be possible to get my laptop?" She held his gaze steadily because she had to be aware this was going to rile him up. "At the very least I could keep working."

The threat to her was real. Giving away their location because she wanted to work seemed like a foolish idea. "I'd prefer to lie low for a bit longer. But I'll consider it."

She gave him a quelling look. "You'll consider it? I knew you'd react this way." Her voice rose slightly. "Don't I have any say in this?"

She had said that her work was her life, had confessed that she really hadn't lived much. "You have a say to a certain extent. I will be the one to assess risk. I don't care if you get mad about it. I say we keep a low profile for now. I haven't even checked in yet." His voice had gone flat.

She set her spoon down. This time her look was peeved and concerned. "Vin, I don't want you to jeopardize your job for me. Isn't there an alternative? A middle ground."

He bristled. "There is no middle ground when it comes to your freedom or your life, Sky. And I'm not worried about jeopardizing my job. Two NCIS agents were killed to get to you. There was a very short list of who knew your location. I don't trust anyone right now. I was assigned as your bodyguard and I'm damn well going to do my job my way."

"Everything else be damned?" Her eyes went stormy.

He rose and walked over to her, realizing that she was being driven by her own need to keep working, keep busy. "I know this is scary and you want some kind of normalcy, but not at the expense of your life." He braced one hand on the table and the other on her chair back, his thumb caressing the soft skin of her neck. His anger was sparked by the thought of losing her.

She was quiet for so long, he didn't think she was going to respond. He'd been tough with her more than once in this conversation, not giving an inch on her safety, and if she didn't like that, too damn bad. But bulldozing over her feelings wasn't right, either.

"I'm sorry I got angry," he said, his voice rough. "I'm…concerned about keeping you safe. It's all I care about right now."

She made a soft sound in her throat, her expression going pained, her eyes softening. She surged off the chair, wrapping her arms around his neck. His arms came around her immediately, crushing her close. She held on to him as the pressure increased in his throat. Her chest expanded raggedly, and he smoothed his hand up the back of her neck. "Dammit, Sky, I'll keep you safe, sweetheart. Just let me…do my job."

She huffed out an impatient sigh. "This is a pretty good tactic you got going."

"What?"

"You know what. Using emotion to manage me."

"If it's working, I'll use it. Anything to keep you from falling into their hands. But let's get something straight. I'm only managing you because of a threat to your safety. I'm not a controlling jerk."

"I get it. I do. I don't want to be in this situation, but I am. I want you to keep me safe. I just want my laptop, Vin. I need it to stay sane."

"I get that and I'll think about it. Trust me in this. I'm a cop, Sky. That's what I do. Before that I was a marine."

"And before that?" The tension seemed to have drained out of her. His honest admission about keeping her safe had soothed her.

His lips tightened and he eased his hold. She folded back down into the chair and he returned to his seat.

"You don't want to talk about that?"

"About my affluent family in Boston? No. Not really." All he had to say about that was how much he'd let his father down. Vin had quite literally escaped by going into the service.

"Boston? That's where you're from?"

Leaning back, he said, "Yes. My family is well-off and paragons of the city. I could have had that life if I had wanted it. Could still have it," he said, the words sounding bitter even to his own ears. "Then I would be my daddy's best boy all over again."

"At least you have a family."

"I'm sorry. I didn't mean to sound insensitive. But when you have these expectations hanging over you, it leads to a lot of disappointment. I'm just setting the record straight."

"I know about expectations. I have the ghosts of my parents haunting me. But you're talking about disappointment? In choosing NCIS over...?"

"The family business."

"Oh, that is tough. Where I come from, family is everything. It's something to sacrifice for. But you're such a good NCIS agent, can't they see that makes you happy and fulfilled?" This was so different from the conversation he'd had with Brittany. She'd urged him to give up NCIS and go back to Boston, take up the corporate life and embrace his responsibilities, as if by working for the agency, he was shirking his duties. Damn, she so hadn't understood him or even accepted him for the kind of man he was. No way to build any kind of lasting relationship. "I don't think my father wants to acknowledge my accomplishments at NCIS because he wants me back on board. Are you happy with your choices?"

She bit her lip and looked away. "Sometimes there aren't choices, especially when you have talents and abilities others don't have. Sometimes there's just a choice, a promise." There was an unnatural tenseness in every line of her body, such a tormented look in her eyes. She was fighting something that was intensely personal. Something that was eating her alive.

"You are the only one who can shape your own life. Relying on expectations and absolutes doesn't really work well. It certainly doesn't make us happy with our choices...particularly if they're not our own."

"I know it can't be easy. I know your work is important to you on a personal level. I need to use my gift and try to do justice to my parents' sacrifice. Aren't those worthwhile goals?"

"Yes, they are worthwhile, but life isn't just about that. Keeping things in perspective goes a long way to making us not only happy, but fulfilled with what we're doing."

"I guess my upbringing and culture plays a big part in how I see it. I can't make it make sense any other way. I lost my mother because of my intelligence and my father last year. I'm sure that I'm not telling you anything you haven't read in my background, so this isn't anything new to you. They protected me with their very lives. That's what scares me about you. I don't want anyone else to have to die for me."

"You lost your parents because the Chinese murdered them, not because of you," he said pointedly until her shoulders relaxed and she nodded. "Yes, I know your background. It was my job to read your file, but I didn't know you then. You were just a designated target then. Now it's different. I care what you went through and feel for you that you lost your parents under such terrible circumstances. It also makes me look at my relationship with my family differently. Sometimes we take things for granted because we really don't know anything else. I'm just trying to point out that people have to make their own choices and not buckle under the pressure of expectations."

She nodded and toyed with her chili. "I try not to take anything for granted. Maybe I have isolated myself in a lab and you think that's wrong. But my parents were very protective of me after I was kidnapped. Fear does that to you. It altered them, and we were never the same as a family. It was always about that damn fear. Sometimes I cursed my intelligence. But, like your parents, they too wanted the best for me. After my mother was killed, my father became increasingly paranoid. When he realized that he was being methodically framed for my mother's death, he knew he had to get me out of the country. The government wanted me, and with my mother and father out of the picture, they would have no impediment to their plans. I wonder if the Chinese..."

"Are after you? That this is just an attempt to bring you back into service for them?"

"Do you think that's far-fetched?" Her mouth tensed up, and her shoulders froze.

"I wouldn't discount your fear, Sky, but it's unlikely. I would wonder why after all this time. Surely they must realize that you've been Americanized. You now value freedom over captivity. You're not brainwashed into thinking that it's all about service to your government. Even here you have the choice on whether or not to serve your country or go into the private sector."

Her shoulders and mouth eased some. His gut instinct told him that they were after her for something she possessed in her navy-scientist brain and had nothing to do with her past.

"I would find working for the Chinese government nothing but aiding the enemy. The United States has my heart and my loyalty. They also really have nothing to hold over me. I can't be coerced into doing what they want."

"Threat of imprisonment or even death is not beyond the tactics they'd use, Sky."

She frowned. "I know. I'm not naive when it comes

to that, but I won't betray my country, not even to save my life."

"Your father got you out of China and away from becoming a slave for the government. His death must have really been difficult to handle."

"It was." She rose and grabbed her bowl and headed for the kitchen.

He should give her some space. He really should, but he was observant enough to realize that she was hurting and she was scared. He couldn't turn away from her.

He set his bowl in the sink as she rinsed hers out. "Sky, I can't imagine what you must have gone through. I also can't imagine what it was like for you to grow up in an unconventional way. Always being too young and too smart in a world of people older than you. I'm sure there was a lot of sacrifice, a lot of awkward and embarrassing moments, but I can imagine quite fully that your parents wouldn't want you to give up any kind of pursuit that would bring you joy. My father didn't care about my aspirations, but look at the lengths to which your father went to get you out."

She turned to him. "You don't understand. I have been told my whole life that it's my responsibility to make sure their sacrifice meant something. So, it's by choice that I have dedicated my life to making sure that I make a difference, no matter the personal cost. I'm honoring their sacrifice."

"By giving up your life, too? Isn't there something that you would love to do? Something that does give you joy?"

She pressed her hand to his chest. "Being with you brings me joy, Vin. Regardless of the circumstances, I care about you, and it's not caused by an adrenaline rush. But I have to be honest. My life is dedicated to science. There's no room for anything else. I need you now, and this thing between us is so potent. I'm not sure how to handle it."

She was such a contradiction. Here she was, admitting she needed him, that she was grateful for his help, the same woman who'd just about undone him in the bathroom, had unraveled him last night. But she seemed cautious, and he had to wonder what it was going to take to get her to open up to him.

Which was insanity. Because winning her over was not the objective here. Solving her problem was the only goal, and when that was accomplished, he'd go back to NCIS and she'd go back to her sterile lab.

He'd be lying if he said he had any regret about what had happened between them. Most likely it wasn't going to be easy to end it. Shit happened in life, and some of it was no damn fun. But being with her was giving him something he'd never had or felt before.

He covered her hand and squeezed, slipped his arm around her waist and drew her close to him. "So, wanna hear the plan with an open mind?"

She rested her head on his chest, and he felt like such a besotted fool.

"We do have a plan?"

He smiled at her wry tone. "Several. I have contingency plans."

"That does sound comforting."

"For tonight, we're going to relax and I'll call in. Tomorrow, I'll lay everything out for you."

She looked up at him with a slight smile on her face. "Will I get to at least make comments?"

"You may put your comments in the suggestion box."

She snorted. "Right. Come on, Vin. Be serious."

He smiled, then did get serious. "You can comment, but that doesn't mean I'll change the plan. Remember, I'm the risk guy."

"Okay," she said with a bit more confidence and a little less wary resignation. "Are you going to call in now?"

He nodded. "I am. Chris is going to tear me a new one, but I know I was right in getting you out of D.C. and Maryland. This was a good move, whether he can see it or not."

She nodded, but her gaze was more intent on him, her thoughts seemingly not as inward now.

"What?" he asked, when she continued to regard him in silence.

"Nothing. I just…" She trailed off, lifted a shoulder. "You're so focused in all this, clearly in your comfort zone, very confident and methodical. On the one hand, it reassures me, makes me feel like I can trust you."

"You can," he said automatically. "Always."

She nodded again right away, and it was almost ridiculous how good that made him feel. "I know that for a fact. You've already proved it more than once." She held his gaze, then looked away.

"Good," he said, trying like hell to keep it business. Which was hard to do when his heart was celebrating what felt like an important milestone in their relationship. A relationship that didn't exist, because it had nowhere to go, he reminded himself.

"On the other hand," she went on, "it scares me. You so clearly see this threat to me and are willing to do anything…." She swallowed and met his gaze. He was sure she was remembering him in that shadowed hallway, the men he'd killed in a heartbeat to keep her safe. "Anything," she said again. "I'm worried about you."

"I can take care of myself, Sky. Believe me."

"I do. It's that *anything* part that worries me."

"I'm not going to lie to you. They have an agenda and they want you alive. I don't think they're going to leverage you for political gain or ransom you. I think they have a job for you to do."

"I won't do it." Her defiance made him smile.

"I'm going to do my best to make that an impossibility, and you won't be placed in that position."

He released her and picked up one of the burner phones he'd bought. After ripping open the package, he dialed Chris's number.

Five minutes later, after a seething Chris had chewed him out, he'd calmed down enough to issue orders.

"Now that I've read you the riot act, get your ass in the car and get back to D.C. with Dr. Baang."

"No."

"I don't think I heard you correctly."

"She's in danger there. We're safer here."

Chris swore for a few seconds. "Convince me."

"Someone knew where she was. They are responsible for killing Strong and Miller. They would have killed me if they could. Seven of them tried. I barely got out of there alive with her. Do you want a repeat performance?"

"No. I don't."

"Do you want my badge?"

"No. I don't."

"Can you trust me on this? Pretend this is a safe house? Let me keep her here until every clue is investigated thoroughly. They're not going to stop coming for her. My gut tells me they want her for something specific. Something that has to do with her research."

"Speaking of that, her boss called. He needs to talk to her."

"Why?"

"Some data he needs for a presentation. A phone call should be fine since you have an untraceable phone."

"She wants her laptop. I could drive to D.C. to pick it up if it's that important. I know the minute I tell Sky about her boss's call she's going to insist."

"No. Don't come to the navy yard. I'll have Beau meet you somewhere. Let me know when you can get away. It'll be safer that way."

"All right."

"Vin, are you sure about this? I'll speak with the director and get him off your back, but he's going to want answers."

"That's up to you guys. I'm doing the heavy lifting here. Get to pulling your weight."

Chris chuckled. "I'm going to kick your ass when you get back here. Make sure you're in one piece."

"Yes, sir," Vin said, grinning. "I'll let you trounce me at darts."

"Let me…"

"Good night, Chris." He disconnected the call as his boss was sputtering about Vin throwing a game or two.

He looked around for Sky, but she'd cleaned up the kitchen and was nowhere to be found. He went looking for her.

She wasn't in the bedroom, and it suddenly occurred to him that they really hadn't discussed the…sleeping arrangements.

Yeah, right. As if he was thinking about sleeping.

He heard the water running in the bathroom and walked up to the open doorway, words on his lips. He never uttered them. Couldn't get them out as he just stared. She was facing away from him, her back toward the door, the long fall of her hair pinned on top of her head. Her back was a delicate expanse of creamy skin. A pink lacy nothing did a poor job of covering her lower half.

He must have made some kind of noise or she felt his presence. She turned her head and looked at him, and her eyes went sultry in response to his gaze. She inhaled softly, her breathing suddenly uneven.

His was downright ragged.

She covered her breasts with her arms. For some insane reason that modest move made him so goddamned hard.

The pink lace panties stretched across her taut butt, hugging her slim hips, coming to a bow just below the small of her back. She was reaching for a nightie but was now immobile.

"Vin," she said breathlessly.

He moved, walking up to her and stopping, his eyes going over her again. He reached out, captured the end of the bow with his thumb and forefinger and pulled. The garment loosened, and he curled his hands around her hips, sliding one over her mound until his fingers delved into the moist recesses of her. She gasped and arched her back, groaning softly. His mouth went unerringly to the soft skin of her back, kissing down the line of her spine.

His dick was so hard against his jeans, it was almost painful. He released her and spun her around, sliding his hands beneath the lace covering each hip and pushing the fabric down her body. He nudged her legs open, lifting one and placing it on the commode for balance, sliding both hands back up each inner thigh while she braced her sweet butt against the sink.

He knelt down, and her head fell back when he found her little bundle of nerve endings with his tongue, sucking on her as she thrust herself against his mouth, and still she kept her arms over her breasts.

"Feels so amazing," she moaned. "Make it a little rough, Vin."

He groaned at her words. He was feeling too damned reckless as it was, but those words slammed into his gut. She did feel amazing against him, and he wanted to hear her cry out his name.

Chapter 11

The exquisite sensation of him was the most erotic thing she'd ever felt in her life. Him on his knees in front of her felt shameless and reckless.

"Vin," she whispered on another soft groan.

His mouth softened on her and the aching liquid feel of him was melting her bones. The pleasure built in her with each sweep of his tongue, with each suctioning swirl of his mouth. A flash of heat washed over her, her hips bucking as the heavy ache increased until it detonated, and waves of bliss undulated through her. He rose in one swift movement.

He groaned, his breathing ragged, as he ripped his clothes off, but when she tried to help, he gently pushed her arms back. He wanted her to keep her breasts covered. It hit her hard. She was turning him on.

That thought sent power through her, and she wondered how far she could push him.

He stripped off his jeans and underwear as he kissed her, his mouth frantic, biting her lips as he kicked them off. Then he pressed her back against the sink, his warm, hard chest against her arms, flattening her breasts. Reaching for a condom, he slipped it on.

His harsh breathing increased as he roughly grasped

her arms, but she resisted. He made a guttural noise in the back of his throat and broke her hold, forcing her arms over her head, sliding his hands there to manacle her wrists, bracing them against the mirror. Her back curved over the sink, elevating her breasts. His eyes were filled with a wildness that made her moan.

"Yes," she whispered as he watched her face when he thrust against her core with the length of his hard, hot cock.

"Say you want me. Say it."

"I want you." She exhaled the words on a moan.

Yoga made her supple, her muscles not even straining. He lowered his head and ravenously took her nipple, scoring it with his teeth. The pleasure and pain of his bite arched her back, made her hips buck uncontrollably.

He sucked hard on her nipple almost to the point of pain, then used his tongue on the tip at the same time. She sobbed with the tingling ache from her nipple right to the center of her.

The rock-hard length of him brushed between her thighs. Her muscles were liquid from the clever mouth that was ravaging her nipple, sucking and licking her.

Then he turned her around and pressed into her buttocks. He pulled her arms behind her, capturing her wrists in one hand, holding them against the small of her back. With his free hand in the middle of her back, he pushed her over the sink. Then his hand was between her legs, opening them wider. With her rib cage against the sink, he slipped his hand over her hip, down into her moist core.

Their eyes met in the mirror. His gaze was dark with need and his face was pulled tight with it. He looked dangerously sexy, his thick, sable hair mussed from her hands. He was so achingly handsome in his need for her.

"Say my name," he demanded, the order a deep rumble in his chest.

"Vincent…Vin…*Vin*," she breathed.

The sound that slid from her was deep and throaty as he pumped into her without warning. She was so ready for him and pushed back onto him. He closed his eyes, his back arching, a fierce look on his face that made her cry out.

His eyes opened at the sound of her pleasure. He pulled out of her and remained still, his eyes challenging her.

"Please," she begged. *"More."*

He thrust the full length in a slow, controlled slide deeply into her, then out, and the rhythm built with each thrust. The connection she felt with him as their gazes held with each thrust was primal, untamed. He released her arms, and she used the sink to anchor herself as he leaned over her, nipping at her ear, while his hands slid up her torso, streaking her with fire.

He covered her breasts, his hands hot, his fingers pinching and rolling her nipples, wrenching groan after groan from her, but nothing matched the low shout of pleasure he wrenched from her when he slid one hand between her legs.

She felt as if she'd fallen into a fever dream. Her world had narrowed down and down to him. There was only him. The pressure of his body against her back, his hands doing wicked, wicked things to her.

She peaked quickly, almost brutally, and he kept his fingers there, slick and clever, kept her quivering and shuddering, until he was shaking with the effort to hold off his own devastating climax. She pushed back against him, craving more of him in some way and yet feeling so utterly full of him, she wasn't sure what more there was to have.

His hands slid back to her hips, his fingers pressing hard as he began pumping harder, faster. She met him thrust for thrust, her hands slipping on the porcelain as she fought to keep her grip. The mirror had fogged completely over, but there was no need to see him. She felt him so thoroughly it was as though she was part of him, as he was part of her. His climax, when he finally let it overtake him, was almost mindless in the tumultuous way he drove into her, body slapping against body, animalistic noises from both of them.

He collapsed over her, and they both fell over the sink. She braced their weight on the mirror, leaving streaks on the streamed glass, as he wrapped his arms around her waist and held her tightly to him, his body still shuddering in the aftermath.

It was hard to breathe in the thick air as their hearts raced and their bodies trembled. She had no idea how much time passed before he finally lifted her up and turned her around, saying nothing as he pulled her into his arms. He shifted, resting his weight against the sink as she leaned into him, still trying to slow her pulse, breathe. He seemed to be doing the same as he stroked her hair, pressed his cheek against the top of her head and just held her.

This was more. It was more than she was willing to admit to herself. She couldn't admit it. It would be too devastating to even contemplate what she so foolishly had allowed to happen. Her heart had been given, and there was no getting it back.

He took care of the condom. Then he picked her up in his arms.

"Wait—"

But it was too late; he was already moving them out of the bathroom and toward the bed. Yes, she wanted to sleep with him, feel the heat of his body against hers. She wanted all the precious minutes she could get with this man before she actually came to her senses.

He folded down onto the bed, rolling to his side and dragging her with him.

She tucked her body against him, her legs tangling easily with his, her head coming to rest atop the beat of his heart as if she'd always slept with him like that. And despite the wonder of what she'd just experienced with him, the anxiety over where this would lead them, compounding the fears about what else lay in store for her in the next days or weeks…the sweet drowsiness of such complete satiation threatened to claim her swiftly. She felt him press a kiss on the top of her head and pressed one against his heart. His arm tightened around her, and she smiled…then let sleep take her.

The first thing that registered in her foggy morning brain was the warmth. So deliciously warm, the tactile feel of hot skin against her—thick, deliciously muscled, perfectly male skin.

She opened her eyes and was rewarded with the sight of Vin. God, he was the most beautiful man. The harsh angles of his face were softened by sleep and the morning's pale light. His hair was thick and the color of midnight. Beard stubble darkened his jaw, his thick lashes lush against his burnished skin.

The sheet was pooled low around his hips, revealing

the hard-packed thickness of his chest and the tantalizing sight of the ridged muscles of his abdomen and hips.

He had symmetrical features, the appealing combination of genes and sex appeal that he'd been born with.

She let her gaze drift over him again, wondering what in the world she was supposed to do now. Hiding was what she usually did, what she'd been doing all her life, and it still seemed like the logical answer, but somehow, she didn't have the heart to hide from him.

She reached out and gently ruffled the hair on his forehead, hair that was normally brushed to the side. The scent of him filled her senses, and she breathed in deep. Watched the gentle rise and fall of his chest. His even breathing was a soft cadence as she did something she never did.

She just lived the moment, absorbed the experience of lying next to him while he slept and dreamed. She greedily captured the memory, holding it in her heart as her eyes went over him again and her fingers played with the ends of his soft hair.

She thought back to her one and only sexual encounter. She'd barely had a chance to feel anything before it was over. Now she realized that she hadn't been the only inexperienced person in the room back then. Was Vin experienced or was it just a natural extension of his personality? His confidence and take-charge attitude were both arousing and annoying.

He shifted, and he took a deep breath. His hand came up and captured hers without even opening his eyes.

He brought her hand to his mouth, kissing her palm. Then his eyes fluttered open, the green of them potent and penetrating.

"Hey there," she said as her heart fluttered.

"What're you doing?" he asked, his voice rough with sleep.

"Staring at you."

He smiled. "You working out some kind of experiment, Doctor? Going to use me as a lab rat?"

"No... Well, maybe, but any testing I would want to do with you would require that you be fully conscious."

He smiled again, wider. "Oh, Doctor, usually in the morning, I'm *fully* up." He drew her hand down his body to settle on his thick, hard erection.

She gasped at the deep visceral reaction she had to touching him. He closed his eyes when she wrapped her hand around him, making a soft strangled sound in his throat. The power of his response settled inside her, and she wanted to see how everything she did to him affected him. She pushed the sheet aside so that she could immerse herself in him. He was so powerfully built, so male, she reveled in the differences between them. She moved then, straddling his hips, and his eyes popped open as the soft heat of her settled against his raging hard-on.

She kissed his temple, burying her nose in his hair, rubbing her cheek against all that sexy stubble. One hand gloved him, and her other hand braced her upper body over him. When she stroked him, he arched his back, his eyes glazing, opening his legs wider, his hips shifting restlessly.

"Oh, yeah, baby," he said softly, his tongue wetting his lips, the look on his face tight with desire. "Use me."

She kissed her way down to his jaw. "Would that be an order, Mr. Special Agent?" she whispered into his neck, the scent of him charging her up. "I really liked your orders last night."

He groaned softly when she rubbed her thumb over the head of his shaft at the same time she sucked gently on his nipple.

"Looks to me like you have the control stick this time, sweetheart."

She giggled, flushing at his teasing words. The man was so much fun. She drew the tip of her tongue down his torso, pressing hot kisses against all that thick muscle.

"You in the palm of my hand sounds so good. But I've wanted to try something else." She lowered herself down the length of his body and took the crown of him into her mouth and sucked. Not really sure she even knew what she was doing, but she remembered what he'd said. Do what felt natural. Chances were he'd like it.

"Oh, damn," he rasped as she took more of him into her mouth. "Sky," he moaned, burying his hands in her hair, tugging gently against her scalp. His chest heaving, his hips lifting, he grabbed her under the arms and dragged her up his body, flipping her onto her back. He made quick work of the protection.

After he slipped inside her in one stroke, she wrapped her legs around him, momentarily worried about his shoulder; but he didn't seem to be in any pain, so she let it go.

He covered her mouth as he thrust deep over and over again, the frenzy in them out of control. His breathing harsh in her ears, she cried out at the thick penetration, his need for her in every harsh breath he took.

She scored his back with her fingernails, and he groaned, pumping harder, faster until he came, stiffening above her, his back arched, his eyes closed, and he looked so magnificent in his release, she couldn't stop looking at him.

Then he collapsed against her for a few moments. With a soft sigh, he dragged her out of bed and into the bathroom, where he turned on the water to the shower. Stepping inside under the warm spray, they lathered each other up, and he tenderly washed her hair.

When they were rinsed off, he pulled her into his arms and kissed her gently on the mouth. "So, do you like studying me?"

She sighed deeply and wrapped her arms around his neck. "Yes, I very much like…um…analyzing all that data. I want to become an expert."

"I'd say the experiment was a success." He grinned.

She looked up at him and couldn't look away. She should keep this on a casual level. It should be casual, but it wasn't. It just wasn't.

"You're staring again." He rubbed his thumb over her moist mouth.

She kissed the pad of his thumb. "I like looking at you. But I bet you get stared at a lot, especially by women."

"I haven't really noticed," he said, pulling back the curtain and grabbing towels.

As she stepped out, he wrapped a towel around her from behind, just as she had for him. He tied the other around his waist. "It's because your face is symmetrical."

She grabbed another towel and started to dry her hair, but he took it out of her hands and started doing it himself. "That's a good thing, huh?" he said as he squeezed the water out.

She wrapped her hair up in the towel and turned to

face him. "It's a scientific explanation of beauty, attractiveness, sex appeal. Movie stars, models and performers usually have symmetrical features."

He snorted.

She moved behind him, grabbed a smaller towel and started to dry his back; interacting with him like this was so far out of her comfort zone, she was surprised it was so easy. "Oh, come on. You've seen yourself. You know what I'm talking about."

He shrugged his broad shoulders and turned to give her a grin. "I just see myself. I don't go posing for the mirror. It's just my face."

She wiped at his damp face and moved back around to his front to dry his hair, saving him having to use his shoulder. "It's a very attractive face, science aside. And it's much more than your looks." She finished and draped the towel around his neck. "Women, on average, tend to be attracted to men who are taller than they are, display a high degree of facial symmetry, and who have broad shoulders, a relatively narrow waist and a V-shaped torso."

He smiled indulgently, and she found that she liked that. She felt it was supportive of the way she viewed the world.

"I know a lot of useless information. When I get nervous, I kind of blurt it out as a buffer, I guess."

He bent his head and kissed her. "You don't have to be nervous with me, Sky. Although, I really enjoy the useless information. You can let go of that buffer. You don't need it."

He stood in front of the mirror and grabbed some shaving cream. Lathering up his face, he picked up his razor and started to shave.

"That's good, because I'm not sure I could control it anyway. I like the way you are comfortable with my intelligence. Many men get antsy around me, as if I'm going to belittle them or something. I'm not like that. At least, I hope I'm not."

"You stimulate me," he said with a wicked grin, and she couldn't help but smile back.

The buffer was all about self-preservation.

After getting dressed, she mulled over his words and wondered if she didn't need a bigger buffer against him. They ate breakfast, and Vin went outside, telling her that he would call her when he was finished with his project. She literally didn't have a thing to do other than clean up after breakfast. She flipped on the TV and let it play in the background. She found some yarn and a set of knitting needles behind one of the chairs in the living room. There was a pattern for a scarf. She wondered if Vin's buddy knit or if it was some other acquaintance.

She hoped the person wouldn't mind, but she desperately needed something to do. She took up the knitting needles and read the preliminary directions. She practiced working with them. It was at first awkward, as it was learning any new task.

It helped to take her mind off Vin and where this relationship could go.

She'd made a choice a long time ago. Her heart squeezed at her limited memory of her mother and father. They were shadows of her past now. The only thing she had of her father was his words. *Stay strong, my sweet child. Make your life have meaning and live up to the potential you have in you, so that our sacrifice isn't lost.* So much had been taken from her at such a young age. The endless expectations that she harbored deep inside her were all generated by her need to honor her parents' deaths. For her.

But did that mean she couldn't be happy? Would she lose something—respect? Value? Herself? Who she had planned to be for all of her life? But that was before she even realized that there was a man like Vin out there. She hadn't known it could be like this, and now her world felt so cold and empty.

No, not empty. She had her honor for her parents and their sacrifice. She'd made a choice.

And yet, despite all of that, or perhaps because that was what she'd been born to bear, she'd always believed that immersing herself in a career that could give something back to her adopted country and honor her parents' sacrifice at the same time would be enough.

Shockingly, she felt a sudden burn behind her eyes and squeezed them immediately, tightly shut to ward off any ridiculous tears that might form.

Even as her mind whispered it wasn't enough, she shut down those mutterings.

Pursuing anything beyond this casual sex with Vin was out of her reach. Completely.

Sacrificing meant exactly that. Heartbreaking, difficult sacrifice.

Dry-eyed, her jaw set, she started to get the hang of the knitting after a while and settled in, determined she would make something. Unfortunately, there wasn't enough yarn to make one uniform scarf, but bits and pieces of skeins that would work.

As the morning flowed into the lunch hour, she found herself looking at the somewhat crooked rows of her half-finished scarf.

When she heard the door handle turn, she quickly put it away, not wanting Vin to see it until she was done.

"Hey, come outside. I want to show you something. We need to talk."

"All right. I'll be right there." She rose as he retreated and closed the door. She bundled up and slipped on boots.

As she closed the door, she saw him moving in the trees at the side of the house. The air was crisp and cold, her breath fogging the air. She went down the steps and walked off the path, the snow crunching beneath her feet. As she approached, he was looking off into the distance. The river rushed past with a soft gurgling sound. It seemed so peaceful here, and she could imagine why he wanted to come here for a break from D.C.

"Did you do more recon?"

He gave her a wry look and looked away. "We're pretty isolated from the road," he said, gesturing. "A lot of good cover. The town is that way and Harrisburg is the other way. Toward the south. There's a nice little town with pretty good nightlife, places to eat and a grocery store. I've got a good amount of cash to last us for a bit. We can stay here for at least two weeks."

"Do you think they will give up after that?"

"They won't give up. I know that's hard to hear, but that's what my instinct tells me."

"The stuff I'm working on is classified. They could be after that."

"I have a top secret clearance. You can confide in me."

"I mostly write algorithms in conjunction with sonar and radar. I'm working on a very top secret project called

Stingray. I'm the only one in the company who is working on this. My boss isn't even privy to the schematics."

"What is Stingray?"

"It's a submarine that uses silent sound waves that can't be detected by conventional sonar equipment. I'm still perfecting it."

"Silent sound waves?"

"A sound spectrum displays the different frequencies present in a sound. Most sounds are made up of a complicated mixture of vibrations, like the fan in your computer, perhaps the sound of the wind outside, the rumble of traffic or music playing in the background, in which case there is a mixture of high notes and low notes, and some sounds such as drumbeats and cymbal crashes, which have no clear pitch."

"That's right. You have a degree in sound. That's what you're working on for the navy?"

"Yes, sonar picks up vibrations in the water and can pinpoint where these sounds are coming from. No machine runs quiet."

"Except your Stingray?"

"Yes, I've developed engines that produce minimal sound. The sub does produce very low-level sound waves intermittently that mix in with the sounds of the ocean until it's almost undetectable."

"Who else knows about this technology?"

"A few select naval personnel. It's really hush-hush."

"Are you sure about that?"

"Yes, I am extremely careful with my research and take my top secret clearance very seriously. I would never have spoken about it to you if you didn't have the clearance. There's a prototype that I helped to fit with the new engines and it's out in the Atlantic right now."

"I need a name."

"Admiral Jackson Bartlett. He is my navy contact."

He pulled the burner phone out of his pocket and dialed. "Chris, it's Vin. I have a name I want you to run." There was a burst of response on the other end. "Yeah, it's Admiral Jackson Bartlett. Could you check him out and let me know what you find?" He listened for a few minutes. "I'd rather not say over the phone." He ended the conversation and stuffed the phone back in his coat pocket.

"What are you thinking?"

"I just have a feeling that this does have something to do with your research. You're working on several top secret projects, but Stingray is technology foreign governments would love to get their hands on. We'll wait to see what Chris digs up."

She nodded, her stomach tying up in knots, racking her brain trying to think if there was ever a breach in her protocol.

He took her arm and pulled her to the base of a wide tree. "I brought you out here to run through the plan if this location is compromised."

She nodded. "What's the plan?"

He gestured to the ground at a pile of leaves. She looked back up at him, frowning. "What? A pile of leaves?"

"In sniper training every recruit has to learn how to camouflage, evade and become invisible to the enemy. That's a blind. I took the concept of my ghillie suit and adapted for this situation."

He squatted down, grasped something and lifted. "A ghillie suit is something I wore as a sniper to make me undetectable in the woods or jungle." The leaves rose, and beneath was a tarp. Sky studied it for a moment, and then her stomach twisted. "There's only room for one person under there."

He let the leaves fall and stood. He set his hands on her shoulders and looked her directly in the eyes. "If we're compromised, this is where you're going to hide."

"What? What about you?"

His gaze didn't waver, his eyes a clear, cool green. She bet he was an amazing sniper, patient, accurate, calm and deadly.

"To protect you from any threat, I need to know that you're safe, and I need to be mobile. I'm going to take them down one by one silently until there is no more threat or lead them away from you. Whichever decision I make, I don't want you to make a sound until they pass by it. Then you run for the road."

"But…"

His hands tightened on her shoulders. "I know this scares you, but I also know you have the courage for this." He pulled out one of the burner phones and a fanny pack. "Carry this with you from now on. I've already entered in the local sheriff's number and my boss Chris Vargas's direct number at NCIS. The number to the other burner is on this phone, as well. If I don't answer, call those other two numbers only. Head toward the sheriff's office if you can't access the car or it's disabled. It's in the town located about three miles from here. Stay close to the road but don't actually travel on it, just in case they are trolling for you. There's an extra set of keys in there for my car. It has a GPS, and the address for NCIS in D.C. is already programmed into it. I'll show you that in a minute. Drive straight there. There's a map in here to show you how to get to the road and where the town and the highway are located, some cash and a few protein bars."

She took the phone, tucked it into the fanny pack and swallowed hard. "Vin," she said, but had to swallow again. "Don't let anything happen to you."

"Sky…"

She covered his mouth with her fingers. "Don't…. I already know what you're going to say. I know I'm all about facts and hard science, but right now I want the fantasy. Screw reality. I want you to tell me everything is going to be okay. We're both going to be okay. I need that."

He grabbed her hand and kissed her fingers, then her palm, sending sensual heat all the way through her. She didn't think she could get enough of this man, and that was a bad thing.

She wrapped her arms around his neck and pulled his head down, planting a kiss on him that was different from what they'd shared in the past. Slow and deep, she felt as if her heart was in her lips, beating with the need for Vin. She fell completely into it, feeling him against her, so strong and sure, her protector, her warrior, her shield.

It was more than her erogenous zones in play. Her heart was all the way out there, and it was both exhilarating and terrifying to think his might be, too. What did it mean? What would it change?

She didn't want to think about any of that. She just wanted to be right where she was, in that particular moment, exulting in the intensity of the connection they seemed to be sharing. Knowing she wasn't in it alone made giving in to it unbearably seductive.

He broke the kiss and said fiercely, "We're both going to be okay."

She traced his lips, the tantalizing strength of his jawline. "Tell me you were a badass, lethal marine."

His mouth came down on hers in a soul-searing kiss; the chilly wind didn't even faze her, she was so wrapped up in Vin's heat and need. He pulled her closer, took the kiss even deeper, until she shivered with the power of him all trapped inside her. They both groaned a little when their lips parted.

He pressed his forehead against hers. "I *am* a badass, lethal marine. There are no former marines. I'm an excellent shot, too," he whispered.

"Good. Don't forget to kill them twice."

He tightened his hold on her. "There won't be anything I won't be willing to do to keep you safe. Just follow my directions to the letter, and it'll all work out."

Tears sprang to her eyes, and her attempts at schooling her emotions failed miserably. She nodded.

"Okay, let's go learn about GPS and practice jumping out a bedroom window."

She stuck her lip out. "I suppose you're going to be a badass drill sergeant?"

"Yes, I am. Now, hup to it, missy."

She walked with him to the car, and her heart wobbled, dipped, but held on with valiant effort. She hoped the men didn't find them. Not because of the danger, not because of the fear, but because it would mean that Vin would be safe, too.

Chapter 12

Standing at the dock watching the water swirl past, Vin was trying to work through what had happened at the blind. The sound of her voice on the verge of tears because there wasn't enough room in the hidey-hole for both of them.

He took a deep breath and let it out slowly. Then there was that kiss. He closed his eyes. It was…beyond words.

Ever since he'd taken this assignment and seen Sky's face on the monitor at NCIS, he felt as if he was continually trying to surface from the deepest part of the ocean. Getting involved with her was exactly the worst thing he could have possibly done in his career as an NCIS agent. Not because getting involved with a woman he was protecting was against the rules. It wasn't. He wasn't even sure if that would have stopped him.

He rubbed at the back of his neck, the cold wind cutting across the dock, making the surface of the water ripple. That was what he was struggling with. Everything with Sky was simply better than good.

Profound. Primal, filling a need in him he wasn't aware he even had. Maybe, just maybe, that was what was missing from all his past relationships?

Because there was absolutely nothing missing when

Sky looked at him, touched him, joined with him. She affected him viscerally on every level.

And that was why it was the worst mistake he'd ever made.

They were in an iffy situation at best. He didn't have enough information about who was after her or why. Yet he had to protect her.

He couldn't fail.

That tore him up. The thought of failing. That was also something new. He never really contemplated failing when he was working a case, just as he hadn't ever considered it as part of his thought process when he was sniping. There was only win in his head.

Losing her just wasn't an option. It wasn't even part of the equation. Protecting her and keeping her safe was all that mattered.

He heard her quick scrabble down the small hill to the wooden dock, then her footfalls before she wrapped her arms around him from behind.

"What are you doing out here?"

"Working shit out," he said noncommittally. He wasn't ready to say anything to her. He wasn't even sure where they stood. The situation really precluded him from declaring anything.

She walked around him and gave him a soft smile. "While you were working shit out, I was practicing jumping out of a window gracefully."

"We don't need any freaking ballerina moves, sweetheart. Just get your ass over teakettle out the window and run like hell."

She gave him a bemused look. "I suspect that my ass over teakettle will be unavoidable because you'll be behind me shoving me out."

He chuckled softly. "I don't shove ladies. I might boost or firmly encourage."

"Like you did this morning?"

His chest filled, thinking about having her mouth on him. "What was it that I said? I was completely distracted at the time."

She flushed but met his eyes directly, and his heart went to mush.

"I believe your exact words were 'Oh, yeah, baby. Use me.'"

"Really. I was that crass. That's not like me."

She giggled. "Oh, no, not like you at all."

He stopped fighting the inevitability of kissing her. Just like from the beginning. He fought a battle in vain. Even as he took her mouth with his, he was still waging that losing battle inside him.

Her mouth was too irresistible, too sweet. The tiny hitch of her breath at the back of her throat unraveled him just a bit more. He figured if he could find some balance, some solid ground, then he might have a fighting chance at focusing on the job at hand and not on how he couldn't get enough of her.

But that little hitch in her breath was a hard push that kept him unstable. And those incredibly soft lips beneath his. He was affecting her defenses, which made him feel a little bit better.

That little hitch sounded again, and he immediately found himself gentling the kiss, soothing rather than conquering. She tasted so damn sweet. She felt fragile and vulnerable, and damn if he didn't want to save her.

He kissed the corners of her lips before taking her mouth once again. He was unhurried in his tasting of her, reveling in the moment, knowing it could end at any time with no guarantees of a future. He kissed her with a gentleness he didn't typically express and carefully avoided examining any further why that particular side of him had surfaced now, of all times. The fragility he sensed was probably temporary at best, no matter what his libido wanted him to believe. But he quickly discovered kissing her like this wasn't just soothing her; it was soothing something deep inside himself, too.

When she sighed into his mouth, urging him on with a little moan deep in her throat, the part of him that was almost out of control for her wanted to take her back to the cabin's bedroom and let her use him again.

But the man who was falling for her found a different kind of contentment, skimming his fingertips over her cheeks, sliding them into the long, sleek strands of her hair, loosening her soft ponytail so he could feel that silken wave cascade over the backs of his hands, all the while taking in her breath with his own.

She was no longer just that beautiful face on a monitor or a brilliant scientist with her life neatly summed up in a file. She was a flesh-and-blood woman who had yet to bare all of herself to him. Something he craved. A woman whose plight should matter to him only in the strictest professional sense. She shouldn't otherwise matter to him at all.

But she did, and there was no going back to impartiality, if he'd ever had it in the first place.

He broke the kiss, and they stared at each other for a few moments as the wind played with her now loose hair.

"What exactly do you do out here when you and your buddy come up here together?"

"Not the same thing I do with you." He grinned.

She laughed and shook her head. She rolled her eyes. "I'm serious."

"So am I," he assured her.

She laughed again, pushing at his shoulder. "Vin..."

He chuckled and nudged her back. "We fish, drink and cut wood for the winter. But mostly fish and drink. Okay, maybe a little more drinking than fishing."

She snorted. "Get in touch with your good-old-boy self?"

"Something like that."

"Do you eat these fish you catch, providing you do actually catch something?"

"Of course we do. I do the cleaning and my buddy does the cooking. What do you do for fun?"

"Fun?"

"You know, when you're not doing something that makes you a living."

"I don't really do much but work."

"No vacations?"

"Um, I present papers at conferences. Does that count?"

He gave her a wry look.

"I don't really have anyone to travel with, and I'm so busy...."

Now he gave her a skeptical look. "Seriously? You don't take vacations or any time off?"

"Not really."

"Not even to the Philippines?"

She bit her lip and looked away. "I've never been to the Philippines."

"What? Okay, that seals it. Before we leave here, you have to do something spontaneous."

"What? Why?"

"Practice for when you go back to your job. Sky, life

was made for living, not working all the time. I saw my father do that, and I didn't want that for myself."

"Tell me about…"

"No. Why don't you tell me about your father? I think I jumped to some conclusions the last time we talked about your family. I'm sorry. I want to understand your culture. Your mom was American. I know all about Americans, but I don't know much about Filipinos."

For a moment she stared at him. Then she looked away. She swallowed, waited a few seconds, then, her voice thick with emotion, said, "It's getting on toward dinnertime. Aren't you hungry?"

He had a sister, a mother and had been in a relationship for two years, and he totally understood that when a woman was ready, she would talk. There wasn't anything he could do to get her to open up. But he was impatient. He'd never felt this way before. Sky didn't know him that well, and he'd been looking at things through his own eyes and not trying to understand them through hers. After his revelations this morning, he wanted a closer connection with her.

He nodded. "I got steaks when I was in town yesterday. Do you eat beef? I didn't even think to ask."

"I don't eat red meat." She smiled at him.

"I'm such a typical guy. But, hey, I got chicken, too."

"That will work. I can make some fried rice."

He turned to head toward the house, and she grabbed his hand. He looked at her, then looked away, smiling to himself, his grip on her hand tightening. They walked up the stairs and into the house.

She went to the kitchen, then turned to look at him. "Do you have my hair tie?"

He'd forgotten about that. It was around his wrist,

and he walked up to her. She held out her hand, but he just turned her slightly and started to braid her hair. She made a soft noise of surprise in her throat, and when he tied her hair off with the elastic, she twisted to look at him, her eyes softening.

"Where did you learn to do that?"

"I have a younger sister, and sometimes she wasn't exactly ready for school on time." He felt a shot of nostalgia and vowed he would call her tonight after dinner. He felt bad for the way he'd acted when she'd called about the damn business. She had to know that he wanted nothing to do with it, and that included discussing it. She'd sounded stressed. But he'd gotten caught up in this case and had been preoccupied with Sky and keeping her safe. The other truth, the one he harbored whenever he saw a Boston area code on his phone, was that he could hear their disappointment, and it was something he wanted to avoid. Had been avoiding for a long time.

"What's her name?"

"Delilah. I call her Lilah."

He didn't press her for any information as she grabbed a frying pan and gathered her ingredients. He pushed up the sleeves of the gray ribbed pullover, leaning back against the counter, his ankles crossed, his arms folded over his chest. The solemn lines around her mouth tugged at his heart.

"Where is she now?" Her tone was nonchalant, but her eyes were very interested. Very curious.

"In Boston, working for my dad."

She got to cooking, and the aroma of the chicken and rice made his stomach grumble.

"Do you have a picture of her?" Once again, her voice had that easygoing tone with the underlying edge to it.

Regret in his voice, he said, "On the phone I dumped, not on me at the moment."

"Oh, that's too bad."

When the food was almost done, she looked over at him, her gaze connecting with his, and for an instant there was an unspoken communication between them that was oddly restrained, yet oddly revealing—one that silently acknowledged his attempt to connect with her. There went his heart again, and she blinked a couple of times.

He noticed how her knuckles grew even whiter, which was saying something, considering she already had a death grip on the frying-pan handle. "I haven't seen him since I was six. I remember him being strong and sure. With dark hair and an infectious smile. My aunt said that my mother fell head over heels for him when they met in college. I loved him and I miss him. But I couldn't risk going back to China, and he refused to let me help by getting involved."

His opening up about his family had put her at ease, it seemed, and she was finally responding to his inquiry about her father. "And you honor him."

"Yes, definitely that. In any Asian culture, honor and respect are very important. Certainly you have that in your family?"

"Yes, I do, but it's a bit different. I rebelled against my parents' wishes and ended up doing entirely the opposite. It's given me a richer life."

"Thank you."

"For what?"

"Trying to understand."

She pressed her hand against her stomach, her face

crumbling, and he was across the kitchen, pulling her into his arms.

"The grief is still fresh. I'm so sorry. I should have just kept my big mouth shut."

She shook her head against his shoulder, her hands bunching the fabric of his sweater in her tight fists. He could hold her like this forever.

"I have no one to really talk to about this. No family. My aunt is sympathetic, but she barely knew him and she's not really my aunt."

"Grief is good, Sky. To feel it, you have to embrace it. Mourning someone is human. You shouldn't have to hide it or bottle up your feelings. It's what gets you through to the other side."

She pressed harder into his chest. "Tell me what you remember about him. The memories are all we really have, but that keeps him in your heart and your mind. That presence."

She lifted her head and looked at him as if she'd never seen him before. "I never thought about it that way." Anguish in her eyes, she said, "He built me things out of paper. It's called *karakuri* in Japanese. He was a mechanical engineer. Very smart, very clever."

He let her go when she pulled away. "He loved math and gave me the same love for it. I was doing calculus when I was six and playing binary hopscotch."

"Damn. I think I was driving fire trucks around and making siren noises at six."

She laughed, and the sound of it, all soft and natural, filled the kitchen with warmth. She shook her head a little as if to say he was incorrigible, then turned to dish out the food.

After eating, he excused himself to make the phone

call to his sister, and Sky sat down in one of the chairs by the fire and pulled out what looked like knitting. She would be surprised to find out that his buddy knit. The craft just seemed too domestic for her, but she didn't have a lot to do here in the wilderness of Pennsylvania.

After going into the bedroom, he entered his sister's number into the phone and sat down on the edge of the bed.

"Hello?"

"Lilah. It's Vin."

"Vinny, I have been calling you, but it never even went to voice mail. There are agents here in the house. They say that you're on a case, and they're here as a precaution. What's happening?"

"I'm protecting a woman, and it's gone a bit crazy. There are agents there? Damn. I wish I could come home and handle this." He had to make it a priority to call Chris and find out why he'd assigned field agents to his family.

She sounded choked up, and she sniffled. "Dad is sick. That's what he wanted to talk to you about. He can't run the business anymore. We need you to come home and help with some decisions. Mom is so upset."

He pinched the bridge of his nose. "Lilah, you know the ins and outs of the business better than I ever could."

"But he wants you to take over."

He sighed. "I can't really discuss that right now. Is Dad in the hospital?"

"No, he's home, but he's going to have to slow down. His doctor insisted."

"I'm sorry, but I won't be able to get home for a while."

There was disappointment in her voice, and he clenched

his teeth. "I understand. I'll handle things the best I can until you get here. I don't have the authority or power of attorney or even a seat on the board."

"I'm really sorry about the timing, but I can't leave this woman. She's in danger, and she needs me."

"Of course. I know you. My heroic brother. Do what you have to do, and come home as soon as you can."

"I will. We'll work this out. Be safe and listen to those NCIS agents. Don't take any risks."

"Okay. Please take care of yourself, too. I love you."

"I love you, too."

He disconnected the call and sat there for a few minutes. He didn't want to take over. But he wasn't sure if he was going to have a choice. Someone had to run the business. It was his father's legacy, and although he didn't really want to be a part of it, he also didn't want to see it fall apart.

Conflicted, he dialed Chris and, after a brief conversation with him, found out that someone had hacked into the NCIS database and accessed his file. He went back out into the living room. He checked the locks to both the front and back door.

He stirred the fire and set another log on it. Settling in across from her, he said, "What are you doing?"

"Making you a scarf. It's either that or go stir-crazy. I really wish I could get my laptop."

"You're making me a scarf?" He smiled, ignoring her laptop comment.

"I'm sure it's not the best I can do, but I just started learning this morning."

He got up and walked over to look at her work. The rows weren't exactly perfect, but that was what made it all the more…sweet. "That's really nice. Thanks."

She smiled and looked up at him. Her face changed. "What's wrong?"

"Why are you asking me that?"

"You look worried. I've never seen you look worried, not even when we were getting ready to step onto that icy death trap of a roof."

He couldn't believe she could see the concern over his family situation in his face. He was good at masking his anxieties. But he didn't want to exactly burden her with any of his own fear for his family. Chris had ordered the Boston field office to respond. He was glad someone was there for his family, but he felt guilt over not being there. He couldn't leave Sky, and he didn't want to make her worry any more than she was already worrying.

His silence didn't sit well with her. Her eyes got increasingly stormy, and her mouth tightened. "Oh, I see," she said, sounding hurt. "I can spill my guts, but you get to keep everything close to the vest."

She rose, set down the knitting and went into the bedroom. He let her go. He wasn't sure how to tell her about the agents in Boston. He also didn't know how she would react to his father's inability to handle the business. With her honor code, she would agree with his sister that he should go home and take over. He had no doubt, and he didn't want to hear that. He wanted her to accept him for who he was, and that included what he wanted to do with his life. He wanted the support.

He spent a few moments banking the fire and knew that he had to go talk to her. He set the poker back in the stand and turned away from the fire.

She was standing in the middle of the living room looking uncomfortable and awkward.

"I'm sorry. I was out of line. Just because I told you all those things about my father and you were so sweet and kind doesn't mean you have to tell me anything you don't want to tell me. It's just…well, it helped to make me feel better. So I thought I could…I don't know… make you feel better. Isn't that what friends do for each other?"

One word of that speech stuck with him, and it momentarily distracted him. Friends? What the hell? He didn't want to just be friends with her. What was he thinking? She'd tied him up in knots until he wasn't sure of his own mind or feelings. "I'm not trying to be evasive, I swear, Sky. It's about my family and the case, and it's complicated." Everything seemed complicated right now.

When he didn't say anything else, she let out a reluctant sigh and turned away, looking so sad and betrayed.

"Dammit," he said under his breath. "Sky, wait."

She turned back, looking hopeful, and he couldn't keep it from her. "Come and sit down, and I'll tell you what you want to know."

She put her hands on her hips, her expression expectant but agitated. "Are you sure you want to, or is this just a pity gut-spilling?"

Even with all the stress tightening his stomach, the way she said *gut-spilling* made him smile. "Just come over here, and I promise to be straight with you, even though I would give you a hundred bucks to say 'gut-spilling' again."

She gave him a dry, wry smile. "Are you making fun of me when I'm trying to be a good friend?"

He didn't move, but his posture, his stance, broadcast that something she'd just said set him off. She made him ache deep inside, where she'd been heading for some time now. She was now embedded there. "Let's get one thing straight right here, right now."

She swallowed and took a shuddering breath. He shifted his hips and tilted his head. She was reacting to his closeness, and it jacked him up. It took all his will-power not to touch her.

"What?" she said, her voice barely audible.

"We're more than friends. I don't want to be just your damn friend."

Her breath hitched. "I know."

Sky was finding it very difficult to breathe with him this close and intense. That was the word. He was using his body and his presence to corral her, and she had to wonder if he even realized he was doing it. What did that say about him? About what he wanted from her?

He didn't want to be just her friend. That was evident. A confident male, he still seemed to need the reassurance.

Really, it was true about all that science of chemistry, because she was vibrating with his closeness, with the way the shadow and light from the fireplace played with the beauty of his face.

"Since you're so good with definitions and useless facts, how about this? Friends don't get this close. Friends don't think about kissing you half the time and wanting to get you into bed the other half. Friends don't feel like they're losing their mind every time they interact."

"Oh, my," she said, completely undone like she'd never been unraveled before. This was something she wasn't quite sure she knew how to handle. "Okay," she said, her voice barely more than a whisper against her suddenly constricted throat.

"'Okay'? That's all you have to say?"

"I'm a little bit crazy myself."

His green eyes intensified. "Sky. I don't know where this is going. But I just wanted to be clear."

"That was very clear. I hope you're not trying to change the subject, because whether you like the word or not, I want to be your friend and listen to you. I want that very much, Vin. You don't have to always be the damn hero. Because, if I'm reading you correctly, whatever you have to tell me is not good. And you're all about protecting people with your NCIS badge and your gun and your deadly marine skills."

"You are used to being sheltered. I guess I was reacting to that, maybe subconsciously."

"Well, stop it. I don't want to live my life with my head stuck in the sand. Not anymore. That's your fault."

"You want brutal honesty?" Energy crackled around him without him even trying. His speaking voice was low, calm, smooth. Only the muscle jumping in his jaw, the gleam in his eyes, gave away his agitation with her.

"If you feel you need to deliver it brutally, well, then, all right, but I'm all for honesty."

"You drive me freaking nuts," he said softly, his voice tortured with something that flowed from him into her, making her feel desperate and not knowing why.

She was the first to move. She cupped his taut face. The contact was every bit as electric as she'd known it would be. He closed his eyes at her touch as if he needed her.

She stepped closer and wrapped her arms around

his neck, flush up against his body. His free arm was instantly around her back, steadying her, keeping her tucked against him.

"I'm not playing games, Sky."

"I know you're not." How was she going to go back to her sterile white life? A life that was akin to a white-noise machine, always on, but in the background, easily tuned out.

He wrapped both his arms around her. "I talked to my sister on the phone just now. There are NCIS field agents at my home in Boston."

Her heart lurched to think that his family was in danger because of her.

"I can feel you thinking, and you can stop it right now. This isn't your fault."

She buried her face into his neck. "How can you say that? This is directly linked to me. They're looking for leverage against you. Oh, God. Do you think they know who you are?"

"I don't know. But that's not all of it."

She released him and pulled back. "What the hell is going on?" she demanded, the adrenaline punch to her stomach like a physical blow. "What do these people want? Now they're threatening your family to get to me. Oh, my God, this is awful. It hurts so badly because I lost my family to thugs who pretended to have my best interests at heart, and they were lying through their teeth. They wanted me to be their slave."

Her eyes widened as the full impact of the situation hit her, and as Vin reached for her, she backed up against the wall.

"I knew how this was going to affect you."

"Me. What about you? What about the thought that

your family could be in danger? What about the fact that they are still looking for me, and if they know who you are, then they have a better chance at figuring out where you might go? They could find out about this cabin."

"They could. That's true. Everything you said is true. But we can't give in to the fear or uncertainty of our situation. We have to take control of it. That's the most important thing I learned in the field. If you don't control a situation, it controls you. I'm going to have to entrust the safety of my parents and sister into the hands of the agency."

"Because you have a job to do. This job. Me. I'm the job."

"You're not a freaking job!" he growled. "This has become more than a job." His expression softened a little and so did his tone.

"You should take me back to D.C. and find someone else to handle this."

"I'm not leaving you," he said fiercely. "So forget it."

"What if I'm being betrayed by someone I know, Vin?"

"We'll figure it out. I'll keep you safe."

Tears stung the backs of her eyes, and for the first time since she'd been ripped from her father's arms and forced onto a ship, her heart was open and vulnerable.

"Let me do my job, Sky," he said and kissed her, this time more gently. "Just listen to me and follow my orders so I don't have to worry about you. Promise?"

When he looked at her like that, and asked rather than commanded, it was beyond her to debate him. It was scary in its own way, how grateful she was that he was here with her. That he was the agent assigned to her case. "All right." She kissed him back. "On one condition."

His eyes narrowed. "What?"

"That you keep that promise you made to me outside."

"What promise?"

She settled her hand over his heart. "That we're both going to be okay."

"We are." He pointed a thumb at himself. "Badass marine. Hooyah."

She smiled. It was almost unbelievable how much she trusted him. Fully and with every bit of her heart. She had no doubt that he would protect her.

What scared the living daylights out of her was how far he would go to protect her.

She was afraid it would be with his life.

Chapter 13

"Wake up, sleepyhead."

Vin opened one eye and groaned. "What time is it?"

"Six a.m."

"What?" He closed his bleary eye. "Why are you up so early?"

"I've done my yoga, and isn't that a prime time to fish?"

His drifting eyes popped open. "Fish? What are you talking about?" He finally focused, and he gaped at her. She was dressed in a flannel shirt that was way too big for her tucked into a set of dark green waders and... He rubbed his eyes, looked again. Yup, she was wearing an old fishing hat with hooks in it, looking freaking adorable.

"You told me to do something spontaneous. Well, this is it. We're going fishing."

"Come back to bed, and we'll do something that will make us spontaneously combust," he said, reaching for her, but she danced out of his reach.

He gazed up at her, and she dropped a bunch of clothes on top of him, including a set of waders that were very cold. He yelped.

"Come on, you big baby. You can get shot without

a peep, but a few cold clothes make you protest like a big sissy."

"Sissy?" he growled. "Did you just call me a sissy?"

"Yes. What are you going to do about it?"

He pushed the covers off himself along with the clothes. With a wary look on her face, she backed up.

"Vin. You're naked."

"Completely."

"You've got a…um…"

"Hard-on."

"Are you trying to distract me?"

"Is it working?" Considering the way her eyes traveled over him, he would say that was a yes. But then she squared her shoulders.

"Stop it and let's go. It's getting late, and all the fish will look at their watches and disappear if it gets past the fishing bewitching hour."

He chuckled and planted his feet on the floor. She bumped into the doorjamb with her back. "You think you can outrun me, sweetheart?"

"Vin," she said, her voice rising an octave as he stood up.

He grinned like a devil and started after her. She squealed and ran for the outside door, but she didn't make it. Vin was way too fast and had longer legs. He grabbed her from behind, and she squealed again when he buried his face in her neck and blew a raspberry.

She laughed and struggled to get away from him. "I'll cook the fish," she said between breathless bursts of laughter. "It's a traditional Filipino recipe."

She twisted away from him, but when he grunted and bent over, the laughter faded from her face. "Oh, my God. Did I hurt you?"

He made a strangled sound. She rushed over to him, and he pounced. She cried out, "You trickster."

"Got you back in my arms, didn't it?"

She stared up at him and smiled. "Aw, that's so deceptively sweet." Brushing the hair off his forehead, she said, "What are you going to do with me now? I can hear the fishes tapping their tails."

He grinned. "Oh, yeah?"

"Yes, they're very impatient."

"A traditional Filipino fish dish, huh?"

"Yes, it's very tasty, but you kinda need fish to make it."

"All right." He let her go and headed back to the bedroom. Before he went through the door, he turned to say something witty, but Sky's eyes were glued to his backside. As he stood there, her eyes traveled up his body until they reached his eyes. He saw her chest heave as a sigh flowed out of her. Her eyes were a hot blue and filled with that unmistakable look a woman gave a man she wanted. "Yeah, baby," he said, his temperature climbing and his hard-on tightening. "Use me."

He growled and went after her. This time she didn't run, but instead of making her squeal he made her moan instead.

An hour later, he walked into the kitchen to see what was keeping her and saw the cooler. "You made a lunch?"

She gave him a half smile. "Yes. Too bad you can't drink because you're on duty."

"Yeah, fishing and drinking go together."

They walked out of the house and down to the dock. He stopped short when he saw the boat already moored and waiting for them along with two fishing rods and a tackle box. "You really got into this. Here I thought I was going to have to do all of this myself."

"Being spontaneous doesn't mean you can't be organized," she said, brushing past him and deftly stepping into the boat.

"You practiced that."

She smiled and tilted her head. He liked it that she was getting so comfortable with him that she could tease him without spouting off some scientific fact. But he kinda liked that, too. Maybe later he'd try to get her nervous enough to get her to nerd-speak.

"No, I'm just naturally graceful."

He gave her a skeptical look, and she gave him a smug, noncommittal one. He stepped into the boat and cast off. She settled down on a seat, and he stepped over her to the motor.

He took the boat down the river to a place where he'd had quite a bit of luck.

"What kind of fish are we hunting for?" She was sitting in the middle of the boat, the wind playing with the ends of her long hair. It fell in a braid over her shoulder.

"Cold water smallmouth, and they're holding not far from here."

"'Holding.' A term that means fish remain motionless and just hover."

He smiled. He never got tired of her agile brain. "They're usually plentiful in areas that offer ample forage and cover, have decreased current speed and receive the most favorable sunlight during shorter winter days."

"Smallmouth, as in bass?"

"Right."

He stopped the boat and anchored it. "Do you know how to fish?"

She gave him a wide-eyed look. "My ancestors may have been very good fishermen, but I'm afraid they wouldn't be very proud of me. Not a whit."

"We'll have to fix that, then," he said, reaching for a rod. "Take this." He shifted, so he was sitting behind her.

She accepted the rod, and their hands brushed. He'd just had her, literally less than thirty minutes ago. But all it took was the brush of her hand to make him think about how she had felt in his arms.

"What are we going to use as bait? Worms are dormant in the wintertime."

"We're going to use lures."

He bent down and reached for the tackle box and flipped the lid open.

She reached out and moved around the lures with her index finger. "Wow, there are a lot of choices."

"Plenty, but I prefer just the plain brown plastic worm. You'll have to work it very slowly," he said softly in a low voice.

She leaned back into him, and he kissed the side of her neck. "Are we going for sexy fishing?"

He chuckled. "Stop distracting me."

She leaned her head on his shoulder, her hair soft against his face. "You're the one who's doing the distracting."

He brushed a soft kiss across her lips. She sighed into him, accepting his kiss, then returned an impossibly sweet one of her own. His heart dipped, then squeezed tightly. "Okay, we'll mutually agree to stop distracting each other. Let's focus on slimy pretend worms. That should help."

"Ick, that helps a little."

"Okay, bait it by threading it on the hook." He handed

her the worm and the hook. "Be careful not to snag your finger."

She sat up straighter, and he missed the weight of her body against his. *Concentrate,* he ordered. Once she'd threaded the hook, he said, "You're going to need to cast it into the area over there. Once you do, you're going to reel very slowly, but allowing the worm to lie motionless and shaking the rod tip occasionally can work, too."

"I'll try both. It'll be an experience."

He slipped his arms around her and leaned his chin on her shoulder as she cast the rod. "That's good, Sky. You can jiggle it every so often."

"Distracting, but it feels good, so I'm not going to complain," she said, her voice indulgent. "How often do you come up here?"

He shrugged. "Not much in the winter, but more frequently in the summer. It's a quick trip from D.C., and it's good to get out of the city and away from the job to decompress."

She shook the rod. "I bet it's beautiful here in the spring and summer."

"It is. Very peaceful. But now my memories of this place will be filled with you."

Her voice hitched a little, and she shifted against him. He tightened his hold on her as if that would keep her here with him. "It was a good place to hide out."

"I'm thinking we might need to find some other place." He was getting increasingly worried. Chris and the team weren't any closer to finding those bastards. Vin was getting antsy. He bet they weren't just sitting around drinking vodka. They had found the safe house once. He still wasn't sure how, and that bothered the crap out of him, too.

"Where?" The rod wobbled a bit, and he wasn't sure if it was her nerves or if she was jostling it to animate the bait.

He kept his voice calm and casual. "I'm not sure. I have an aunt who has a beach house on the cape and I know Chris and his wife have a place in Norfolk."

"Virginia? That's a trek."

"We probably shouldn't stay in one place too long."

"You're probably right. Is this ever going to be over?"

"It will, Sky. We just have to figure out who is behind it and then track them down."

For a full thirty minutes they sat together and fished. Well, she fished and he held her, the stillness broken only by her movement when she cast again or jogged the rod. He thought about what he might do once this was over and she was safe. He tried to get his head around not being with Sky. He couldn't. Made him not want this moment to end. He'd avoided telling her about his family difficulties. He'd had preconceived notions about how she would react. Maybe part of it was that he didn't want to go back home and have to make decisions. He had no intention of giving up what he was doing to take over. But he also didn't want to see his family's business fail.

She twisted her head to meet his gaze over her shoulder. "What's wrong?"

She was picking up body cues he didn't even realize that he was sending out. It brought home to him not only that he felt comfortable with her, but that he was still distracted. The obstacles to any kind of relationship with Sky were dragging at him; he wasn't sure if she would accept not only what he did, but who he was. And he couldn't bear to disappoint another woman he loved. His mind stumbled over that thought. He groaned inwardly. He'd said the L word to himself. Either it was a momentary lapse or he was in love with her. And that did make it doubly bad about their situation. He didn't want to see disappointment in her eyes when he had to make the choice that was best for him. "Why do you think something is wrong?"

"You keep tensing up. I thought fishing was about relaxing."

"It is." He should tell her what he was holding back. If he couldn't trust her with his heart, what was the point?

"Is there something you're not telling me?"

"Yes."

Trepidation thick in her voice, she said, "What?"

Suddenly the line pulled, and she jerked upright. "Oh! What was that?" It pulled again, and the reel started to grind. "Oh, I got a bite! What do I do?"

"Pull back," he said. "Set the hook."

"It doesn't feel small," she said. "I thought you said these were smallmouths."

"Supposed to be."

"Feels like a whale."

"Just start reeling," he said, chuckling.

She did, and he watched as the pole bent toward the water. "Ease up or you'll snap the line. Geez, maybe you do have a whale there."

"Wow, he's a fighter," she said, looking at him, the excitement of catching her first fish bright as fireworks there.

Something leaped from the water, and the powerful body thrashed against the surface, sending water splashing all around. The light caught the scales, and

Sky gasped. Rainbow? he thought. Trout here? There was only one ginormous rainbow in this river.

He looked down at her, and she was momentarily struck by the beauty, and the rod dropped, the line tautened and the fish started to run again.

"Sky, the line…" She came back to her senses and grabbed the spinning reel and stopped the fish's momentum, but now she would have to fight him all over again.

"Take it slow. I think you've got Monster on the line."

"It sure feels like a monster."

"No, not *a* monster. *Monster*."

"What are you saying?" she asked, carefully pulling and reeling.

"It's a rainbow trout and huge. Everyone around here who even thinks to call themselves a fisherman wants that fish."

"Really? Wow."

Finally she got him close to the boat, and he scooped up the twenty-pounder. "You caught Monster."

"That's awesome! He's beautiful."

"He's exhausted. He put up a tough fight, but you landed him. Way to go, baby." He carefully removed the hook from the fish's mouth.

She took the trout from his hands. "Get a picture of me with him. I want to remember this."

"Dammit. These burner phones don't have picture-taking capability."

"Oh, darn. That's okay." Before he could stop her, she bent over the boat and set him into the water. He floated for a few minutes and swished his tail. It looked as if he was looking up at her; then with a power flick, he disappeared into the murky depth.

She turned the reel and he could feel her shaking. "Are you all right?"

"I had no idea fishing could be this much fun."

"Not as relaxing as you thought, huh?"

"No. It was exhilarating fighting that fish. Just him and me against the odds. One mistake and he would have been gone. You were great."

He shook his head. "All I did was bark orders. You did all the work."

After that excitement, they caught several smallmouth bass and headed back to the house. He filleted them, and Sky made her delicious dish.

"What do you call this again?"

"Fish Adobo, and it's cooked in adobo style, which means soy sauce, vinegar, garlic, pepper and bay leaf."

"I can't believe you've never been to the Philippines. It's where your father is from. Why wouldn't you want to go there?"

She looked away, got up and walked to the darkened window overlooking the front porch. He immediately regretted his words. He got up, thinking he should give her some space, but he couldn't. There was a battle that she fought inside. He knew it. "I'm sorry."

She stood with her back to him, and he wasn't able to sit there when it was obvious she was in pain. "No, it's all right. You're right. My father was born in this small fishing village in Donsol. It's beautiful.... Well, the pictures on the internet are, anyway. They have whale sharks that you can swim with. How cool would that be?"

He crossed the room. "Pretty cool." He touched her shoulder, but she didn't go into his arms. She turned to look up at him, her eyes shadowed by some emotion he could only guess at. There went his heart again, rolling over and twisting hard. "Were you afraid that you'd somehow feel worse if you connected to the country where your father was born?"

She shook her head. "I was afraid that it would only make me miss him even more. I was afraid of those feelings."

He slipped his arms around her rigid body, and she finally relented and went into his arms. He felt her shudder as his arms closed around her in a comforting embrace. He realized then how lonely she must have been. How lonely she really was. It was her emotions that she'd buried right along with her parents. Because feeling them hurt too damn much.

He drew her over to the fire and pulled her down with him onto the couch. "Someday, you'll go," he said. "When you've worked it all out. I'm sure of it."

"You're more confident than I am. Ever since I met you, I've been floundering, confused and insane."

"That makes two of us."

"Are you just being a gentleman? Because I can't imagine you being anything but."

All he could remember was the way she had clutched at him this morning, holding on to him so tightly, and the way her body had taken his, holding him there so tightly, too. He wanted more, so much more, already knowing it would be, between them, the way it had never been for him with anyone. Sky was one hell of a woman.

But could she be his?

It was getting late; they were both tired. Although they were safe, that didn't alleviate the stress of being hunted, even if they tried to ignore it.

"Only with you," he whispered.

"Right. On bad guys you use a very scary knife and a gun."

"That's right. Is that a comfort, or does it cause you nightmares?"

"A little of both."

"Damn," he said. "I didn't mean to…"

She covered his mouth. "Shh. You did what you had to do. Nothing about this whole situation is easy. I'll get over it." Her eyes focused on his mouth. Her thumb pressed there. "I can easily say that you are also giving me fever dreams." She kissed the corner of his mouth, then moved her fingers along the line of his jaw and softly kissed his lips. "I had a really good time today. Thank you for making me have fun."

He smiled. "You're welcome and thank you," he said, never more sincere.

"For?"

"Trusting me. I know it's not easy for you."

"Actually, it's so damn easy with you."

He smiled and brushed her mouth with his lips.

"Come on. Let's get to bed. Somebody woke me up at the crack of dawn."

She yawned then, and they both laughed.

"That was a very inconsiderate person."

They laughed again, and he felt as if he was falling. He caught the doorjamb and spun into her as he backed her against the wood, taking her mouth again, this time not as softly or sweetly.

It was only later after they were satiated and warm and cozy under the blankets that he asked her the question that had been at the back of his mind ever since she'd caught Monster.

"Why did you let him go?"

She stirred beside him, but he couldn't see her face in the dark. Her voice was pensive and quiet. "Because he'd survived for so long. I just couldn't eat him. Is that dumb?"

Cradling her against his chest, he smoothed her hair back off her face and kissed her temple. "No, I don't think that was dumb at all."

He wanted her to be his, but was their concept of how to live life too divergent?

He knew her intimately and she knew him. But was that enough?

Fighting against the attraction and the chemistry because she was dedicated to a promise she'd made when she'd been young and vulnerable. Lost and alone. It hurt his heart to think of her like that. He wanted her to get in touch with everything she'd shunned. All those feelings that made a person alive and strong and real.

Denying them wasn't healthy.

He wanted to change her mind. He wanted to make her understand that what they were building was solid, so solid it could last a lifetime.

If she would let it.

She could be his, if she let her past go.

He wasn't sure she could.

He wasn't sure where that would leave them.

Chapter 14

"Dmitry?"

The younger man rubbed the back of his neck and sat back from the computer.

"Anything?" Alex growled in Russian, so frustrated he wanted to punch something.

"I broke into his personal email, and there was correspondence with a friend of his about a cabin."

"Where?"

"I'm still going through the emails, but so far there has only been a reference to it. It's possible he's already deleted the emails that described it in more detail."

"Shit!"

Dmitry typed on the keyboard and stared at the screen. "I'm trying to backtrack and find out who the friend is. Then I can search for properties. I need more time."

Alex grabbed him out of the chair and slammed him against the wall. "We're running out of time! We are supposed to deliver her tomorrow. Find that damn cabin. I am not going to be bested by some smart bitch and her lapdog! Find them!"

Dmitry started to sweat. That was a good sign—he realized that Alex was dead serious. "Agent Fitzgerald graduated from MIT. I'll try to find an address in their database. That will at least lead to his family, where we might get some leverage."

"His name is way too common to search for him that way. Where is MIT?"

"Cambridge, Massachusetts."

"Massachusetts? Do we have anyone in that area?"

"Not at the moment."

"Hack the university and see if you can find a home address for him. And his parents most likely paid for his education. Track them that way, too. There's always a money trail."

"Yes, sir," Dmitry said, looking as if Alex had given him the incentive he needed.

"I'm going to contact our employer for any insight from him."

Alex walked away from the kitchen table, leaving Dmitry to work. They still had the possibility that Dr. Baang would act true to form, demand her laptop with the hidden microdot that contained a GPS tracker that would lead them right to her, but so far she hadn't. Alex wasn't any closer to tracking down Agent Fitzgerald's family. That could be a damn dead end. If he put stock in Dmitry's skills, then getting leverage against Agent Fitzgerald would be in the bag, as the Americans said.

He dialed and waited for the call to go through.

"It's me," he said.

"Do you have her?"

"*Nyet.* Can you do anything to speed up process? You know girl better."

"I tried, but I haven't heard from her. They might get suspicious if I push. She's got to be getting pretty antsy right about now."

Alex heard a phone ringing in the background. "Speak of the devil. Got you, sweetheart."

"This is good news? She grabbed bait and will lead us to her. Call if you have lead."

"You're lucky, Captain Andreyev."

"*Da nyet*. I feel better when I have girl and turn her over to you to get paid."

He disconnected the call and went into the kitchen to the freezer and pulled out a bottle of vodka.

Dmitry looked up from his computer and smiled. Alex smiled back, knowing that Dmitry was aware if Alex was drinking, it meant they were celebrating.

His computer beeped. Alex walked up and looked over Dmitry's shoulder. He was into MIT's database. He grinned. They did have something to celebrate as Special Agent Vincent Fitzgerald's personal information flashed up on his screen.

When Russell picked up the phone, Sky breathed a sigh of relief. She had to at least touch base with him, and the phone was untraceable, so she felt safe calling him.

"Russell?"

"Hello there, hon. How are you holding up?"

"Not very well. I wish I could go back to work." She set the scarf down and rubbed at her forehead. The day had dawned, and Vin was outside again doing a perimeter check and making sure his map was accurate before he was satisfied. But she'd heard him shouting, and she guessed that he'd been talking to his boss. He wasn't happy.

That was one man she wouldn't want as an enemy.

She'd had a good time with him yesterday, but today

she was feeling restless. It hadn't been until he was fast asleep that she'd remembered she'd asked him if something was bothering him. He'd replied yes, but in the excitement of catching Monster and the rest of the fun, relaxing day, it had slipped her mind.

Being in his arms seemed to make everything better. But she didn't want to get too used to it. There were still barriers to their understanding of each other. She'd read something in a journal once about how couples got used to sleeping with each other, so that it was hard for them to sleep without their partner.

She had to wonder if that was going to happen to her when she and Vin parted and went back to their own lives.

Her heart ached at that thought, but how could she reconcile her oath to honor her parents' sacrifice and take this happiness for herself? Guilt tightened her chest and her throat hurt. She could barely remember what her mother looked like. She'd had to leave everything behind when they had fled. No pictures of her mother or father. Nothing to remember them by except for the solid foundation of her vow.

How many times had her father told her how important it was to make the gift of her intelligence count? How many times had her aunt reinforced that, mentioning how much her parents had sacrificed for her?

She was jerked back into the conversation when Russell said, "Well, you know you can't. Not until this threat against you has been neutralized. But having your laptop with you will at least allow you to work some. I'm depending on you, Sky. Could you thank Agent Fitzgerald for relaying my message to call me back?"

"What? When did you call Agent Fitzgerald?"

"A couple of days ago. Actually, I called his boss. I'm assuming he relayed the message. I need the data on the Stargazer project."

"It's on my laptop."

"Don't you have that with you?"

"No. When I ran from the safe house, I had to leave it behind, but it's secure with NCIS."

"Well, are you close enough that you could get Agent Fitzgerald to get it for you? I'm desperate here. I need that data for a meeting I have at the Pentagon at the end of the week."

"I'm almost finished analyzing it. It shouldn't take me more than a couple of hours."

"That would be stellar."

"I'm sorry about all this, Russell."

"So am I, Skylar. Thank you for handling that for me."

She disconnected the call.

Vin came into the cabin then, and she turned toward him. He saw the phone in her hand and toed off his boots, frowning. It looked as though he was already in a bad mood. Part of his argument with his boss? Partly what he wanted to spill to her? "Who were you calling? It would be best if you didn't call anyone."

"I thought you said this phone was untraceable," she said bluntly as her temper began to snap inside her like a live wire.

He walked up to her, already doing that observant once-over of her, scrutinizing her pose, her expression, the passion in her voice. "It is, but you could let something slip. We can't trust anyone."

To his credit, he didn't try to placate her, but she

almost wished he had. "I'm not an idiot. We can trust Russell. He's my boss and has a high-level clearance."

His gaze intensified, sharpened, as if he had sensed something in her. Slowly, he leaned forward until he was just a little too close. "Not high enough to be a part of Stingray. I don't trust anyone at this point."

Annoyance flicked through her, and her chin came up. "When were you going to tell me that he called?"

He rubbed at his temple, and his eyes hardened. "It slipped my mind, Sky. I had other things occupying my attention."

"You had no right to keep that from me. This is my job."

He stared at her a moment, then paced away, his tone flat. "Right. Your life. How could I have forgotten?"

She folded her arms, her anger jumping up a notch. "Don't use that tone. My job is important to me. I have several high-level projects I'm working on. I want you to go get my laptop."

"Sky—"

She marched up to him and poked him in the chest. "No, Vin. I'm going crazy here. All I've got to do is knit, and that is not stimulating my brain. I'll be jumping out of my skin by the end of the week."

"Why don't you use your meditation CDs and do some yoga to relax?"

His dismissive tone only made her dig her heels in deeper, her stomach turning at the change of subject to something that she didn't want to discuss. "Yoga is exercise, and meditation doesn't take up a significant amount of the day. I didn't start Espiritu to be a substitute for other pursuits, Vin."

"What? You started Espiritu? That's your business?"

She bit her lip. Damn him for distracting her. Now she'd let the cat out of the bag.

"Yes. In college as a project I was interested in sounds and how they soothed people. So I experimented with them and came up with a regimen to complement my yoga routine." She looked away, trying to cover how much she didn't want to talk about this.

"You love yoga, don't you?"

Dammit, the man was too observant.

"Don't you?" he pressed.

"Yes. I love yoga. Your point?" She said it calmly, but she wanted to shout it.

He studied her as if her anger didn't even faze him. His eyes were intent and deep. They narrowed, and he said, "No, you really love it, like in you'd like to teach it."

"That's a frivolous pursuit," she said, guilt twisting her up inside. It also happened to be true, but she'd put aside her own dreams of owning a studio for family obligations. "My time is better spent serving my country."

"You have really done a number on yourself."

She bristled. "Vin, I'm not in the mood right now to debate my choices. Right now I need you to get in the car and get my laptop. Russell needs the data for a meeting."

"No."

"What? You can't refuse to do this for me. I'm not a prisoner."

His expression eased. "No, you're not. Back to the question on the yoga, I'm trying to understand. I really am, but I don't buy into this theory that your parents wanted you to give up everything so you can use your big brain. That's what my family wants me to do."

"What? Is that what you were going to tell me yesterday? Is that what's bothering you?"

"I'm torn between protecting you and worrying about my family."

He seemed evasive, as if he didn't want to tell her the meat of the issue. As if he was holding back from her. She was hurt and shocked. She'd been so open with him. More open than she'd been with anyone in her life. "What is it you're trying really hard not to tell me?"

"My father is ill, and he can no longer run the family business that is their sole income. That includes my sister, who works for the company. My father wants me to come back home and take over."

She stepped closer to him. She softened her voice. Antagonizing him wasn't helping. She tried to get control of her anger, but once she let it have free rein, it bubbled up from a dark well she'd kept a lid on. "Vin, please do this for me. Make it work. I know you can. I just want to stay busy."

"No, you don't. Working, for you, is all about maintaining your family's honor. You feel if you're not working, you're somehow failing. It's all tied up inside you together. You can't separate them. Admit it."

"What would you know about that? You're turning your back on your family. I may work all the time, but I hold my family in esteem."

"You're getting me all wrong. Why can't you understand what I'm saying to you? I love my family, but just because I don't do what they want me to do, it doesn't mean I don't care about them."

"You don't want to do this to honor your family? Make this sacrifice? At least you have the opportunity to make a difference in their lives." She wrestled with trying to understand his point of view and getting him to understand how maintaining family honor to her was more important than either individual freedom or individual achievement. Something both her parents had done without hesitation. How could she do anything less?

"That's not fair and exactly how I expected you to react. How can I put this so you'll understand? What I do at NCIS protects everyone, including my family. It makes my life worth living. I don't want to give it up."

"I don't understand you, Vin. I can't conceive of not helping out your family in their hour of need."

He blinked a couple of times as if her words cut him to the quick. Sacrificing was something that she understood, but Vin's need to find his own way without consideration of his family's needs was very alien to her. Her emotions were tying her up, confusing her. Maybe it was her own personal failing, but the values had been ingrained in her from birth and that was all she could see. His face tightened, and the glimmer of hurt glistened in his eyes.

He stepped within inches of her, leaning down, meeting her at eye level, his nose almost touching hers. In the bright light, his green eyes were as hard and unrelenting as agate. "No, you don't get me, Sky. Taking what you want in life honors yourself. I don't know the situation yet. I don't know what is going on at home. I'm conflicted about the choices I have to make, and you siding with my family doesn't help."

She was in full panic mode now. It was better to make it clear to him about where she stood. She couldn't do this. She didn't know how, and it already hurt more than she could stand. "It's obvious to me that we have different mind-sets when it comes to how we view our families. You don't understand me, and I don't understand you. Family honor is the foundation of my culture."

"And freedom of choice is the foundation of being an American. So we are of two different minds when it comes to this. Or are we? You're holding on to the past. You were just a child then, and it must have been terrifying to lose your mother, then be separated from your father. You're afraid of real emotion like we're sharing. It scares you because it brings all of that back. That's why you isolate yourself from living, and work has become so important to you. You're afraid of life. You haven't even visited the Philippines. You aren't embracing your culture. You're running scared."

She straightened, her heart lurching at his words. The hurt in his eyes having a profound effect on her, but she stubbornly held on to what she knew, afraid to walk into that unknown black void and deal with all the stuff he'd just mentioned. It wasn't true. She was doing something important with her life, just as they'd wished it. She wasn't afraid. She wasn't. "And it seems we're incompatible. I would lose respect for you if you don't do what is right for your family. I just see it as dishonor. You disappoint me, Vin."

He grasped her upper arms, and the feel of his hands sent waves of electricity through her. His eyes tormented with unexpressed emotions, he said, "Why can't you just see me as a man who's trying to make the right choices for his own life? You should make your own choices and stop holding on to the past, sacrificing everything for your deceased parents, who aren't even alive to judge you."

"I'm alive to judge me. My foundations are all I have left of them."

"Are you alive? Do you live?" He got closer and the tension around them increased tenfold. She couldn't help responding to him; her whole body yearned for him even with her anger and her disappointment wedging between them. She shivered at the way he looked at her, the desire melded with the pain and the tension ratcheting up with each breath they took. Longing welled inside her when he reached out to touch her, and the feel of his fingertips on her face eased an ache in her, filled the hole in her heart. He framed her face with his palms, his fingers combing back into her long hair.

He leaned down, his voice nothing more than a whisper. "I bet you've lived more while on the run these past few days than you have your whole life." His mouth descended to hers, his lips trembling.

She couldn't fight it. She sank against him, shivered against him, savoring the feel of his strong arms around her, the vulnerability in his kiss. Her skin alive with awareness, she tingled at the slightest brush of his fingertips, the sensations swirling in her like stardust.

"Feel that?" he said. "That's genuine. That's intimacy. That's *living*."

She wanted so much to yield, but she couldn't. She pulled away, backed up and put distance between them. "You don't know what you're talking about."

He sighed, looking as if he wanted to pursue her, but he didn't. "Yes, I do. I know the truth hurts. So here's a little more. I think you're afraid of letting go and living, because with life comes pain and indecision and a whole host of chaotic and difficult emotion. I think that scares you because you've lived in this sterile life.

You've lived in your head all these years, finding it hard to connect to people too mature for you at such a young age. Pain is living. Hard choices are all about living. Making your own decisions is living. What you're doing is just marking time until it runs out. Will you have regrets then? Because there's one more thing that's all about living. Love."

"I'm so glad you have me all worked out, and it's not about me. It's about you and your choices."

"No. This *is* about you. But you're the only one who can work that out. Obviously, what I say doesn't really matter. I've been down this road, Sky. I've loved deeply, and my previous girlfriend couldn't accept me for who I was. She didn't value me for who I was, just who she thought I should be. What I'm looking for is acceptance, and the last thing I want is to be with a woman who thinks I'm not good enough."

That stabbed like a knife. Her heart squeezed painfully at the thought, but she pushed the pain away. She had to go with what she knew and ignore her gut instinct. These feelings were too new, too sensitive, to be explored, so she reeled back away from delving any deeper. "I do value you, and I've struggled with my feelings for you. I have. But I don't see how I can reconcile my heart. It's being torn in two."

"I know that feeling," he said, his eyes telling the story of the same kind of issues she struggled with. He set his hands on his hips, then dug in his pocket for the car keys and the burner phone he carried. She pressed her lips together to keep them from trembling. "I'll go get your laptop. I'll make it less than an hour. Why don't you come with me?" It was an olive branch, but she was smarting from their disagreement and was afraid she would cry.

"No. I'd rather stay here," she said in a small voice.

He sighed and she ignored it. "Keep your phone with you at all times, then."

She ran to lock the door and, as her knees threatened to buckle, she collapsed onto the couch and dropped her face into her hands in despair. She gulped down tears and struggled to snatch a breath that didn't catch in her throat.

She tugged her composure tight around herself. Damned if she let him make her cry for what she knew was right.

So why did it feel as if she'd just lost her whole world?

Chapter 15

He clutched the wheel in a white-knuckled grip and felt sick. His stomach twisted at her words. *You disappoint me, Vin.* They played over and over in his head. His fear was realized. She couldn't accept him for who he was, and she used her parents' sacrifice to keep from really living life. They were at an impasse. He wanted her understanding; that was really it and pretty simple. But her past and her sacrifice colored everything. Until she let go of that, he didn't see they would even have a chance.

He set his GPS for the address Beau had given him. He was coming from the navy yard, where they had Sky's laptop safe and sound, and rendezvousing not far from here. Beau was taking a clean car, and no one was aware where he was going. This wasn't really risky, but Vin planned to be vigilant regardless.

He stared out of the windshield and could be happy about only one thing in that fight. She was mad and hurt. That wasn't lost on him. Maybe once she calmed down, she would see what he was talking about. Her anger wasn't a bad thing. It gave her away, telling him that it could only be fueled by passion. If she hadn't cared, he wouldn't rate that kind of response from her.

All he had to do now was convince her to let go.

And hold fast to the knowledge that while she was saying no and constructing walls, in that moment when she'd looked into his eyes, there had been confusion and longing plainly there for him to see. He was good at guessing what was going on in people's heads, and the closer he got to Sky, the more he knew. She just had to figure it out.

There was no guarantee that she would, and the fact that he didn't quite trust her didn't deter him. He was a marine and an agent, confident in his own abilities. But this time he had to rely on her to come to her own conclusions. There was no way he could force the issue.

He had to accept that she might just disappear after this was over.

The short trip flew by because his mind was occupied with Sky. When he pulled into the gas station where they were supposed to meet, Vin parked his car and turned off the engine. He got out and did a quick perimeter check, not that he was worried that there were any bad guys in the vicinity. It was routine, and he embraced the chance to get his mind off Sky.

About fifteen minutes later, Beau pulled up. He got out and walked over to where Vin was waiting, braced against the driver's-side door of his vehicle.

He pushed away when Beau was almost to him.

"Hey, man. You doing okay? Heard you got shot."

Vin rubbed at his shoulder; the pain was still there but dulled. It wasn't as sharp as the pain in his heart.

"I'm still upright and breathing."

"I had Math disable the GPS," Beau said, studying him as he handed him the laptop. "You look like shit."

"Thanks. It's good to see you, too."

"Is that beautiful *fille* putting you through your paces, *mon ami?*"

"She's not a girl, my friend," Vin said wryly.

"*Mais oui,* dat be true."

"How goes the investigation?"

Beau's expression changed, and he dropped the good-old-boy Cajun speak. "We've identified most of the bodies, and we know they're all mercenaries, when they came into the country and what they're doing here. That's about it at this point. I've been following up every clue I have, but these bastards are ghosts."

"How about the leak? Any luck there?"

"If there's a leak, I couldn't find it. The safe-house database wasn't breached, and only Miller, Strong, me, Amber and Chris knew where you were."

"Do you think Miller or Strong was dirty?"

"If that was the case, I would expect to find money deposits, but I found nothing out of the ordinary in their bank accounts, and for the record, Chris made me investigate him and Amber while he investigated me. We all came up squeaky clean."

"Then they found Dr. Baang by some other means."

"Her phone, maybe. That has GPS."

"That's possible, but seems unlikely. The company she works for must have that in deep encryption."

Vin opened his mouth. "Before you even ask, yes, I looked into Admiral Bartlett. No red flags on him. I delved into Russell Coyne like a pit bull into a juicy T-bone. There's nothing to indicate that he's involved in any way. He's got a large number of navy contracts in addition to corporate ones. What would he gain from kidnapping his own employee?"

"Only one thing I can think of. Sky's working on a top secret project. How did his financials look?"

"Tight. He's leveraged, but what business isn't? I couldn't find anything suspicious there."

"Sky called him. That's why I wanted the laptop. He says he needs some data from her for a meeting he has at the Pentagon at the end of the week. Check that out for me and let me know what you find out."

"Will do. What about her, Vin? Could she have gotten herself into something she couldn't get herself out of and she's using our shiny shields...or...um...your shiny shield to hide behind?"

"I don't think so."

"And which head are you thinking with?"

Vin clenched his teeth. "Not the same damn head you were thinking with when you got involved with that lovely JAG friend of Amber's."

Beau surprised him by laughing.

"What is so damn funny?"

"You like that hot little scientist. Can't say I blame you."

"That's not exactly professional," he said, though he knew Beau could see right through him with bro-radar.

"That *belle femme* is going to change your life."

"Thank you, Dr. Phil."

"This gives me ragging rights, *mon ami*. At least you'll have someone to console your tears."

"Very funny."

Beau laughed. "I know. I can't wait to tell Amber."

"Yeah, you'll get a lot of help there. She thinks you're a womanizer, especially after the JAG friend of hers got her heart broken."

"Hey, that's her fault. I'm always up front. Women just sometimes don't choose to hear what I'm saying."

"You keep telling yourself that, *mon ami,* and when you get tagged and bagged by some little cutie you can't resist, the tables will be turned." Vin thought back to how he'd left things with Sky. "I've got to get going."

"Be careful. This was a well-thought-out mission using a deadly merc force. They want her for something big, and they're not going to stop coming for her. Watch your back and call us if you need us."

Vin nodded and said, "Call me as soon as you have information on Coyne. Dig into him deeper."

"All right. I will. I don't disregard your hunches. They've panned out too many times. But maybe I should look a little deeper into Dr. Baang?"

"You can, but you won't find anything."

"How can you be sure?"

"She might be one of the smartest women on the planet, but she's a terrible liar—her face gives away everything she's thinking."

"Maybe she rehearsed it."

"My gut tells me no."

"Are you sure it's your gut...?"

"Don't finish that sentence. I don't want to have to shut you up."

Beau chuckled. "You're sure there's not a remote chance she's playing you?"

"If she is, then I should hang up my badge and gun."

Beau turned to go, then smiled and turned around. "I've got your back."

"Thanks."

"Don't thank me yet. Thank me when this is over

and I can get on with giving you shit for… Oh, a few years ought to cover it."

"You find out who's after her, you can rag on me as long as you like."

"Then I guess I better make sure that not only do the good guys win, but that you get the *belle femme*." He waved goodbye as he walked away.

Vin got back in the car with Sky's laptop, setting it on the passenger seat. He wished that Beau could make it possible that he would get the girl, but right now, he wasn't so sure the girl would cooperate.

When he got back to the cabin, it was close to noon. Sky was sitting by the fire, staring into it. As the door opened, she started and met his eyes.

Hers were sad and conflicted. He breathed a sigh that they weren't cold and distant. She reached down in her lap and stood. The multicolored scarf in her hands, she came up to him and took the laptop case, walking over and setting it down on the coffee table. She returned to him. Without a word, she draped the scarf around his neck.

He grabbed her hands and squeezed. But she only pulled away. "I made lunch. Just some soup and a sandwich. Help yourself."

"Thank you, but I'm not hungry." He left the living room as she was plugging in and booting up her laptop. Inside the bedroom, he stripped off his sweater and picked up a long-sleeved flannel shirt. He rolled his shoulder a few times. Going into the bathroom, he pulled the bandage away from the wound. It was still tender but looked pretty good. He discarded the bandages and pulled on the shirt and buttoned it.

Walking through the living room to the front door, he could see that Sky was already deeply immersed in her data analysis.

How he had fallen for another woman who couldn't let him be himself was beyond him. His heart twisted as he pulled open the door. He stretched out both shoulders and his back. Going down the stairs, he headed for the woodpile and grabbed up the ax sitting next to two big piles of wood.

He pinched the ax between his legs and rolled up his sleeves. It was nippy out, but once he got going he would get hot. He'd been inactive too long. It was time to get his blood flowing and get his mind on something else besides the woman in the house.

Was she as conflicted as she said?

As the ax came down, splitting the log in two, Vin took it slow until he warmed up. Hours later he'd split all the wood, and it was getting dark. He'd taken off his shirt because he'd been overheated, but now that he'd stopped he was feeling the chill. He shrugged into the shirt, gathered up an armload and went back inside the cabin.

Sky didn't even look up. He cleaned out the debris from the smoldering fire and took it out back to dump it.

Once he was back inside, he reset the logs and tinder and started up another good blaze. He was good and hungry now. Since it looked as if she wasn't interested in stopping what she was doing, he took a quick shower and heated up the soup, eating in the kitchen what she'd prepared for lunch.

His shoulder was throbbing a bit, and he took some painkillers, sat down in a chair by the fire and placed his gun on the side table. Sky's head came up when the steel hit the wood with an audible sound.

Her gaze went to the SIG, and the glaze over her eyes receded. She looked momentarily scared, as if she'd forgotten where she was. She must have gotten lost in her work.

"You expecting company?" she asked, eyeing his weapon.

"I'm always prepared," he said, rubbing at his shoulder.

"Does it hurt?" she asked, remorse and concern in her voice.

"It's fine," he said and dropped his gaze. He could see that she stared at him for a few more moments; then with a resigned expression on her face, she went back to work. He hoped that it sustained her. He doubted it did, but the decision to change her life wasn't in his hands.

He drifted off to sleep to the sound of the *rat-a-tat* of her keys.

When he started awake, he wasn't sure what had brought him out of a deep sleep. But then he heard it. A footfall. He looked to the couch to find Sky sleeping, and then his gaze went to the laptop.

Fuck. That was it. He didn't know how they had done it, but it was the laptop. Her need for her work had given them away.

He was up and moving before he completed that thought. He slipped his hand over her mouth, and when her eyes popped open and she registered that it was him, he pulled her up, grabbed their coats off the hook near the door and ran for the bedroom. Handing her coat to her, he shrugged into his own. The scarf she'd given him in the pocket, he draped it around his neck as she pulled on the black knit hat and a pair of gloves. As they passed the bed, she grabbed up the fanny pack.

Tucking his firearm into the holster at the waistband of his jeans, he silently opened the window and looked out. He picked up a faint rustling and the sound of hushed voices. They had very little time. He picked Sky up, dropped her out the window and followed her, taking the time to close the window behind him.

He took her hand at the same time he reached for his gun. They rounded the house, and he holstered his weapon, pulling her tight against the house to hide in the shadow. A man crept up the back steps. Vin reached for the knife in his pocket and released the deadly blade. The bastard had a semiautomatic slung over his shoulder, and Vin was sure there were more mercs ready to explode into the cabin. He turned to her and put his index finger against his lips. Her eyes were wide and terrified, her breath shallow. He stealthily stepped around the edge of the porch, staying low, moving like a sniper with a target in sight. He waited, his nerves drawn to a lethal edge. As soon as he heard the door crack from force, he leaped at the guy and took him down without a sound. He stripped him of his auto and slung it over his shoulder. Then he vaulted the porch railing, landing with a thud next to her.

He grabbed her hand and bolted for the car, but as soon as he saw it, the hood up and the engine disabled, he changed direction. Dragging her into the woods with him, his keen sense of direction honed from all his perimeter walks, he got to the blind in moments.

He lifted it as he heard a loud, foul stream of Russian come from the cabin. The guy was pissed. Sky gasped, and her head whipped toward the cabin. "Get in!"

"Vin."

"Now," he growled.

She scooted forward, and he crouched, draping the blanket he'd jerry-rigged with tinfoil to temporarily block the infrared scope any smart merc would carry as part of his gear and tucking it over her. "As soon as they pass, hightail it for the road. Use the map to find the sheriff's office and lie low until I get there. Do you understand?"

She nodded, her breathing too fast. "Don't hyperventilate," he ordered. She made an effort to calm her breathing. She looked up at him with scared, pain-filled eyes. With a reassuring look, he let the blind fall.

He sidestepped into the woods and took cover as six big silhouettes poured out of the cabin's back door; the frantic yelling started up again as they tripped over their buddy.

He ran down to the river's edge and hid to the side of the boathouse. As he coated his face with mud, he pressed Chris's number, but Beau answered.

"Beau, it's me. I think the laptop was bugged. Listen…"

"You were right. I checked on that meeting at the Pentagon. There wasn't one. Coyne lied to her. Chris and Amber went to pick him up. I found out other—"

"There's no time for that, Beau. Dammit. They found us." Vin rattled off the address where they were. "Get a chopper fast and get here yesterday." Vin stepped closer to the boathouse to hide his heat signature. "We're heading to Newport and the sheriff's office."

"On it!"

Sky used every trick she knew to keep her breathing even, but the terror inside her threatened to overtake her. Vin was good at his job. That she already knew.

But, oh, God, she thought over and over like a litany in her head. *Let him be all right*.

She heard footfalls near the blind, and then men passed her by. She waited several seconds more. She was just about to lift it and escape to the road, when she heard an inhuman sound of pain.

"Dr. Baang, we have your Special Agent Fitzgerald. Come out now or we'll kill him."

"Sky! He's lying. Stay where you are!" Vin's voice.

There was a spate of automatic gunfire, and she was frozen in place. They had made him give away his position. She couldn't lie here anymore; she had to do something.

She pushed the blanket off her and lifted the blind. All she saw were shadows running toward the boathouse and then heard more automatic gunfire.

In the distance, she could hear a helicopter drawing closer. She hoped that was the cavalry.

Should she stay put or go?

Then she heard a pain-filled cry and a triumphant laugh. Her heart sank. Through the crack in the blind she saw them drag an unconscious man into the clearing not far from her hiding spot.

Vin!

He was only a few feet away from her. Close enough for her to see the blood on his face. The whooshing of the helicopter blades drew closer and closer.

Death Head. She could see him clearly. He crouched down and put a gun to Vin's head. He stirred awake and grabbed the gun, rolling and getting it away from the leader. He shot one of the men point-blank before one of them kicked him in the head. The gun went spinning out of his lax grip and Death Head grabbed it. Swearing at the top of his lungs, he walked toward Vin. She had no doubt that he was going to kill Vin.

"No!" she shouted and ran across the open ground and threw herself across Vin's prone body.

"If you kill him," she screamed, "you'll get nothing from me, ever!" She felt something wet and sticky and pulled her hand back. It was covered in blood, his shirt soaked in it.

The helicopter landed in the front of the house, and Sky prayed it was NCIS. But it was a lone man, and as he drew near, her heart sank and shock rolled through her like a Mack truck.

"Hello, Dr. Baang," her boss, Russell Coyne, said.

Chapter 16

Splintered silvery pieces of awareness filtered through Vin's consciousness, and he drifted in and out for how long, he couldn't say. Then pieces of reality flowed through—the hardness beneath his head, feeling weightless and the sensation of bobbing, the rough texture of something immobilizing his hands, the piercing light above him and the jumble of voices. He heard them as if he was underwater.

"...hurt him...you...anything."

He took a deep breath and came fully awake. "Sky!" He tried to rise, but his hands were flex-cuffed.

At first glance, it looked as if they were in the captain's stateroom aboard a ship, but if it had been a ship, there would have been portholes. There were none that he could see. There was a desk with compartments and a table that extended from the wall with two chairs and a bed. He was lying half in and half out of the tiny stateroom.

"Vin!" Then she was there, beside him, but someone pulled her away. He twisted and tried to come to his feet, even as his side screamed in agony. Someone put a boot in the middle of his chest.

He looked up into Sky's boss's face. He'd met him

briefly the day he'd gone with Sky to her lab. He looked to be in his forties, salt-and-pepper curly hair a little long for a man of his age and ruthless blue eyes. "Coyne, you hurt her and I'll rip your fucking heart out."

He crouched down. His face was tanned, and the sun had left its mark in deep lines around his eyes and across his forehead. "Wow, Agent Fitzgerald, you wake up really grumpy. You look worse for wear than the last time I saw you."

Vin stared at him and the man's smile slipped a bit. "Cut me loose and make it a fair fight." His wrists throbbed, his fingers feeling numb.

He snorted and eyed the flex-cuff around Vin's wrists. "'Fair'? You're wounded."

"I can still kick your ass," Vin said, menacingly low. "If you want, you can leave the flex-cuff on."

Coyne rose and backed up.

"What happened to your Russian wolves?" Vin asked.

"They got paid, and I sent them on their way. Andreyev is ruthless, but they were much too expensive. I simply don't have the technology or skill to pull off a kidnapping and they were good at misdirecting attention onto a foreign government, keeping NCIS busy. That allowed me to stay under the radar. What I didn't bank on was a highly trained, resourceful agent like you mucking up the works. Thankfully, I had a contingency plan in place. I knew she couldn't stay away from that laptop." He smirked. "I've got many foreign governments on the hook for this technology. These are my security people."

"Leave him alone. I told you I would do whatever you want. You can stop gloating," Sky said. Vin looked at her as she struggled against the hold of one of Coyne's goons. When he connected with her gaze, she smiled.

Relief rushed through him and an emotion so strong he knew he was deeply in love with her. "Are you all right?" he said.

She nodded, giving him a reassuring look, trying to mask her fear.

"Let her go," Coyne said. "Remember what I said, Sky."

"And you remember what I said. I'm not doing anything for you until I tend to Vin."

Coyne's mouth tightened. He looked at the goon and said, "Take them down to the infirmary. If he so much as twitches, shoot him. When she's done patching him up, separate them."

Sky rushed forward and put herself between him and Coyne. "No! He stays with me!"

"I don't trust him."

"He's bound. What could he possibly do?"

"He took down a lot of mercs carrying automatic weapons with one handgun. I don't trust him."

"Then you don't get the algorithm or Stingray."

"It galls me that you have a higher clearance than I do. Bitch. Otherwise I could have stolen your plans without all this shit. It would have been nice to be able to frame you for treason. I'll kill him, Sky."

"Do that and you don't get what you want, Russell. Good luck finding that silent submarine in all of the Atlantic Ocean!"

"Sky…" Vin said. She looked at him, her expression set. He wasn't going to change her mind, and he had to trust her in this. There was no way Coyne was going to let either of them walk away from this no matter what he promised Sky. He was leverage against her, but she had Coyne by the short hairs. They would have a much better chance to escape if they were together.

He pointed a gun at Vin.

"Go ahead," she said, her gaze unwavering. "You'll be killing any chance of getting what you want from me. I'll work better knowing he's not being mistreated. We stay together."

Coyne grabbed her hair and pulled her head back. "You try anything and I will put a bullet between his eyes."

"I already said I'd give you what you want. You have armed guards and we're defenseless."

Coyne nodded and let her go. As soon as she was loose, she fell to her knees. "Vin," she said as she helped him to rise into a sitting position. The agony in his side screamed, but he bit back a cry of pain.

"Careful," she said. "I don't know how badly you're injured. They wouldn't let me check."

"Let's go," the goon said.

"Can you walk?"

"I'm going to get you out of this."

"I said move." The man nudged Vin with his automatic weapon. If only his hands were free.

Sky helped him stand, and the guard motioned for them to precede him into the passageway. Sky slipped her shoulder under his arm. His head was starting to clear.

Very low, she said, "I need you to distract the guard when we get to the infirmary. Can you do that for me?"

He nodded slightly.

"Good."

"This is about Stingray?"

"Later," she said.

He noticed she was limping. "Did they hurt you?" he growled.

"No, later, Vin."

At the infirmary, she supported him up onto an examining table and helped him to remove his shirt. She bent down to his side, and when she pressed on the wound, his vision went gray, and he started to slump over. "Catch him!" Sky shouted.

The guard moved forward and caught Vin. He played it up but not by much as the guard manhandled him back onto the examining table. He met her eyes and she nodded that his fainting spell had been effective.

She swabbed the wound and breathed a sigh of relief. "It's just a bad graze. The bullet missed your rib, too. Lucky."

"Still hurts like a son of a bitch."

"I bet," she said with sympathy, her touch gentle.

She cleaned the wound and bandaged it, then moved to his face. She stood close to him as she cleaned the blood off. "This is getting repetitious."

"I agree."

"I'm sorry I didn't follow your orders. I couldn't let him kill you. I couldn't."

"It's okay." He gave her a brief smile. "I can't complain that I'm alive, but I'd rather you were safe."

"This doesn't need stitches." She put on a couple of butterflies and helped him down. The guard escorted them back to their stateroom and closed the door. They both heard it lock.

She helped him to sit on the bed.

"You're giving him Stingray?"

She pulled a chair up and sat down. "I'm giving him an algorithm. I don't know where the sub is. For security reasons, the navy wouldn't give me the coordinates of where they were testing the sub, but I have all the training data, and with data fusion, I can extrapolate. Russell knows that."

"Why doesn't he just take the plans?"

"He already made me send those to his computer, but he wants the prototype to show off to his buyers."

"Buyers. Damn."

"I know. I can't believe I'm working for a traitor."

"It's all about money, right?"

"Yes. He's broke, or he was until he made them ante up half a million dollars apiece for the privilege of viewing the submarine and bidding on the technology." Her eyes filled, and she looked so ashamed and guilty. "He found me by using my laptop. There's a microdot on it. It was up under the casing, very hard to detect. He knew me, Vin." She sat forward. "He knew I couldn't keep away from my work. It's my fault we're here. I'm going to get you out of this."

"By giving him the algorithm? He's going to kill us anyway. You have to know that."

She clutched his forearm. "He couldn't risk letting us go. But the longer we stay alive, the better chance we have. He had to bring us on the sub. He intends to use the algorithm to make sure it works before he takes care of us." Her eyes chilled. "It's a good place to dump two bodies."

He raised his bound hands. "Let's make sure that doesn't happen. Can you release me?"

"No. Russell forbade it." She looked at the door and lowered her voice. "I have your knife."

"What?"

"When I was lying across your body to keep them from shooting you, I got it out of your pocket."

"You're a miracle."

"I'm resourceful." She eyed the door again. "That's why I was limping. I slipped it into my boot."

"Didn't they search you?"

"Yes, they did, but when I took my boot off, I held it against the sole of my foot, and then when they gave me back my boot, I just held it again and slipped my boot back on."

"That was brave and clever, Sky."

She flushed at his praise. "I've been hanging around with you so long, your ability is rubbing off on me." She smiled. "Listen. The algorithm should take a couple of days. It'll give us some time to plan how we're going to get out of this."

He nodded. "We are going to get out of this. I promise."

"With you going all commando on them, I have no doubt. But we'll have to time this carefully."

He raised his bound hands and brushed the backs of his fingers over her soft cheek. "You tell me when."

His heart soared when she leaned into his caress.

"Right now, you need to get some sleep. How is your head?"

"It's okay. I think I have a concussion, but not a severe one. I know what that feels like, courtesy of an explosion in Afghanistan."

"All right. Let's get some sleep."

He made room for her on the double bed and she turned off the light.

"When you passed out in the infirmary, I grabbed a bottle of sedatives and I palmed two hypodermics, too."

"Sweet," he said as he lifted his arms and put them around her. She snuggled up to him, careful of his wound.

"I'm tired of seeing you get shot, Vin."

"I'm kinda sick of it myself."

"I think Russell peed his pants when you gave him that crazy Rambo look. You scared the hell out of me. I'm glad you don't want to hurt me."

"Never."

"You're not really going to kill Russell, are you?"

"As long as he's not stupid, no. I'm not a cold-blooded killer. I might hurt him a little."

"For treason?"

He snorted. "No, for putting you through all this."

He felt her mouth brush against his. "I'm so thankful that you're alive." She pressed her mouth against his a little desperately. He tightened his arms and kissed her back.

She relaxed against him, and her breathing slowed. He stared into the dark. He knew nothing was guaranteed. Just because they had a knife and a sedative bottle didn't mean getting out of this alive was a given. They were under thousands of pounds of water, in the middle of nowhere, and held captive. But he vowed, whatever it took, he was going to get Sky off this sub and out of danger.

The next day they were woken up by the goon who had taken him to the infirmary. They actually brought them breakfast. Vin moved a little slowly getting off the bed. He was actually feeling pretty good, but he didn't want the guard to know that. A seasoned guy would be vigilant, but Vin noted this guy seemed to be more of a rent-a-goon than a seasoned merc.

At the table, Vin ate his eggs and drank the coffee. Sky was given her laptop to work on. She was seated at the desk. There was no connectivity, so she couldn't send or receive any messages.

She worked all day while he napped on and off, building up his strength. She carefully changed his bandages, and when they were back in bed, she said, "I have a plan. After I give Russell the algorithm, he's going to try it out before he does anything to us to make sure it works."

"That makes sense."

"I know him. He's cautious. He'll make sure he can find Stingray before he kills me." She swallowed hard. "There are two guards outside the door. I can cause a commotion and inject the first one if you can handle the second one."

"I can do that."

She laid the plan out for him, and he listened. "Sky, are you sure you're not the navy's secret weapon?"

She blushed. "So we'll do this tomorrow after I give Russell the algorithm."

He nodded.

She slipped out of bed and wedged a chair under the door handle.

"What are you doing?"

"I want some private time with you, Vin. Is that all right with you? I know we had that terrible fight and we don't really agree. For all I know, you don't want to have sex with me again."

"You want to have sex? Now?"

"Yes, tomorrow is it, and there are no guarantees. I want to be with you again before…"

"Ah, sweetheart," he said, his voice ragged.

"Please, Vin."

"There is so much that's complicated between us."

"I know. But tonight let's just make it simple. There may be no tomorrow."

He pushed himself up with his bound hands and pressed his back against the headboard. "Have your way with me. Wait! Shit! Protection."

"I scoured the cabin and found these." She opened her hand to reveal three foil packets. "Must have been expecting a good time on shore leave, huh?"

Meeting her gaze, he reached out and grabbed a long ribbon of her hair and ran it through the fingers of his bound hands.

"I wish I could release you."

He nodded, following the fall of her hair as it settled against her upper body. So long and inky black. He leaned forward and grazed her jaw with his teeth, felt her tremble. A shuddering sigh left her, and he felt her hips rise against him with an undulating slide.

"You are the most beautiful woman I have ever seen," he said.

She made a soft sound in her throat and fused her mouth to his, kissing him with a desperation that he felt in every pore of his body. She straddled his hips, and he could feel the heat of her against his erection.

Adrenaline and a hot and willing woman was a lethal combination. The fact that their captors could come into the room at any moment added another danger element to what he was already feeling. The danger to his heart.

She dragged her mouth from his, and he felt her slide his zipper open. Their eyes met in the darkened interior, and he knew it didn't matter if they were shamelessly desperate. Her gaze was hard with need, her hand roving over his chest, down to his cock and back up. All he could do was watch her face—so beautiful, her silky long hair, her eyes so exotic, so thickly lashed, so intensely focused on his.

His heart filled with so much love he thought he might die from it.

A guy gave that away only once, and he thought he had, but he'd been so wrong. He'd never given it away to anyone but Sky.

He loved her.

She loved him.

Oh, God, she had no idea of the potency of that feeling. How it would fill her heart to bursting. She wanted to cry, but she couldn't catch her breath. He kept stealing it with his eyes and his mouth.

No man could ever taste like Vin, darkly delicious, primal male, answering a need in her that she hadn't known she had until the first time he'd kissed her. She'd wanted him so badly all day, even more than she'd wanted that first night she'd thrown herself at him.

She remembered the first time she'd laid eyes on him. Fresh from saving her, covering her body, protecting her. His eyes so green, his hair mussed, looking both elegant in his impeccable suit and so street tough.

She'd seen him at his rawest, his most brutal, and she still loved him. All six incredible feet of raw, lean power, silky dark hair and sharp cheekbones. His self-assurance in standing up to Russell, beaten, shot and so confident it made her shiver inside at his bravery. She knew for a fact he could back up that claim.

They had too many complications, and at this point she didn't care. She needed him.

She reached down and pulled off his jeans and underwear, running her hands over him with abandon. His chest heaved, and he closed his eyes and groaned. He cupped her face between his bound hands, his mouth closing over hers, hot, wet, tongues touching and twining, lips rubbing and pressing, consuming.

His hands were hot on her face, and she got rid of her clothes without breaking the kiss.

She wanted him, desperately. But no one had more control over himself than Vin—just the thought of all that control was enough to make her melt another degree.

"Slide all over me, Sky. Oh, baby, you feel so good."

She moved over him, and he groaned hard as she unbuttoned his shirt, pressing her breasts against his chest. Rising up, she reached down, slid on the condom and guided him into her. She gasped, almost a sob, and a huge crash of pleasure waved over her. She cried out against his mouth as she increased her tempo. She felt his hands against her stomach, then cupping her breast, his thumbs rubbing over her nipple. He pressed her back and lowered his head to take her aching tip into his warm, wet mouth.

And as he sucked on her, the pleasure built until she came in a torrent, going deep on him, her soft cries and trembling shudders rolling over her.

His hips rose to meet hers and his thrusts were powerful and penetrating, getting more rapid until he stiffened and moaned, his back arching and his head twisting.

She buried her face into his throat, her breath fast and heavy just like his.

He pushed off the headboard with his back, grunting a little in pain until they were lying against each other.

They would have to get dressed soon, but right now she reveled in being against his naked body.

She couldn't think. She could barely catch her breath.

Love. It was so beautiful, just like he'd told her. The essence of life.

Her resolve to sacrifice her life for her parents was shaken, the very foundation cracking. All because of Vin.

"Vin," she whispered against his neck, tightening her arms around him.

The next morning when they came for them, they got up and ate breakfast, and Sky booted up her computer. The algorithm was almost done. She worked on it for an hour, put the finishing touches on it and knocked on the stateroom door.

The guard opened it, and she said, "Get Russell. It's done."

When he closed the door, she looked at Vin. He gave her a reassuring smile and said, "We're ready for this. Just keep it cool."

She nodded as the door opened again, and Russell stepped through. The guard closed it behind them. She gave him the flash drive. "Here it is. I hope you choke on it."

He grabbed her by the hair, and Vin rose from the bed, but the guard shoved him back down.

"You little bitch. It should have been me who got the Stingray project. Beaten out by a woman."

"That's why you hired me."

"I had plans for that project, and one of them was to

shaft the navy, who has been so proprietary with their contracts. It was all about you. But now I've leveraged the company into so much debt, I've got to bail. The sale of this sub to a foreign government will make me rich and then I'll retire."

"You are despicable, Russell."

He backhanded her across the face, pain exploding in her cheek. She hit the wall of compartments, covering her cheek with her palm.

"Coyne," Vin said, and her blood froze at the tone of his voice.

"You only have the time it takes for me to check out this algorithm. Then you're both dead."

He turned and walked out of the stateroom, but the guard didn't leave and Sky's heartbeat accelerated. How was she going to cut Vin free? She really had only one choice. She'd have to do this herself.

She'd already filled the syringe. It was just a matter of getting close enough to the guard to inject him. Since the space was so limited, it wouldn't take much.

She reached up, rubbed her temple and stumbled toward the guard. He reacted by bringing his gun up, but she was close enough. Holding the syringe like a knife, she jammed the needle right into his chest and pushed the plunger. He cried out, backhanding her. As he lunged for her, he stumbled and Vin rammed into him. The downed guard hit the bulkhead and didn't move.

The door opened and slammed against the wall. She was hurriedly kicking off her boot to pull out the blade to cut Vin free, but they were out of time.

The guard brought up the semiautomatic weapon, and it was as if everything slowed down. Vin was already moving. He hit the guard on the side of his knee with his boot, and Sky heard bone crack. The guard cried out and listed to the side. Vin rushed him and dropped his arms around the man's neck. With his bound hands he lifted up, and there was another audible crack and the guard collapsed at his feet.

She hurried up to him and cut the flex-cuff off him. He rubbed his wrists, working the feeling back into his numb fingers. He crouched to grab up one of the semiautomatics. She grabbed his arm and pulled him out the open door. "We've got to get to the engine room before he plugs in and tries to use that algorithm."

They paused at the corner to the passageway, and she handed him the knife. He closed it and dropped it into his pocket. "Why? Won't it take him time to find Stingray?"

"I didn't write a program for Stingray. All Russell is going to find with that flash drive is a pod of whales."

Vin grinned and she laughed. "Come on. He won't think it's as funny as we do." She looked around as if she was getting her bearings. "Come on. The engine room is this way." She ran down the passageway.

"How do you know your way around a sub, sweetheart?" he asked, covering her as they ran.

"I studied a lot of schemata when I was designing Stingray. I know most sub models like the back of my hand."

They didn't meet anyone, but when they reached the engine room, Vin slipped inside first and pulled out his knife. "Stay here."

He disappeared from view, and she heard absolutely nothing until he returned back to her, startling her.

She made her way to the life-support system. "Grab

those breathing masks." He opened the compartments and took out two, handing her one. She put it over her face and started the flow of oxygen.

"When we breathe in air, our bodies consume the oxygen and convert it to carbon dioxide. Exhaled air contains about 4.5 percent carbon dioxide."

Vin nodded. "A submarine is a sealed container that contains a limited supply of air."

"Exactly. There are two crucial things that must happen in order to keep air in a submarine breathable—oxygen has to be replenished as it is consumed. If the percentage of oxygen in the air falls too low, a person suffocates. Carbon dioxide must be removed from the air. As the concentration of carbon dioxide rises, it becomes a toxin."

"You're going to knock everyone out. Clever."

She worked as she spoke. "Oxygen is supplied from these pressurized tanks and is released continuously by a computerized system that senses the percentage of oxygen in the air. We're going to reprogram the computer to lower the release of oxygen so that just enough is supplied, but not enough for them to regain consciousness. They won't even know what hit them. Then we will have free rein of the sub."

"And move to step two."

She smiled through the mask. "That's right. Distress signal. I know how to do that, too."

"I don't think Coyne even had a clue what he was up against."

She tapped on the keys to the console, did the math in her head, using the size of the sub and the amount of oxygen a body needed to maintain its bodily functions, and made the adjustments.

Then she looked down at her watch. Vin moved closer to her, and she welcomed the warmth of his presence. She realized that he was making sure she was covered, but it felt good just the same.

When a sufficient time had passed, they left the engine room. As they made their way to the bridge, they stepped over collapsed bodies.

On the bridge, they found Russell slumped over the console. He'd plugged in her algorithm, and she saw that he would have realized she'd written it to find a pod of whales. She laughed softly as she put out a distress signal.

Chapter 17

Vin leaned against the ambulance that had pulled up to the navy-yard dock where the coast guard had escorted the sub. The men inside, including Coyne, were taken into custody. An EMT was examining his wounds.

"You look good, sir. Whoever patched you up did a great job."

Sky was sitting on another ambulance, talking to his boss.

When Chris walked away, Sky looked over at him. Then she slipped off the back and crossed the distance separating them.

"Your boss is going to take me home."

"Sky, wait. We need to talk. I need to tell you something important." He glanced at the EMT, and he moved away.

She looked at him, her eyes bruised. "Don't say it. I'm not the right woman for you, Vin. I almost got us killed because of my oath to my parents. I don't think they would be very proud of me right now. It won't work for me, Vin, and you deserve someone who isn't obsessed by her past. My family's honor…"

"Honor? That's your argument against anything we could have together?"

She shook her head and cupped his face. "No, Vin.

It's not that. Their deaths have to mean something. They have to. I can't turn my back on that."

"What are you talking about? Their lives already have meaning, and I'm not asking you not to honor them. I'm just asking you to let me in. Look at you. So beautiful, so smart. It's all about you. Not about them. They're gone. But you're alive. Do something with your life."

"I gave it away. I promised. I can't go back on it."

"You're afraid to live. That's what it is. You're using your parents' sacrifice like a crutch, a barrier to embracing life because all you've known is fear. I'm offering you something else here. A chance, Sky, to be together, to live and to love. I love you. I love you more than I've ever loved anyone. Please, take my hand and we'll work through this."

"I can't." She backed up, and he tried to come after her, but he collapsed against the side of the ambulance.

When she shook her head, his heart sank. "Sky. Don't go."

But she turned away from him. "It's me, not you. You're the most wonderful man I have ever met. Please, take care of yourself."

She ran then, away from the chaos and the flashing lights and the sirens.

She ran from him.

Sky couldn't spend one more day in her empty house. She was barred from Coyne Industries until there was a thorough investigation. It pretty much meant she was out of a job. Her boss had committed treason, and she would have to testify. But it didn't change the fact that she was unemployed.

Vin's face, on the day she'd run from him, haunted

her sleeping and waking hours. But she couldn't let him near her. Couldn't let him touch her or she'd crumble. She would get lost in him, and then the honor, the sacrifice her parents had made would be for nothing.

They had clashed over his lack of family honor and her abundance of it. Her need, so all consuming that she had almost gotten them killed. He was better off without her. Her work had to be her life. Even her enemies knew her better than she knew herself. She had to run. Run away from the one man she would have died for.

She loved him and she'd broken his heart.

That was the sacrifice that hurt so, so bad.

She arrived on her aunt's doorstep, and as soon as she opened the door, Sky burst into tears. Her aunt dragged her inside, her weathered face crinkled in concern.

After she made some tea, they sat at the kitchen table.

"Why are you here, child? What is so very wrong?"

"I fell in love."

Her aunt's face registered her confusion. "Shouldn't that be a cause for celebration?"

"But I promised I would give up my life to make a difference, so that my parents' sacrifice meant something."

She patted Sky's hand, handing her a tissue. "What kind of notion is this?"

Sky wiped at the moisture on her face, dabbing at her eyes and sniffling. "My father's. He told me to use my gift to make a difference. You told me all my life the sacrifice they made."

Her aunt frowned and sat back in her chair, distress clear on her face. "Oh, no." She bit her lip and looked away. "I have been an old fool and kept something from you all these years. Now I see what a terrible mistake I've made."

Everything went dead still for Sky: sounds, her hands, her heart. "What have you kept from me?"

"Letters. Your father's letters. I think it's time you read them."

A sudden ache constricted her throat, and she clenched the tissue in her hands. Drawing a deep shaky breath, Sky sat back and said, "Letters? How could you have kept them from me?"

Her aunt's expression softened. "I didn't want to upset you, and then it got easier to just conceal them. But I was wrong in keeping them from you. Read them and you'll understand what I'm talking about."

Sky followed her aunt up to her bedroom and waited while she pulled a box out of her closet. "Here they are. Take them to your old room and stay as long as you like. We'll talk again after you have read them." She squeezed Sky's arm. "I'm sorry, Sky."

She set the box in Sky's arms and left the room. Making her way to her old bedroom, Sky set the box on the bed and closed the door. Shrugging out of her coat, she threw it on a nearby chair. With trembling fingers, she pulled out the first letter. When she saw her father's neat handwriting, a sob caught in her throat. She'd been denied so much of him, denied his comfort and guidance. She resented her aunt for keeping these secret. She had a right to his correspondence, no matter how it made her feel.

But that was it, wasn't it? Just what Vin had said. Her stomach flipped over. Had he been right?

She started to read, and she read until she got to the last letter, the one dated just before his death.

Malaya,
I'm very ill, my child. I don't think I will see an-

other day. I've spent my life in this prison, but it
hasn't been in vain. I've written several books
that will probably never be published, but that
doesn't matter. I did something good with the time
that was given me. You are a young woman now.
Grown up. I know that your aunt has not given
you my letters, but eventually she will. I know
that you are a navy scientist working on top secret
projects for the United States. It is fitting, as your
name Malaya means *free*. That was your mother's
idea. It was her birthplace, and I'm proud to know
that you have embraced the country that values
freedom. My wish is that you have understood
that freedom is all I've ever wanted for you. Your
right to choose. The Chinese would have taken
that from you. I fought to give it back to you. You
are free to choose to do with your gift as you see
fit. Don't let what your mother and I sacrificed
trouble you. You were our child, and it was our
responsibility to make sure you were safe. She
loved you and I love you. You would honor us
if you begin your own legacy with a home, husband and children to bring you the joy that you
brought to us.

Your loving father

She set the letter down, covering her face with her
hands, and mourned him and her mother, let the feelings she'd always kept separate in and overwhelm her
with grief and loss. Vin had taught her how. He had
given her so much, and in her foolish belief, she had
discounted it and him. After all that had been burned

away in the aftermath of her grief, all that was left was her love for her family, for Vin. Her sacrifice had been easy. Too easy. Cutting off emotion and living a life of a martyr was what she had really done. She could see it clearly now.

He had been so right. She was scared. Because taking what he offered would open her up to emotions that frightened her as a child. Love, need for reassurance, fear of abandonment. Dealing with everyday life as it happened was something that she'd avoided, and the one time she'd let a man in, she'd ruined it by being so stiff and cold. He was right, she realized as she sat there and absorbed her father's words. He had wanted her to be happy. *Happy.* Not give up everything to their memories. He'd spelled it out in black and white.

He wanted her to start a new legacy, a family of her own, using her skills and abilities as she saw fit. Something that had rubbed off from her independent and beautiful mother and the reason he fell in love with her. He'd given her back her family in the words that he'd written on these pages.

Tears streamed down her cheeks as she felt finally, inexplicably free. She also felt terrible remorse for how she had ended it with Vin. Hoping against hope that it wasn't really over. That her actions hadn't killed any feeling he'd had for her. Because she loved him. It had sneaked into her heart like a thief and stolen it away for him.

This kidnapping had changed her life, had been the catalyst that had drawn her away from her isolation and her loneliness to something more fulfilling and now ingrained in her heart. In her terrible ordeal, she'd found herself and realized that she could let go of her past. She'd found Vin, and she never wanted to let him go.

As the sun rose, she told her aunt that they would talk later. There was something that she desperately needed to do.

She drove over to NCIS and went up to Vin's office, but when she approached his desk, it was empty.

Amber smiled at her and said, "Hello, Dr. Baang. You looking for Agent Fitzgerald?"

"Yes. Where is he?"

"He took personal leave."

Tears pressed on the backs of her eyes. "Please, Amber. Tell me where he went."

Amber studied her face, and then her eyes softened. She pulled a piece of paper off her notepad and wrote something down. She folded it and handed it to Sky.

Sky clutched it in her hand and left the building. Out front she unfolded it and looked at what was written there. She smiled, and, for the first time in a week, she felt lighthearted.

Vin sat back into the cushy chair of the conference room in downtown Boston. His sister sat next to him and his father and mother on the other side. His shoulder still ached a bit, and the two bullet wounds on his torso and the one on his shoulder were healing well. He'd gone home without Sky. The loss of her was almost more than he could bear. He'd come home to help his family. He'd assembled them to work out the future of the company and his future at NCIS.

"Lilah, what's really going on? I've gone through every piece of paper in this place, and it looks to me like you've been running the business for a long time."

He covered her hand. Lilah glanced at their father, and Vin saw his mouth tighten.

"She's been saving it for you, Vincent," his father said.

"No, Dad. I've told you so many times that I'm never running this company, but Lilah, who's graduated with honors in business administration and then went on to get her law degree, has been dedicated and sacrificed so much to keep this place running. Why can't you acknowledge that and just be proud of both of us?"

"Yes, Dad, Vinny saves lives. He just saved a woman from being kidnapped and protected our national security. He's a decorated marine. Why can't you just accept that it's not what he wants? I'm so amazingly proud of him. I love him so much. That's all that should matter."

His mother put her hand on his father's arm. "Patrick, I don't want Vin to come home during family crises. I want him to visit us when he wants to and not be guilt-tripped into doing something that doesn't make him happy. Lilah's right." She looked at him with tears in her eyes. "I'm so proud of you, Vincent. I burst every time I think of your dedication and service to our country. Tell him, Patrick. Tell him now or I will never forgive you."

His father looked at him, and he cleared his throat. "Of course both of you are totally right. I'm extremely proud of you, son. But I've never been dead set against Delilah taking over here. She's an asset and would make an excellent CEO. But I wanted this company to benefit you both. It's your legacy, too, Vincent. I couldn't see any other way to get you involved than to insist that you take over. Perhaps there is some way you could be a consultant and be involved with the decisions that Delilah makes. Who knows? Maybe someday one of your children will be interested in the business."

Stunned, Vin sat there and stared at his father. It was a revelation to him that Sky was right. There was something to honoring his family, and the offer his father had just made suited him just fine. Touched by his dad's speech, he could only nod his head.

Vin pulled into the driveway of his parents' home. His side twinged as he got out of the car and headed for the front door. His father, mother and sister had gone out to lunch, but he was more interested in getting changed, packing his suitcase and going after Sky. It was a relief that his father had accepted retirement. Vin wanted to talk to Sky in person and tell her that he understood what she was talking about. Maybe they could stop arguing and really talk about their differences and the similarities. But if she wasn't willing to change to accept him, he would have to figure out how he was going to live his life without her. His thoughts trailed off as he saw a woman standing at the front door with long, dark hair. His heart leaped in his chest. It couldn't be…Sky.

She turned and her gaze caught and held his. Her features softened and she smiled. His heart skipped a beat as he walked up the stairs.

"I was just about to jump on a plane and fly back to D.C. to find you."

"You were? I came here hoping you'd tell me it's not too late." She stood there looking scared and hopeful at the same time.

His voice wobbled a bit, his throat constricted and his chest tight. "Here I was, trying to figure out how I was going to get through the rest of my life without you."

Her face crumpled and she lunged into his arms.

He held her close. "I love you. But you have to explain to me what happened. What changed?"

She raised her head, her eyes warm and alive. "I went to my aunt, and she had all these letters from my father. You were right. I misinterpreted their meaning. They never wanted me to sacrifice anything. They wanted me to live, and all this time I haven't. I've been marking time just like you said. So, to fulfill my family's honor, I must live. I choose to live with you. I love you, Vin."

He crushed her to him. "Then it's time to live, Sky."

She wrapped her arms around his neck and lifted her face up to his. He dropped his mouth down onto hers, making a soft moan of relief as she kissed him back.

When he broke the kiss, she said, "It is important to honor your family. The thing is, we all have to decide what that honoring consists of. I realized that I needed to trust your judgment about what was right for your family. It isn't up to me to say how involved you should be. I misjudged my own father's wishes, so I shouldn't presume to know what you should do, either. I was wrong to insist that you follow my path, which ended up being so misguided. I don't care what you do, Vin. NCIS agent, CEO, just as long as that is what makes you happy and fulfilled. You wanted acceptance. You have it unconditionally."

"I just needed you to let me in. We'll do great together now. And I'm going to be both NCIS agent and work for the family business when I can. My sister is now the CEO and is going to run the company, but I'm going to be involved with major decision-making."

"Well, that's good news because I have to let you know that I'm unemployed."

He tilted his head. "Are you? Well, then, that gives you a chance for a new beginning."

"Yeah, I could scope out suitable yoga studios by myself, but it wouldn't be as much fun as having a friend and a lover along with me."

"Is that an invitation?"

"Do you need it engraved?"

He chuckled and opened the door, pulling her inside. "My parents aren't going to be home for a while. They and my sister are having lunch."

"Oh, is that so? Then I guess we could get down to the business of living."

"I have some business I want to share with you."

He pulled her into his arms and picked her up. Heading for the stairs, he climbed them two at a time, their laughter echoing all the way to the ceiling.

Epilogue

Sky caught her breath as Vin kissed her neck. She cuddled up to him as the boat they were on traversed down the Donsol River, not far from the sleepy fishing village where her father had been born. It was stunning here, simply paradise. Located in the province of Sorsogon, the village was a place of pristine beaches, stunning waterfalls and unexplored caves; their days had been all about exploration and their nights had been more of the same, only on a much more intimate level. A level they wouldn't have attempted in public. Well, except for his soft lips on her skin right now. Luckily they were the only ones on this particular trip. She suspected that Vin had arranged it.

The boat meandered as she took in the palm and mangrove trees. They stopped and the boat left them off.

As it putted away, she looked at Vin.

"Don't worry. He's coming back for us."

He bent down and lifted her foot to slip off her sandal, and she caught herself on his stooped shoulder, balancing on one foot, then the other. He slipped off his shoes and gathered both in his hands. He curled his free hand around hers, and they walked a little ways along the beach, the lazy waves lapping at her bare feet. She stopped when she spied the double wide hammock, the table and chairs all set up in a copse of palms as if it was waiting for them.

He pulled her toward it, festooned with bright pillows in hot tropical colors and a couple of comfortable throw blankets to match.

He dropped their shoes and pulled her down onto the hammock with him.

"What is this?" She met his twinkling eyes.

He pressed his mouth down on hers, and she gave herself up to his kiss, making room for him between her thighs; she wrapped her arms around his neck.

"This is a secluded island that we have all day and all night. Just the two of us."

"We're going to sleep outside under the stars?"

"Yeah. How do you feel about that?"

"Oh, my God, Vin, that's so romantic and so spontaneous."

They sunned and swam in the warm water, then ate and dozed on the hammock. As the sun went down, Sky woke to a million sparkling fireflies lighting up the night sky.

She reveled in the decadence of lying with Vin on the comfortable hammock as the soft ocean breeze blew across her bare skin. The day before they had swum with whale sharks, and the day before that they'd participated in catching shrimp in nets for their dinner.

"I can't believe my father would have ever wanted to leave here," she said as she smoothed her hand over Vin's bare chest. "Thank you for this. For coming with me to the Philippines to this village where my father was born."

"It is beautiful, but he must have had ambition.

Wanted to be a mechanical engineer and not a fisherman."

She was content to nod. She'd started up her yoga studio and named it Espiritu like her company name. It fit so well: Espiritu was Tagalog for *soul*—mind, feeling, body. She loved teaching yoga and doing several consulting projects when the mood struck her.

She loved loving Vin every day and night while he saved the world. The navy had nominated her for the Presidential Medal of Freedom. Before they had left on the trip, she'd been notified she would receive it and the president of the United States was going to present it to her. Vin had been so proud of her and she already knew her parents would have been so proud of her. Vin would receive the Department of the Navy Meritorious Civilian Service Award and a Commendation for Meritorious Civilian Service for his part in keeping Stingray out of enemy hands.

He turned toward her, propping his head with his hand, giving her a sultry look, and then glanced down to where her hands were playing with the ridges of his abdomen. "You going to keep that up?"

She grinned at him. "Why? You got somewhere to be?"

He chuckled. "Um…no… Could you do it a little lower?"

"I could." She slipped her fingers between his waistband and his hard-muscled waist, teasing his skin, and then she slipped her hand into his swim trunks to wrap around him. His eyes drifted closed on a groan. Then he kissed her and moved his hips forward, thrusting into her hand.

"Sky," he murmured between kisses on her mouth,

and her cheek, and her ear, and that very sensitive spot on the side of her neck, "we met under the craziest of circumstances."

"We sure did, and you saved my life in more ways than one." She was melting under all those kisses and the very gentle exploration he was making with his fingers between her legs. Then with two pulls he had her bikini bottom off.

Her body overloaded with wonderful sensations. "So, what are we going to do for excitement without bullets flying and adrenaline rushing?" she whispered, running her hand over his chest all the way to the hardest part of him.

He kissed her, a sweet stunning kiss that had her melting all over again.

"How about this for starters?" He pulled something out of his pocket, and her breath caught when he held it up to the torchlight. A ring box right in the middle of making love. A very spontaneous marriage proposal.

"Will you marry me?" he said, his voice rough-edged with emotion.

She rolled to face him, and he lifted his head to meet her gaze. Her hands went over the scar on his shoulder and the two on his side. He shucked off his shorts and slid all that sun-warmed muscle over her, the hot and welcome pressure of his body seeking entrance into hers. She could see it in the darkening of his eyes and in the not-so-innocent curve of his smile.

He opened the box, and her breath caught at the beautiful, square-cut sparkler inside as the shine of it vied with the moonlight.

She lifted her head and whispered in his ear and he shivered. When she lowered her head and met his eyes, she plucked the ring out of the box, handing it to him. Then she offered up the ring finger of her left hand. "It's yes to infinity, and I can tell you how long that is."

"Oh, you can?" he said, his eyes moist and so, so green as he slid the ring all the way to her knuckle. "How long?"

"Oh, Vin, my gorgeous love." She lifted her hips and accepted him deep inside. "That's easy. Forever."

* * * * *

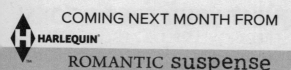

COMING NEXT MONTH FROM

HARLEQUIN®

ROMANTIC suspense

Available December 2, 2014

#1827 THE MANSFIELD RESCUE
The Mansfield Brothers • by Beth Cornelison
Falling for smoke jumper Amy Robinson is the last thing grieving widower Grant Mansfield has in mind. But when his daughter is kidnapped, Grant and Amy must work together to save his little girl. Now, if only he'd let Amy rescue his lonely heart...

#1828 COLTON HOLIDAY LOCKDOWN
The Coltons: Return to Wyoming • by C.J. Miller
To save Christmas in Dead River, Dr. Rafe Granger is working overtime to cure the deadly virus quarantining his hometown— while fighting his attraction to nurse Gemma Colton. But when someone sabotages their research, can this reformed bad boy win the day and get the good girl?

#1829 LONE STAR SURVIVOR
by Colleen Thompson
"Soldier" Ian Rayford returns from the dead, but can't remember anything but his former fiancée—PTSD psychologist Andrea. As an element of his past targets her, spy secrets become deadly secrets!

#1830 LETHAL LIES
by Lara Lacombe
With his cover blown, agent Alexander goes on the run with the alluring Dr. Jillian Mahoney. Yet with the FBI and a dangerous gang after them, separating the lies from the truth becomes a matter of the heart.

YOU CAN FIND MORE INFORMATION ON UPCOMING HARLEQUIN® TITLES, FREE EXCERPTS AND MORE AT WWW.HARLEQUIN.COM.

HRSCNM1114

REQUEST YOUR FREE BOOKS!
2 FREE NOVELS PLUS 2 FREE GIFTS!

ROMANTIC suspense

Sparked by danger, fueled by passion

YES! Please send me 2 FREE Harlequin® Romantic Suspense novels and my 2 FREE gifts (gifts are worth about $10). After receiving them, if I don't wish to receive any more books, I can return the shipping statement marked "cancel." If I don't cancel, I will receive 4 brand-new novels every month and be billed just $4.74 per book in the U.S. or $5.24 per book in Canada. That's a savings of at least 14% off the cover price! It's quite a bargain! Shipping and handling is just 50¢ per book in the U.S. and 75¢ per book in Canada.* I understand that accepting the 2 free books and gifts places me under no obligation to buy anything. I can always return a shipment and cancel at any time. Even if I never buy another book, the two free books and gifts are mine to keep forever.

240/340 HDN F45N

Name	(PLEASE PRINT)	
Address		Apt. #
City	State/Prov.	Zip/Postal Code

Signature (if under 18, a parent or guardian must sign)

Mail to the **Harlequin®** Reader Service:
IN U.S.A.: P.O. Box 1867, Buffalo, NY 14240-1867
IN CANADA: P.O. Box 609, Fort Erie, Ontario L2A 5X3

Want to try two free books from another line?
Call 1-800-873-8635 or visit www.ReaderService.com.

* Terms and prices subject to change without notice. Prices do not include applicable taxes. Sales tax applicable in N.Y. Canadian residents will be charged applicable taxes. Offer not valid in Quebec. This offer is limited to one order per household. Not valid for current subscribers to Harlequin Romantic Suspense books. All orders subject to credit approval. Credit or debit balances in a customer's account(s) may be offset by any other outstanding balance owed by or to the customer. Please allow 4 to 6 weeks for delivery. Offer available while quantities last.

Your Privacy—The Harlequin® Reader Service is committed to protecting your privacy. Our Privacy Policy is available online at www.ReaderService.com or upon request from the Harlequin Reader Service.

We make a portion of our mailing list available to reputable third parties that offer products we believe may interest you. If you prefer that we not exchange your name with third parties, or if you wish to clarify or modify your communication preferences, please visit us at www.ReaderService.com/consumerschoice or write to us at Harlequin Reader Service Preference Service, P.O. Box 9062, Buffalo, NY 14269. Include your complete name and address.

HRS13

Returning to Dead River is anything but welcoming
for Dr. Rafe Granger, who lands himself in the middle
of an epidemic...and discovers a connection to the
powerful Colton family he never anticipates.

Read on for a sneak peek of

COLTON HOLIDAY LOCKDOWN
by C.J. Miller

Dr. Rafe Granger would never escape this rotting purgatory.
His return had brought with it a terrible series of events:
an unidentified virus was claiming victims by the dozens,
the virus research lab had been trashed and a murderer had
escaped the local prison and was adding to the terror and
paranoia of every person in town.

Rafe entered the clinic through the single metal entry
door. The smell of smoke hung in the air. Behind the recep-
tion area, the clinic's patient files had been pulled from the
shelves and littered the floor. The culprit had done much
worse to Rafe's office and the lab.

Dread pooled low in his stomach. What had been taken?
The most critical work had been stored in the lab.

Rafe checked over his protective gear, pulled it on and
entered the lab, noting the lock was broken on the door.
Anger and frustration shook Rafe to his core. The inside
of the lab was a disaster—tables overturned, equipment

thrown to the floor and petri dishes and beakers smashed on the ground. But the most alarming thing was what had been done to the samples. The small refrigerator they'd been using to store the carefully labeled Vacutainer tubes was open and emptied.

Rafe let loose a curse he almost never used. This situation was beyond all repair.

He felt a hand on his back and whirled around, coming face-to-face with Gemma Colton, one of the clinic's registered nurses.

"Where are our samples?" Gemma asked, sounding shocked and panicked. Her green eyes were filled with concern. As many times as he had looked into those green eyes, the vibrancy and beauty of them struck him every time. "Who would do this?"

"Not sure. But that virus is deadly on the street," Rafe said.

"We already have an epidemic and now we have to worry about someone running around with vials containing the virus," Gemma said, her voice shaking.

Rafe heard shouts and banging from the clinic. He and Gemma exchanged looks. What else could go wrong?

Don't miss COLTON HOLIDAY LOCKDOWN by C.J. Miller, available December 2014 wherever Harlequin® Romantic Suspense books and ebooks are sold.